I0524730

THE NINTH HOUR

THE NINTH HOUR

BOOK ONE OF IN MEMORIAM

DANIEL POPPIE

Daniel Poppie

Waukesha, WI

Copyright © 2018 Daniel

All rights reserved. No portion of this book may be reproduced in any form without permission from the publisher, except as permitted by U.S. copyright law. For permissions, contact:

dan@danielpoppie.com

Cover by Kyle Julian.

ISBN: 978-0-9994705-1-0 (Paperback)
ISBN: 359-2-85933-609-1 (Ebook)

First Edition 2018.

Daniel Poppie
Waukesha, WI 53189
danielpoppie.com

For Sarah

Part I

New Year's Eve

"You want to understand the bicentennial of the United States? Have you ever bit into a rotten apple?"
– Samuel Judah, *American Autumn* –

ONE

————

"They say history is created by giants, not mere men."
– Samuel Judah, *American Autumn* –

James was a slave.

Although slavery had been outlawed since Lincoln's Emancipation Proclamation, James' essential situation was slavery. Although legally classified as a servant, through familial debt he had come into the unpaid employ of the House Karling. Because of his young age when 'sold,' his labor was appraised at minimum value; the interest upon the debt compounded until he became useful, and he would be forty-three when it was fully paid. Although Society, with its superficial moral preening, talked of enslavement as a savage and abhorrent act, even the most upright members maintained at least two of these unpaid servants, and most maintained dozens.

————

James never knew who incurred the debt, and with more than half his life spent as a servant, he no longer cared. He had little memory of freedom, and he had little desire to spend his precious free time finding who was at fault. Others were in far worse situations. Others were in far better, but it was no use to look at the lives of these others. The poor would remain poor. The rich remain rich. He would reach forty-three, pay off his debt, and either stay in the employ of the House Karling or find another great house willing to hire him on for food and board. Life would not change for him because life could not change for anyone. Sometimes older servants would talk of their youth when a pauper could become president, but most dismissed these comments as the gilded memories of the aged. Cobblers begat cobblers. Anglers, anglers. Tailors, tailors, and that was the way of the world.

"Don't you listen to these businessmen who tell you they started on the streets," George the cook, would tell him. "No pie-in-the-sky fairytales. Stick to what you are. That's where you belong. That's what you were made for."

James was a slave. They called him servant, and he saw no reason to waste his time wishing he were something else. Life was hard enough, and those few and fleeting covetous daydreams always filled him with the miserable awareness of his own impotence. He saw neither the pleasure nor practicality of dwelling on the disparities between Society and himself, and had mastered the art of enjoying his own meager and bland sustenance after serving at one of the House Karling's elaborate feasts.

His early boyhood had been filled with fantastical ambition, but it took only a year or two before these notions were beaten out of him and he had accepted the bitterness of reality in full.

And life isn't changing anytime soon, he thought as he stared up at the dark ceiling.

A servant shifted on the other side of the dormitory as James studied the textured plaster above. His companion on the bunk below whispered out an exhale, and an old servant who had almost passed the days of his usefulness filled the room with the buzz of a snore. Having spent two hours in his bed tossing and turning and hoping sleep would come, James was once more filled with the nocturnal frustration of consciousness as the clock at the end of the hall tolled eleven.

James sighed again and sat up in bed. He glanced about the room at the sleepers and over to the large French windows. Beyond the windows a tree twisted up an arms-length away. Beyond the tree, a fountain sat empty and lifeless three stories below, and beyond even that, the estate house sat far on the other side of the property.

The snore paused for a moment as James stared at the gnarly tree branch, but just as he began to hope for its end, the snore filled the room once more. And James, giving up on sleep for the night, slipped from his bed with his blanket wrapped about himself, trotted over to an old, worn-out armchair an old, worn-out servant had placed by the window, fell into it, and looked up at the moon, opalescent in the dark sky. Snowflakes, caught in the lunar light, drifted down like soft cotton balls.

George told him if there was ever an atomic war, the snowflakes would not be white.

"They'll be gray when it happens. The ash from the blast'll go up into the atmosphere. We'll have winters, long, hard winters. The crops'll die. People'll starve. Those gray snowflakes'll fall from the sky, and we'll have a gray world."

George always talked this way. He would be kneading dough or scrambling eggs or putting the finishing touches on a plate, and he would go on rambling about Armageddon. "God's judgment on the world is a thousand atomic missiles lighting up the globe red hot."

The other servants rolled their eyes and mumbled at the remarks, but James always saw the hint of doubt in their eyes, especially the older servants. Summer had lasted only a month following the conclusion of World War Two, and most blamed it on the nuclear activity. The Nazis had been the first of the nuclear powers to use the weapons. They had vaporized London, bringing Britain to its knees, established bases in Canada, and began a nuclear assault on the Atlantic coast. The United States responded with a no-prisoner policy, liberated the British Isles, and lit up Germany with radiation until the countryside was rendered uninhabitable. When Japan refused to surrender even with an all-out assault on its home islands, it was bombed into the stone age.

As soon as total victory was achieved on both sides of the globe, Russia swept through Europe and, from the Bering Strait to the Strait of Gibraltar, established the United Soviet Socialist Republic . . . save Britain, which somehow remained with its sovereignty intact.

And humanity limped along. And the summer that year only lasted a month.

~~~

The room filled with the static cadence of snores and the loud *tick–tock* of the clock at the end of the hall. James stared at the bright winter moon in an insomniac's stupor, and though he had expected it for fifteen minutes, the smiling ghostly apparition on the other side of the window sent shivers up his spine.

The apparition waved a bundle of something at James. The feeling faded, and the window swung open, allowing in the frigid winter wind.

Mackenzie was not a slave. It was true his mother had come to work off debt at the House Karling before Mackenzie had memory, that she had caught and succumbed to rheumatic fever, and left Mackenzie in servitude until the debt had been paid. It was true that another dictated the way in which he spent his time, his clothes were well-worn and the green of the lower class, and his schooling was minimal. It was true that Mackenzie was in the same extended servitude as James and wore the same mark of this servitude: a small ring through the tragi of his ear, but Mackenzie was not a slave. His life was devoid of all the privilege and pleasure of the emancipated, but he was the furthest thing from a slave James could imagine.

Mackenzie was a slave, but he did not see himself as one. He did not see himself as part of the lower class. Some rule amongst the servants had never gotten through to him to make him understand his place in society was permanent and his situation stationary.

James watched as the other boy slipped through the large window, and stood on the window seat to survey the room like a general looking over the devastation of a battlefield. "Ladies and gentleman," he called out to the sleeping bodies, and jumped as high as he could into the air. The window remained unclosed, and the winter wind still pricked at James' exposed skin.

Mackenzie's shoes, golden brown, pointed down as he fell toward the floor. Perfectly pressed, rich blue pants scrunched at his bent knees. His suit jacket billowed, and diamond-studded gold cufflinks glimmered as he brought his arms above his shock of blonde, almost white, hair. At seventeen, James Mackenzie Jacobe was handsome, carefree, and—although a servant—was a ubiquitous name on the lips of the city's youths.

Mackenzie was not a slave because he did not believe himself to be. All obstacles before him were minor inconveniences. Servitude was merely a temporary situation he would soon be rid of, and he saw the rigid class system as a challenge to be overcome and bettered by on his path to victory. What was his victory? What was the hope of his hope?

"Why couldn't I be president? What would stop me?" he had shot back when an older servant girl had scoffed at the verbal expression of his hopes and dreams.

"There's no changing what you are, Jacobe," the girl had said.

"I am going to be the president," Mackenzie had answered, relaxed surety filling his voice.

The girl laughed. "Talk to me in twenty years. We'll see how that's going for you. Hell, talk to me in fifty; we'll still both be here."

James did not laugh when Mackenzie expressed his aspirations. He was perhaps the only one who did not. He did not laugh, because he believed them. He believed them in part because Mackenzie said them with such confidence, but in greater part because Mackenzie as the president of the United States made sense to him. It fit into James' perception of what ought to be within the world.

Mackenzie was the best of the servants, excellent in his work not only because of his innate intelligence but also because of the careful dedication he put towards making it and himself excellent. When others saw no reason to speed through simple tasks, Mackenzie completed them as quickly as possible to free up even five minutes so he could study the etiquette of Society or hone a skill most saw as unfit for a servant to possess. When others coveted their sleep in the wee hours of the morning, Mackenzie would slip into the library and read every book he could get his hands on. Where others took little care, Mackenzie took the greatest care, as if even the most mundane and insignificant tasks would achieve him victory in the end.

And he had been rewarded for his hard work and unseen dedication by being given the honor of replacing Master Karling's personal servant when the age of his retirement became apparent. Mackenzie was the youngest to ever possess the station, and he was the youngest by more than a decade.

Mackenzie was filled with surety when he said he would be president and James was as well, because Mackenzie possessed something that James had never and could never hope to have. James could only ever describe it as greatness, a quality that bathed even the deepest places of the boy's being and ensured the success of even his fever-dream aspiration of becoming president.

It was for this reason that James never laughed, never scoffed, never leered in annoyance when Mackenzie said those words he said again and again as he did now:

"Stand and meet your new king!"

Mackenzie said he would be president, and if one knew him, there was no reason to doubt this statement. Mackenzie was bound to the House Karling, essentially a slave in situation, but Mackenzie was a free man where it mattered most.

"Shh, shh," James answered his proclamation. "Quiet, Mack," he whispered out. "You're going to wake everyone."

"Not you," Mack smiled over at him. "I'm a bit surprised you're awake."

"If I had anything to say about it, I wouldn't be," James replied. "There's too much noise to fall asleep in this room."

Mackenzie laughed and shook his head. "Sleep in the house," he answered. "The room next to mine is empty, and if you talk to Janice, she'll avoid putting guests in there for you. I've told you this before."

"Janice doesn't like me," James responded. "She'd rat me out for sure."

"I'd even talk to Janice for you," Mackenzie replied.

"Not worth getting caught. I'll wait until they invite me into the house like you," James said.

"Well, you better become a personal servant or get better at cooking, because those are the only two types of servants that the lunatic Karling lets live in the house these days." A smirk curled up on Mackenzie's face as he said the words.

"Mackenzie," James' voice held the acid of a rebuke, "that type of language'll get you whipped."

Mackenzie laughed through his nose. "What can I say? The man's gone nutty," he answered. "Maybe he'll take to riding as much as he's taken to eating at night, and he'll keep a stable servant somewhere in the house, if you have any luck."

James hushed him again and wrapped his blanket around himself more tightly to try to combat the winter wind that was blowing through the gaping window. "Can you shut the window?" he asked, but Mackenzie was preoccupied with dropping the bundle he was holding in James' lap.

"What's this?" James asked, cold wind still blowing across his exposed skin.

"Your clothes for the night," Mackenzie answered.

"I've already got clothes," he replied. "Can you close the window?" he asked again.

"Do you?" There was a lilt in Mackenzie's voice as he asked the question, and he walked over to James' chest of drawers and squeaked one open.

"Do you have any clothes that aren't green?" Mackenzie continued. The first drawer clapped shut and another slid open. "Or brown?" he continued. The second drawer shut, and Mackenzie opened a third. "Green. Green. Green, green, green." The drawer clanked shut. The final drawer opened. "Green. Green, green, green." Mackenzie chuckled under his breath. "Ope! Another brown." Then he sighed. "And five more greens."

"Your clothes are just as green. Besides, I like green," James said as he pushed himself to his feet, reached over, and pulled the window shut.

"No one likes green," Mackenzie replied.

"What's wrong with green?" James asked.

"James, James, James." Mackenzie reached over to the window absentmindedly and opened it with a quick flick of his wrist. The frigid wind blew in once more. "Green's the common man's color, and you can't be wearing commoner clothes tonight, James."

"I am a commoner," James replied.

"The question is, do you want to be?" Mackenzie answered. "All you need to do to not be one is put on these clothes and take out your slave ring."

"Servant identifier," James answered Mackenzie with the correct legal terminology for the ring in his ear.

"Well, James, I don't want to be a commoner," Mackenzie said as he pointed at his own ear. James did not see the ring that was always there, and he could not make out the hole in the ear where the jewelry should have been. "And tonight, James, I won't be."

James let out a quiet laugh. "And you call Karling crazy," he said.

"Master Karling," Mackenzie corrected. "A bit loose with the lips for one who's avoiding a whipping."

James shook his head and rolled his eyes. "I hate you," he said, turning to look out the window.

Mackenzie merely smiled. "No, you don't," he said, reaching into his pocket and retrieving a small, flat, rectangular object. "This is makeup," he continued. "Make sure you put it on your ear and try your best to blend it with your skin. But don't worry too much. Even if it is a bad job, no one will care. They all wear some type of makeup, and most do a terrible job with it." He placed the makeup on the arm of James' chair, reached back into his pocket, and pulled out a single cigarette. "Now," he placed the cigarette in his ear, "it's been fifteen minutes since the last time I've smoked. I'll be waiting at the bottom of the tree." With those words, Mackenzie slipped outside and out of James' sight without closing the window.

James sighed, swore, stood up, and slammed it shut. He glanced down the tree and saw Mackenzie already half way to the bottom with the cigarette already lit. James glanced back at the chair. The dry-cleaned tuxedo was draped over the back, and the makeup rested on the arm.

~~

James swung onto the tree with little trouble and perched on the branch just outside the window. James had never worn a tuxedo before and never imagined climbing a tree in one. The makeup had been the easiest part of the outfit; the bow tie the most difficult, to the point where it now hung around his neck untied.

And now I'm climbing a tree, James thought. *Of course.*

"I should grab a coat," he called down as he slid the window shut.

"No need. You'll be fine. Any more of a wait and we'll miss all the fun."

James shook his head, sighed, and hung a leg down in search of the next branch.

When they were twelve, nearly thirteen, they had made their first trip down the tree. On the final branch, Mackenzie had slipped and broken his arm. Despite his broken arm and a large cast, the next week Mackenzie climbed to the third-floor window, woke him, and made the precarious climb past the peeling paint of the servants' quarters to the ground.

James enjoyed the view from the top of the tree. In the distance was the Karling woods, once filled with boyhood forts and the cries of children. Closer was the drive and gardens which were beautifully manicured in summer but now covered in a thick blanket of snow. At one end of the drive was a large garage; at the other was the House Karling, stretching high into the moonlit night with its spires draped in snow and decorated for the Christmas season. Before him was the servants' quarters, a dorm-like, brick building tucked behind a row of pines which always reminded him of frail, old men with long, wispy beards.

To the west of the house and in front of the servants' quarters was the fountain inside the circular drive. James stared at the dry fountain as he dropped from the final limb to the ground. It had bubbled brilliantly the first time he had seen it, and he had once thought it one of the most wonderful things in the world.

Where's Dad? The question floated through James' mind.

"Where's Dad?" he had asked his mother on that long car ride.

"Gone on a trip," she lied, all emotion hidden in her face. "Gone on a trip," she said again, "and for the time being, you'll be staying with friends."

He remembered the rest of the car ride as a blur. The next clear link of memory was the car coming to a crunching halt next to the fountain and a small boy with a shining blonde head and a silver tie fluttering over his shoulder running past. James' mother left, never to return, without so much as a goodbye, and he did not sleep at all that first night.

Ten years, James thought. *Arrived in fall, so it has been a little longer than ten years.* James swore he still caught the sweet scent of blushing maple leaves. The day had been wet, the sun bright, the breeze warm.

As James reached the last branch of the tree, the memory unraveled and fluttered aimlessly like a flag on the desolation of an old battlefield.

Mackenzie sat on the stone bench at the foot of the tree. He stared across the yard at the lifeless fountain. A cigarette was between two of his fingers, and smoke twisted up into the branches above. As James hung from the last branch and dropped with a crunch to the ground, Mackenzie burst into loud laughter and stood up.

"What?" James asked. "I can't tie a bow tie."

"It's not that," Mackenzie said, shaking his head as he lit a new cigarette off the end of the one in his mouth.

"Wasn't expecting you to come." He flicked the remaining stub of the cigarette toward the fountain as he placed the new one in his mouth and paid no heed to the other as it came to rest after skittering across the crust of snow. James looked at the boy who, at six-five, towered over him and everyone else. "I had hope that you'd come, but I didn't think you actually would," Mackenzie continued with a smile.

"Well, I'm here, and I can't tie a bow tie to save my life," James answered.

Mackenzie motioned to the other boy. He reached out for the tie that hung around James' neck and tied it as he spoke. "It's not too big of a worry. Half of Society doesn't know how to tie a bow tie properly. Bit of a shame," he continued as he made a final few adjustments to the tie. "You look good otherwise. Feel free to relax."

James laughed. "Relax when I'm risking a fine for impersonating a member of Society? I'd like to be free before I turn seventy. I'm surprised you haven't been caught yet."

Mackenzie smiled and nodded. "Need a cigarette to calm your nerves, James?" he asked with a gesture toward the one in his mouth.

"I quit smoking," James said.

Mackenzie shook his head as he motioned for James to follow him, and the two began walking toward the driveway.

"For the new year?" Mackenzie asked.

"Since December 10th," James answered.

"And I haven't offered you a cigarette since then?" Mackenzie pulled the cigarette out of his mouth and tapped the growing ash into the snow.

"Guess not," James replied as the two boys stepped onto the drive. James noticed a long, black car idling with its lights off.

"I've heard of the scientific studies," Mackenzie said as he pulled open the driver's door. "But why in God's name would you give up the most perfect pleasure in existence?" Mackenzie slipped into the idling car and James was unable to reply until he had taken his seat on the passenger side.

"I've got a thing about dying," James said as the vehicle began to move.

"And I've got a thing about living." The car shifted into second as Mackenzie swung from the driveway onto the boulevard. "James," he spoke the name with a sigh, "you picked the worst time to quit smoking."

"You got me to come with you tonight. I don't see why it should bother you," James interjected.

"Yes," Mackenzie continued. "But tonight of all nights, on this New Year's Eve, the Bicentennial of the United States of America," he put great emphasis on the country's name, "it is proper, I say, right, I say, your moral obligation as a human being, to smoke with me. How many chances do you get to enjoy the ultimate pleasure on such an occasion?"

James shrugged and rolled his eyes. "Not many, I suppose." His words came out in a sarcastic drawl, and Mackenzie broke into laughter at the comment and glanced over.

James grunted and looked at the snow as it hit the windshield and melted into droplets. "Why did I climb down that tree?" he asked himself.

"Why?" Mackenzie answered. "You climbed down that tree because you're ready for a change. You're tired of the same old. Because you're sick of being a slave, a slave up here." Mackenzie pointed to his temple. "You climbed down that tree because this is a turning point for you, James, a ninety-degree turn to a different life that you cannot even begin to fathom."

James sighed. "No." He shook his head as he answered.

Mackenzie ignored him and continued.

"And why did you have to climb down that tree? Because nothing would change if you weren't the one to step out, if you weren't the one to change your behavior, to change the dead-end pattern you've been living in for sixteen years."

"No." James shook his head as he said the word again, but the word was swallowed up as Mackenzie continued.

"And what a wonderful evening it is, the moment of your rebirth. One day, when you're old and surrounded by grandchildren, full of age, full of wisdom, filled to the brim with all life has had to offer you, you'll look back on this moment, and you'll think, 'Mack was right. I could be whatever I wanted. I was only limited by my imagination,' and you'll know that you have to credit me with every accomplishment you ever made."

"You're insane, Mackenzie," James answered. "And going out tonight is insane. Take me back to the Karlings'."

Mackenzie's eyes opened wide. "Why would I take you back? We're almost there."

"Almost where? Where is this party anyway?" James asked impatiently.

"To the Phis'," Mackenzie answered as he nodded to a driveway in the distance.

"To the Phis', hmm? Why the Phis? Who are the Phis?" James asked. "How do you know the Phis?"

"They are extremely wealthy members of Society," Mackenzie answered. "Extremely. I know their son, Amadeus. And they throw the best parties around."

"You've been here before, then?" James asked as they turned into the driveway.

"No. I am responsible for planning the party. Every aspect of the party had to be okayed by me," Mackenzie answered.

"So, you and Amadeus are friends then?" The house came into view around the next bend, and James could tell in the dark that it was at least four times the size of the Karlings'.

Mackenzie laughed. "Amadeus Phi," he said the words slowly, "he is perhaps the worst person I have ever met in my entire life."

James squinted in confusion, and Mackenzie glanced over with a big grin on his face.

"But," Mackenzie continued.

"But?" James replied.

"Have you ever met an angel, James?"

James sighed as he felt the car slow as it approached the valet.

"Amadeus' sister is perfection personified. I can't even speak when I'm around her," Mackenzie finished.

"That'll be the day," James answered with a shake of his head.

The car crunched to a halt, and after the boys had exited the car the vehicle quickly disappeared down the drive.

When Mackenzie rang the doorbell, they heard a soft, muffled ding, but no one answered even after thirty seconds. The boys glanced at each other. Mackenzie rang again. Once more, no one answered.

James clicked his tongue and absentmindedly tapped his foot. "I'm guessing no one in the house can hear the doorbell." His foot stopped tapping.

"Amadeus would make someone wait whether he heard it or not," Mackenzie replied.

"You two must be amicable if you planned this party together." James' words bit with sarcasm.

"Amadeus is incapable of amicability," Mackenzie answered, his own foot beginning to tap with impatience.

The door swung open at the final word Mackenzie

spoke, and both boys turned to see a short, fat boy standing in the doorway. The fat boy squinted at the two through thick, Coke-bottle glasses, then slammed the door with a loud bang.

"Was that Amad—?"

"No," Mackenzie interrupted, "That was fat kid."

TWO

"The biggest mistake Society ever made was acting as if the rest of the country didn't exist."
— Alexander Viccor —

The servant who greeted them at the door with a "Masters," and bowed as they passed into the foyer was only a few years older than themselves and avoided eye contact at all costs. James understood the avoidance. His ears had been boxed more than once for failing to use the proper greeting or for staring at attractive female dinner guests.

"Masters?" James muttered as they stepped into the room.

Mackenzie smiled.

It was not the first time Mackenzie had been addressed as such, but before James walked through those doors he had never been called master, never been bowed to, and was only beginning to glimpse the vast differences between his world and Society's.

A servant was to be silent, to speak only when spoken to. Though a few members of Society engaged some to make sport of them (by asking one for a drink only to send it back five, six, seven times; or to ogle another and make comment after suggestive comment until one became bored, distracted, or got what one wanted—though it was seen as improper for a gentlemen to proposition any woman in public, a rash of scandals tore through Society in those latter years), most acted as if the servants did not exist, and servants were severely punished if they spoke even one unneeded word. A servant was to be unseen. If one was a good servant, one would go unnoticed until a need arose, take care of the need, and slip back into nonexistence. James knew this. Mackenzie knew this. Every servant knew this.

A servant's world was invisibility and toil; Society's was celebrity and leisure, and all those around basked in the slow pleasure of the place, especially Mackenzie. As a servant, these Society youths would not have given him a second glance, but here the whole room stopped as he entered. Every servant greeted him with the required bow of the head and "Master," and each Society youth turned toward him and paid some sort of homage as he passed, whether a mere nod of the head or his name on their lips: "Mackenzie Jacobe," always his first and last name.

"Isn't it wonderful?" Mackenzie asked as he put a big

arm around James' shoulders and swept him forward as they walked.

James pursed his lips as his eyes swept over the young faces. "They all know you," he replied.

Mackenzie nodded his head. "And why shouldn't they?" he answered.

"By your real name?" James continued.

"Why not?" Mackenzie shrugged, and a big smile curled across his face. "I am Mackenzie Jacobe. My parents live out west on a big estate in the middle-of-nowhere Montana. We're a small Society family, value our privacy, and I'm in the city for my education." Mackenzie rattled off the string of lies as if he believed them himself.

"But what if they check?" James asked. Nervous hesitation filled his voice.

Mackenzie shrugged. "No one ever checks, James. And I've been around long enough that no one ever will."

Mackenzie had been attending the parties of Society's youth since he was fourteen years old. It began on a whim. He wanted to experience a party as a Society member, so he had stolen a tuxedo that fit him and attended a party near the city center. The first three times he had merely observed the party-goers, studied them to learn how they functioned around one another, what language they used, their etiquette, and so on. By the fourth, he was playing drinking games with a group of girls. By the fifth, going to the parties had become a compulsion. Just as none of the youths knew him to be fourteen because of his stature, none knew he was a slave due to his charm. And in only a few short years, a party was not seen as legitimate unless Mackenzie attended.

"But what if someone does?" James continued.

"James, James," Mackenzie replied. "You are at the most extravagant party ever conceived by the adolescent mind. You need to figure out your Society name, not whether I am going to get caught. Unless you prefer to use your actual name, but I don't think Anderson is a very good alias."

"You use your real last name," James answered. "What's wrong with mine?"

"It's all in the auditory aesthetic. Jacobe has a ring to it, especially if you emphasize the French J, but Anderson? People believe a lie more when it sounds good," Mackenzie shrugged.

"Well, I've got to figure it out quickly, don't I, then?" James asked. After a moment of thought, he shook his head. "I don't know," he said. "I'm not good at this."

"Well," Mackenzie answered. "You could be a Dalimore . . . but no, being related to the president might actually raise some questions." Mackenzie grunted, and his hand went through his blonde hair in thought. "Heep? Hmm, but there's Heeps in the city, so that would be no good. There is a family who lived in this area until a few years back, had a boy who looked like you, friend of mine, members of Society. Rumor his father murdered him. You could be him back from the dead, really rock the boat. That would be good."

"What about another Jacobe?" James asked.

Mackenzie's mouth rolled down in a frown of thought, and his head danced back and forth with a bob as he considered the suggestion. "Could work." His head continued to bob back and forth in thought. His eyebrows went up. He looked over at James, and his mouth opened in a slight smile. "James Jacobe you are then, but we can't be brothers. I've already told everyone I'm an only child, but . . ." Mackenzie pursed his lips and put up one finger. "You're my cousin from Colorado."

"I'm your cousin from Colorado," James replied in assent.

"Then for the love of God, let's mingle."

The foyer swallowed the two boys, and James gaped at the grandeur of the room. Every surface gleamed with the blinding, heavenly radiance of marble, and a fringe of intricate gold trim displayed both the mythology of antiquity and a detailed journey of United States history from its founding to the present. Columns as big around as redwoods rose up out of the floor with the gentleness of water to meet chandeliers the size of small cars. High above, painted heavens fooled the eye into believing the room went on forever, and the gleaming, stoic eyes of great men from history stared down in uncaring curiosity, as if they were making quick inspection of how the living were managing the world they left below.

How's us being on the brink of nuclear annihilation for the past thirty years? James wondered up to them.

"The room has the same effect on everyone on their first visit," Mackenzie muttered into his ear. "You're not supposed to stare, but what is the point of the room, if not to look at it?"

"Did you stare your first time?" James asked.

"I never stare unless alone," Mackenzie replied. He laughed before continuing. "Society's got an odd habit of surrounding itself with beauty, ignoring it, and fawning over artistic monstrosity. You're respected more when you're apathetic about all this stuff." He motioned to the magnificence of the room.

"But why do they stare when they first walk in, then?" James asked.

"Why did you?" Mackenzie replied.

As they moved farther into the room, James noticed the walls were filled with countless paintings and the center of the room with countless display cases bearing any number of antiques: busts, blunderbusses, military uniforms, manuscripts, mummies, the legendary Franklin kite, the teeth of George Washington. Every step plunged them farther into the sea of bodies past oddity upon oddity.

Feels more like a museum than a home, he thought as they turned a sharp corner to where the room opened up, and he was confronted by a terror that would have certainly sent him running if not for Mackenzie's hand grabbing his forearm.

A shark. James told himself. *A shark.* He took a deep breath in as his heart thumped inside his chest. James' breath slowed, but a nervous tickle remained in his throat as he stared at the fish. Its tail propelled it forward. Its gills fluttered in and out, and its teeth stuck out of its mouth in an enormity of cluttered knives. James, of course, had seen pictures of the animal, but until now he never understood its size or the mindless ferocity in its glassy eyes.

"They have a shark," James breathed out to Mackenzie.

"They have a whole ocean," Mackenzie said, nodding to the aquarium that stretched the entire length of the wall. It teemed with the bright colors of ocean life, and James saw a dozen species of fish at a glance.

"Why a shark?" James asked as the shark moved out of his vision and the anxiety disappeared from his chest.

"They've got everything," Mackenzie replied. "Sea turtles. A dolphin. A squid."

"A squid?" James throat filled with thick fear as he imagined himself looking over the handrails of a ship and watching a beaked face rise out of the water followed by an enormous tentacle that wrapped the boat in its terrible embrace and pulled the whole vessel and himself under to those abysmal depths and a thousand unseen monsters.

"A squid, yeah," Mackenzie replied. "We can find it if you like."

James shook his head. Mackenzie shrugged in response

and led him to the other side of the room and out a door into the luscious green of a domed garden.

Smooth-faced boys in black tuxedos mingled with girls wearing colorful dresses. A dance floor was filled with couples in the midst of slow, leisurely, sensuous movement. Servants, barely noticeable even to James, flitted this way and that serving drinks and hors d'oeuvres to the partiers, and the music, a slow, rich jazz descendent of Benny Goodman and Glenn Miller, stitched the entire ensemble together.

"James Mackenzie Jacobe!" a boy called out across the garden as soon as he spotted Mackenzie.

"He knows your full name?" James asked as the boy moved toward them through the crowd.

"Well, it is my full name," Mackenzie replied.

James sighed and shook his head, knowing the decision had been made long ago and nothing could be done about Mackenzie's indiscretion.

"James Mackenzie Jacobe!" the boy said again, though this time he emphasized each name.

"Ami," was all Mackenzie gave him in reply, but the boy seemed satisfied with the greeting.

"James," the boy continued. "The party's been on for three hours. I expect you stylishly late, but I was beginning to worry you wouldn't come."

"I wouldn't come to the party to which all other parties will be compared?" Mackenzie replied.

The words made the other boy's face beam with a smile of pride.

"My cousin thought the time was an hour earlier," Mackenzie motioned toward James, "and I had to wait for him to get ready. Amadeus Phi, meet James Jacobe," Mackenzie continued.

As James and Amadeus shook hands, James became aware of the size of the other boy. Though he stood several inches shorter than Mackenzie, his arms were thick with muscles and his hands easily dwarfed James'. His shoulders were square, his chest barreled, and a large ugly head topped with thick, black hair protruded from his body.

"Another James Jacobe?" Amadeus' eyes rose in surprise. As Amadeus said the words, several boys who appeared to be Amadeus' entourage and others who had noticed Mackenzie stopped and sought to ingratiate themselves with him.

"My cousin," Mackenzie replied. "Named after the same grandfather as myself."

Amadeus nodded to James, "Pleased to meet you." His voice was slithery with ulterior motives. "Your cousin surprises us with you. It seems a special honor to meet one of his blood relatives."

"You'll find Mackenzie full of surprises," James replied.

Amadeus responded with a patronizing chuckle and turned his conversation to Mackenzie as if James did not even exist. It appeared it mattered little to Amadeus whether he was at the party or dead in in a ditch, even if he was Mackenzie's cousin. At first James felt the bite of annoyance, but soon saw that as others piped into the conversation, Amadeus never even glanced toward the sound.

I've been given a special honor, I suppose, he thought as he began to understand Mackenzie's distaste for the boy, who was only concerned with exploiting the lesser and impressing those in power. James, along with the rest of those around him, were of no use to Amadeus and thus ignored, but Mackenzie...

A smile grew on James' face as he watched the exchange between the two boys. Mackenzie replied with the refreshing, calm humility of a beloved emperor, and Amadeus danced about in sycophantic display as if Mackenzie was that emperor. James took great delight as this smug Society youth earnestly pandered, not to an emperor but a slave; but if Mackenzie derived any enjoyment from Amadeus' ironic groveling, none could be found in his expression.

"Did you hear of the Russians' program to shoot missiles out of space?" Mackenzie asked him.

Amadeus tilted his head in thought and looked as if he were choosing his words carefully "*If* it is true," he replied slowly. "They've got turmoil going on in their satellite states. Even if they do have the capability to nullify our nukes, I don't think they have the organization to do it."

Mackenzie paused to think and nodded his head. "Their satellite states aren't cooperating with them, but a stable Soviet government is better than an unstable one. No one wants a maniac or someone with ambitions of world conquest to seize power."

Amadeus stared off into the crowd in thought and nodded his head gently, reluctantly.

"Predictable people, Ami," Mackenzie continued his charade. "We want predictable people in the Kremlin, otherwise there's no knowing the damage they'll do."

"But wouldn't it be better with an unstable Russia?" a boy who had been listening asked.

Mackenzie brought up his hands in a half shrug. "In this current political climate, it would be a waste. The United States does not have the ability to exert influence in Russia. An unstable Russia can go anywhere with an unready America. It could crumble, or a leader like Churchill could come to power. Basic human psychology places people in the position to follow. One man with brains enough could throw our progress with Russia years into the past. We want a sure, strong future for the United States."

"And how do we do that?" another boy asked.

"Humans." Mackenzie placed a hand on the boy's shoulder. "Have you not heard of the pyramids, the roads of Rome, Europe's cathedrals, the Model T?" Mackenzie smiled. Those around nodded. "We are on the cusp of a revolution," Mackenzie continued.

They nodded for him to continue, hanging onto his every word, and Amadeus along with them.

Mackenzie's lips parted into a big smile of gleaming white teeth. "Humanity takes part in the creation of the world. Through our perceptions, thoughts, and actions, we conform the world to our image. We do not stumble into revolutions; we run headlong into them. The natural movement of mankind is forward."

"And what can we expect of this future?" James, who had so far been a bystander, asked. Though he had never doubted Mackenzie's capability to rise to the level of Society, he had never seen it, and was baffled by how well Mackenzie directed the conversation.

Mackenzie glanced over at James and raised his eyebrows slightly, betraying surprise. "Well," he said, "instant communication from anywhere on earth and maybe even from space. Cars running off water. The ability to regrow limbs. The entire library of human knowledge accessible to anyone from anywhere. Free energy. The abolition of poverty, starvation, and death."

One of the younger boys who had been listening stifled a laugh of surprise at his words and was quickly cuffed by an older member of the group. Mackenzie smiled at them with eyebrows raised. He laughed. "You think I'm going crazy," he said to the boy. "Within the next fifty years, you're going to see many of these become reality. All of them and sooner if I have anything to do with it."

James smirked and tilted his head. His eyes moved slowly across the glamor around him. "Mackenzie," he said. Mackenzie turned to face him. "How long do you plan on living?"

Several more boys echoed the sentiment before Mackenzie responded.

Mackenzie's eyes squinted in thought. A smirk still played across his face. "I wouldn't be doing very well if I didn't make it to a hundred and fifty. At least a hundred and fifty, if not more. My potential is only limited by my imagination." His eyes met each of theirs before catching James'.

"Jim," he said, "I think it is about time we find some more attractive and intelligent company." He gestured to a group of girls standing near the dance floor.

James shook his head and smiled as they left the other boys.

"Hello." Mackenzie's features softened as he addressed the girls. His face, no longer commanding, was that of one asking for an invitation indoors on a cold winter's night.

The girls looked at him all at once as he addressed them. Some smiled, while one or two whispered to each other.

"I haven't been here before," he continued, "and I was wondering if any of you happened to know where I can get a drink. The estate's a maze and quite confusing."

One laughed, and big smiles spread across the rest of the faces. "Mackenzie Jacobe, we know who you are," one of the girls replied.

"That doesn't work on us anymore," another continued. "Just like it didn't work last time."

"It didn't work, did it?" he asked, a smile flitting through his fiery eyes. "From what I recall, we had a great time."

Several of the girls laughed.

Mackenzie shrugged. "How are you alone right now? Ten beautiful girls and no guys. I can't believe it."

"Oh, Mack, you tried that last time too."

"But it's true." Mackenzie's face was filled with incredulity. "And it's a shame."

The girls smiled at him.

"No one's gotten drunk enough," a blonde girl in a red dress said.

Mackenzie shook his head like a disappointed parent and sighed. "Well, I guess I shouldn't complain." An arm went around James' shoulders. "Have any of you met my cousin yet?" he asked.

The girls shook their heads.

"Call me James." James nodded toward each one of them with a smile. Anxiety thickened in his chest as he spoke.

"We were named after the same great-grandfather." Mackenzie interrupted. "He's out to visit, thinking of moving here permanently."

James shrugged. "We'll see." He swallowed and glanced up at the soft, inspecting eyes staring back. Pleasure bubbled from his feet to the top of his head.

Although he enjoyed their smiles and nods, he felt like he was a small boy who had suddenly slipped into deep water and had never learned to swim.

"Where are you from?" one of the girls asked. James looked over and, stunned by the girl's beauty, did not know how to respond. Mackenzie nudged him. "Um," James shook his head. "Denver," he said and forced himself to smile at the girl.

"Oh," the girl answered quickly. "We go skiing in Colorado at least twice a year. Do you ski?"

"My parents ski, but I've never been very good at it. They go all the time and want me to come, but the skill has always eluded me," James answered.

The girl laughed. "Well," her eyebrows raised, "Mackenzie always refuses me. Next time I'm in Colorado you should take a weekend with us, and I'll teach you."

James laughed back at her. The nervous tightness in his chest began to leave. Lying was surprisingly easy. He found solace in the fantasy. No one wanted to (or could) know about James, servant in the House Karling. But James, cousin of Mackenzie, was an interesting, never-mentioned mystery.

"If Mackenzie gets his way, I won't be in Colorado much longer," he answered the girl.

"Why should that stop you from coming?" Her eyes gleamed over at him, and the knot in his chest returned.

He laughed through his nose, but the enjoyment he felt only a moment before began to fade. "I suppose I could." His voice lacked the same ringing interest as before. He knew little to nothing could come of it, and he knew even if something did, it was a dangerous road to travel.

"Why hasn't Mackenzie ever mentioned you before?" she asked.

James looked around to solicit Mackenzie's help, but he was nowhere in sight. James shook his head and swore aloud, though relief filled him. "I'm sorry." He looked into the girl's eyes, studied her face one last time, and wished reality away. "Mackenzie does this all the time. I've got to find him because he tends to leave me places when I visit. I'll be right back."

The girl nodded, and James moved through the crowd pretending to look for the other boy. He was in no danger of being left behind. Mackenzie had given him the keys when they arrived for this very reason.

James knew he did not belong here. This was not his music. He had never tasted food so rich. These were not his clothes. He was the servant. These were the masters. These were the protagonists, he was an extra: barely seen, unheard, and unnamed. A million thoughts, perhaps more, had been focused on each one of these young people. Every need, every wish, every hope and dream had been attended to, but he had no parent to give him even one word of direction in life and had fed from the disregarded detritus. He was a nobody in a flood of somebodies. They would go down in history, and he would be forgotten a week after he was lowered into the ground.

James let out a loud sigh when he was out of sight of the girl and leaned against a wall. He had seen the door to his left and recognized it immediately. *A slave passage,* he thought, and he felt comfort in the thought. His mind eased as he studied it, smaller than the main doors, unadorned, inconspicuous. Familiar. He glanced at the crowd before he reached for the knob, but he realized no one would care if he entered the passageway. He was a Society youth tonight, and the limits he had were very few. The door opened to a narrow passage. The image of the girl passed through his mind. Anxiety rose up in his chest, and he shook his head again.

After several twists and turns in the darkness, the passage opened to a wide, bright, carpeted hallway. A boy and girl passed as he exited. The girl led the boy by the hand. Her eyes were sharp. Her voice laughed out. Both disappeared into the first room they found.

James followed the hallway until he no longer saw any partygoers. He ascended the second set of stairs he found, and, after opening several doors he stumbled onto a landing that overlooked the garden and had a small spiral staircase that seemed to twist all the way to the roof.

Filled with delight, he tramped up the staircase with his eyes studying the party on the far side of the garden and was startled to see a girl leaning on the handrail at the top.

"I'm sorry. I didn't realize anyone was up here," he said and stopped two steps from the top.

She smiled at him.

"I can leave you alone," he continued.

"No," she replied gently, "it's fine," and turned to look below at the crowd.

As he ascended the final steps of the staircase and leaned against the rail near her, he took note of her appearance out of the corner of his eye.

"I love it up here, especially during parties," she said. "I thought I was the only one who knew about it." A hand went up to push her hair out of her face. "I suppose I'm not."

She was not beautiful but the charm in her voice was so rich James barely noticed. She wore a scarce flirtatious smile. Her eyes examined the garden in eager wonderment. She hummed a few notes and then sighed. "The music is better up here. It's always better up here." She hummed a few more notes with the band.

"Why's that?" James asked after a few moments.

He saw her look over with a thought-filled face. She bent her upper body, rested her chin on her hand, and smiled. "Sounds like a dream." She let out a tiny laugh. "It sounds like the wind is singing."

James grunted and glanced over at her. She caught his eye. "You don't agree?" she asked.

He answered after a moment of studying her face. "I

don't know," he replied. "I've never really thought about it."

"I had a nurse whose husband would play the violin, and you could hear it from the house. It always reminded me of some long-forgotten story. I wasn't at home; I was looking out of a little window over sprawling Napoleonic Paris."

James forced a smile at her comments, but he had no idea what she meant. What was Napoleonic? Where was Paris? How did Paris look? He almost laughed at his own ignorance.

"Scarlet." She nodded toward him. "My name is Scarlet."

James swallowed, deciding whether or not he was going to lie. "James." He nodded back.

"We must have missed each other the other times you were up here." She looked down at the party.

"I've never been here before," he answered and followed her eyes down to the dance floor.

"Well, you don't look like anyone I know." A delicate hand reached up to her temple and curled a small lock of hair around a forefinger as if she had drifted away into her thoughts.

"I'm not anyone you know," he laughed.

"I must know someone you know; I know most everyone," she replied.

"Mackenzie Jacobe?" James asked.

She smiled big and cocked her head. "Everyone knows

Mackenzie." James nodded. "How do you know him?" she asked.

He laughed through his nose. "We're friends."

"Not from around here though?" She glanced over to James as she asked the question. Her dark hair was still curled around a finger. "I'd know you if you were from around here."

James pursed his lips. He shook his head. "I don't feel as if I'm from much of anywhere."

She laughed. "I've never heard anyone in Society make a comment like that."

James smiled back. *That's because I'm not Society,* he thought, but he knew he could not tell her that. Though he had not lied to her yet and found he did not want to lie to her, he could not tell her the truth. With the other girl far below, the one concerned with skiing, the lie was a thrill, but with this girl . . . She had a certain quality in her voice, in her bearing, a certain pure sincerity in her eyes. He wanted to tell her nothing but truth. But the truth was that he was a slave, and it was a truth he could not tell. In another world, truth would abound. Perhaps something more would come of the serendipity of their meeting, but not in this reality, only in his dreams. *That's because I'm a slave,* he wanted to tell her. "That's because everyone in Society knows where they belong," he said instead.

She laughed again and once more turned to look at the crowd. "Where do you belong?" she asked.

"I don't think I'd be up here if I knew the answer." He forced a weak smile.

"What's your last name, James?" she asked.

James sighed. He did not want to say Jacobe, because it was a lie, but he knew he couldn't tell her it was Anderson.

"Why are you up here?" he asked, as if he had not heard the question.

"I don't enjoy crowds." She shrugged.

"A member of Society who doesn't enjoy crowds!" James could not help but smile.

She looked at him again. "Speak for yourself." She gave him a gentle nudge.

He shrugged at her, and both looked back at the crowd.

As they each studied the people below, James was disappointed to hear the click of the door closing and the soft tap of feet climbing the stairs. Both turned to see Amadeus appear around the bend in the stairs. "Scarlet!" He shouted as soon as he saw her. "I've been looking everywhere for you! You've given me a heart attack!"

She gave James a final grim glance. "Well, we'll meet again, James, and I'll get that last name from you then. For now, I need to attend to my date," she said to him softly, so Amadeus would not be able to hear.

James nodded, and the girl moved swiftly toward the steps.

"I just needed a break, Amadeus," she said to the boy.

Amadeus said something rough under his breath and

gave James a brooding glance, but no recognition flashed in his eyes.

The two clattered back down the stairs. The door slammed, and James sighed as the final tonic of the song drifted through the night like a dream, just as the girl had said.

"Friends!" The word from the other side of the room was clear and distinct to James. "Tonight!" James watched as the crowd parted, and the tall, thin figure of Mackenzie climbed onto a table and turned to study the crowd.

James swore under his breath as he saw the boy, and the crowd quieted to less than a whisper. "This is unbelievable," James muttered to himself, and a smile formed on his face.

"Tonight," Mackenzie continued in a voice like a bright trumpet, "we will celebrate the first moments of our bicentennial. From 1776 to today, we stand as the greatest hope of freedom for the world." The emotion began to build in his voice. The crowd cheered.

Two hundred years, James thought as he glanced into the past. It stretched behind him like a tunnel of small stages. Most were blackened by ignorance, but several played out in lively color. American rebels dumped tea into the Boston harbor. Washington crossed the Delaware. "Four score and seven years ago ..." Dalimore elected. "With great heaviness and sorrow, I regret to inform you that the Nazi war-machine has made nuclear strikes on New York City and Washington D.C." Finally, victory in Europe.

Nuclear annihilation of Japan. Two hundred years wrapped up in now. Every hour not existing without the last.

"Our futures are bright." Mackenzie cleared his throat. "As the mob says, 'There's only one way to swing a cat.' And there's only a way to swing an inheritance of millions." The crowd laughed. Mackenzie's face beamed with a smile. James wondered whether Mackenzie found more pleasure in the positive response to his words or that fact that he, a slave, had such a vast influence over Society's youths. "This future we hold in our hands is one vastly different than that of our parents and grandparents. Two world wars? The threat of a nuclear holocaust? Soviets on the moon? But let's not be so grim." A chuckle filled up the garden.

"Let us not see our future as some do, as a cloud of uncertainty, because the future is not uncertain. We know the future. It is in us. It is in our hearts. It is in our minds. It is in our dreams. By our vision, with our hands, through our inspiration, we shape the world. We steer the ship in the direction we deem fit. We are divinely appointed to guide the nation and usher in a new age. Let us make it a good one. Let us make all our dreams a reality: instant communication, mass travel as fast as sound, simulated reality, limb transplants, human augmentation, and perhaps even the abolition of death."

Mackenzie smiled and pointed to the clock. "Now, join me in ushering in another year and another age for this great American Republic." The whole crowd cheered, and all waited for those final seconds until the new year.

James watched as Mackenzie reached into his coat to retrieve his cigarette case. His face was filled with calm as he lit one. His eyes were hopeful. As the crowd stood there with their thoughts, Mackenzie took his time. A tall cloud of smoke ringed his head like an infernal halo as he lifted his hand and pointed at the grandfather clock built into the brick wall above the crowd. For a moment, there was complete silence.

~~~

"Ten!"

The air in the courtyard was as warm as summer. Above, the snowflakes settled on the dome. The cold moon beckoned from a distant, icy world. The courtyard itself glowed in the firelight.

So, this is the bicentennial, James thought as his tongue pressed against the roof of his mouth. *Two hundred years?* His eyes glanced at those below him. Bodies were coiled springs, limbs animated with electric emotion. James sighed and shook his head.

~~~

"Nine!"

Mackenzie stared across the crowd. Faces gleamed with life. They—by birth, by status, by upbringing, by wealth—would be the next generation of kings. These hundred or so youth would wield power the lower classes could not conceive of, and yet here he was. And that was something.

"Eight!"

History led up to this point. The first men established cities. Hammurabi wrote a law code. Civilization sprang up along the Fertile Crescent. Empires rose. They became masters of the world. Romulus killed Remus. The barbarians sacked Rome. The barbarians became Roman. The barbarians became Christian, and Rome once more became an empire until people, ordinary people, toppled it and with words, no less.

And welcome to the modern era.

Men sought liberty. Men sought freedom and sailed to an unknown land of unknown people. History, a divine domino line, had progressed from a rebellion against the most powerful empire on earth through a civil war and two world wars to this point, to this pinprick of the present.

~~

"Seven!"

Mackenzie watched as each of the dominoes fell. He imagined his family, poor, arriving on boats. His great-grandfather worked himself to death. His grandfather was a scholar. His father bankrupted them and killed himself. His mother sold herself into servitude. And now here he was, another link in this long chain of individual minds.

He was another domino falling, trying to build something lasting before he fell flat.

An exhilarating, lightning-speed ride from birth to death, and he was enjoying every minute of it.

~~~

"Six!"

James' eyes turned away from the crowd and back at the clock. Memories spun in his mind: the image of a man standing above him. *A father?* he thought. *My father?* But the man's face was a blur. This father was glimpsed through the curved, clouded glass of time.

Life was not a neat arrangement of dominoes with one pushing over the other to create an intricate pattern. It was not parts in a great cosmic machine. As James saw it, it was cold, savage elemental forces, unfeeling chance. The wind tore his father from him. The cold killed his mother. He never had grandparents. He came from nothing and nowhere. The universe was not orchestrated. It played no tune. And the greatest artist in his life was death.

~~~

"Five!"

Mackenzie allowed his eyes to wander to the crowd once more. His eyes paused on each person he knew as he replayed the memories he shared with them. One to another to another his eyes moved, brief cinematic features in his mind, before moving on. A patchwork of souls sewn into his own.

Happiness shot from the tips of his toes to the top of his head. He could not help a smile curling up on his face, and he broke into a loud laugh.

Everything had led up to this moment, and everything was beautiful.

~~~

"Four!"

And now we are here, James thought. *All the chaos has led to more chaos.*

~~~

"Three!"

And the future is open. Mackenzie plucked the cigarette from his mouth. A fantastical vision of the future played in his mind, bright gleaming, gold and glittering.

And the future is free.

~~~

"Two!"

James looked to the place where the girl had stood. He thought he still smelled her perfume in the air. *Life is just this moment. Nothing before, nothing after.* His lips pursed. *One spinning, continuous, unchanging moment.*

~~~

"One!"

The future is mine. Mackenzie's teeth broke from beneath his lips as if the words were the thunderous crack of sudden inspiration.

~~~

"Happy New Year!"

The room exploded with a scream. James' mouth did not move to speak the words. His eyes focused on the clock even as its second hand ticked on past the new year.

Nothing else exists except that moment. His eyes stared up through the dome, past the clouds and the atmosphere, into the frozen blackness surrounding the world on every side, a blackness punctuated by the lonely, blazing light of the party.

THREE

———

"We are all looking for an escape. There isn't one."
– Eli Torte –

Dogs barked. He heard the men laugh. "We've got a fast one here," a voice said.

Have they started? he thought. David's legs were becoming stiff and heavy as he ran. His breath wheezed in and out. Each inhale was a hand grabbing his lungs and tearing. A world of cold and snow, of howling wind and swimming shadows, spun before him. The night was ferociously cold, the mercury dropping at least ten degrees below zero. The whipping wind folded the temperature in upon itself until it grasped the negative-thirty-degree mark. Sweat ran down his neck, back, and face in freezing rivulets.

Although he ran in an open field, he felt the clutch of claustrophobia. He was still stuck in a cell, still running in circles. Though he fought with all his might to escape, he ended where he started. Hope felt like an illusion. The dark behind was overpowering. The city lights ahead were only bulbs stuck into a cardboard prop piece.

David looked from the ground to the skyline. His eyes began to water from the whipping wind, and the horizon turned to streaks of hidden dark and blinding light. His eyes returned to the ground, and he reached up to wipe away the tears and sucked in a deep, sobbing breath as his heart spun with fear.

He had not felt fear in a long time. After he was thrown into the cell, his life was uprooted. A low buzz of fear wormed its way into his stomach, and he slowly shrank until he would barely be noticeable inside a thimble.

And then nothing.

He was gone. Life, the world, all of existence was a thin veneer painted over a charred frame. There was no hope of reprieve. Every night was followed by another day of agony and then nothing. The fear disappeared and everything else with it.

One of the men laughed. The laugh echoed in his mind, tranquil autonomy juxtaposed against miserable, anxious subjugation.

Should I stop? he asked himself. His eyes filled with liquid lamentation. The frigid, mindless, whipping wind answered, and for a moment, anxious fear overwhelmed and gnawed at him.

One leg seized into a cramp. His side split from

dehydration. Pain tore into his lungs like a barbed hook. He had eaten only a crust within the last twenty-four hours, and he felt faint. The wind seemed to whip stronger and the cold grow harsher. Together they grabbed him until it felt as if even his bones were exposed to their icy hands.

I could stop, he thought. *I could lie down.*

A gust of wind whipped his face.

Won't they catch up eventually?

He closed his eyes.

A quick fifteen minutes of agony and then sleep, deep, ignorant, and eternal. The thoughts flickered in his mind like an old, worn light bulb, like a frail radio signal in a storm.

His legs stopped.

He looked up at the dark sky. He stared at it for a moment and shook his head slowly as the dogs snarled nauseatingly close.

No. The word was a firebrand. The thoughts plaguing his mind scattered as he gritted his teeth and ran toward the city lights up ahead.

FOUR

———

"The United States is divided into four classes. The first class is Society, a small group of elites consisting of only a hundredth of a percent of the population, yet controlling 99.99 percent of the industrial complex and 100 percent of the government."
– Amherst Rhodes, *Life in the USA* –

The garden was exuberant with shouts. Tambourines rattled. Noisemakers bleated. Confetti and balloons fell from the ceiling, and one youth let out a long blast on a trumpet he had found in another room.

James leaned against the handrails of the balcony and watched Mackenzie down below as the boy carefully, quietly dropped his cigarette in one drink and lifted another drink to his lips. The boy looked up at the blackness of the dome above and appeared to wink before saying those few unheard words: "Ladies and gentlemen," and then he leapt from the table. The tails of his coat fluttered up. Alcohol sloshed from the glass; a smile was painted on his face. James swore he could almost hear his feet hit the dance-floor.

Ladies and gentlemen. Ladies and gents. Gentle lady-men. The finest of my people. And Mackenzie's favorite, *Girls, girls, girls.* The variations on the phrase flashed through James' mind. Mackenzie had used them all on different occasions and surely made up more when James was absent, but even though those three words of greeting often varied widely, the phrase that followed varied not in the slightest, not even in inflection.

"Stand and meet your new king!"

James saw Mackenzie say the words, though he could not hear them from his lips. And James knew Mackenzie had said the words because he always did and always would, to the end of time, to his dying breath, whether he had a mind to speak any other intelligible thing or not.

For now, the words were trapped in the irony of a slave's tongue, but James knew that they would one day be spoken by a ruler. On that future day, Mackenzie's past would not matter. It would not matter whether anyone knew he was a slave or not. No one would care where he came from; they would only care who he was. Yes, one day James would taste those sweet words on his ears and a king would be crowned. As he watched Mackenzie land, as he watched Mackenzie speak, as he saw the slight grin on his face, he believed it would be the case. At least for Mackenzie.

Of course, for Mackenzie, he thought. *What other future could possibly exist?*

As James watched the other boy pick another cigarette out of his pocket and his blonde head disappear back into the mansion, the thought of the future lingered. As James made his way from the balcony, as the slow drawling jazz of the old year went away and was replaced by the fast rhythms of 1976. As he passed youths of Society, as their calculated conversation was replaced by joyous shouts, as decorum was replaced by drinking contests, sobriety by drunkenness, and order by disarray, he was left to choose his fate. Society did not exist, and he was not a slave. A future existed where he could go anywhere, say anything, do anything, sweep the girl on the balcony off her feet. In those moments, he watched the youth of Society slip ever into entropy, and he tasted a little of a daydream he had sworn he would never allow himself to taste. And for that brief vaporous time, he understood the hope of Mackenzie.

The feeling did not last long, and, as he turned back into the gleaming foyer, he saw the stark reality of his place in Society and the laughable quality of his fantasy.

"The strongest drink you've got," he told one of the servants as hope turned to ash in his chest.

And if my wishes are laughable, aren't Mackenzie's? James' face turned dark at the question as he received his first drink. He was both disturbed by the insinuation and surprised he had never asked it before. If his wishing was absurd, did Mackenzie dwell in a constant absurdity?

James threw back the drink and beckoned for another. He pursed his lips as he gagged down the liquor and a cloud of depression descended with the thought. Mackenzie was perhaps the best of anyone he had ever met. If anyone deserved to be president, he did; and if anyone could reach beyond his station, rise above the rigid Society structure of this age, it was Mackenzie.

James was alright with never being more than a servant himself, but he realized that he was not alright with Mackenzie remaining one. If Mackenzie could make the leap to be something else than what he was, it was hope enough for him, but if Mackenzie could not be anything other than what he was . . .

An image filled his mind as he finished one drink then another and another, and he saw Mackenzie grow into an old man. He still wore the clothes of a servant. His back was stooped. His walk was tired. The hope had escaped him, and those fiery, intelligent eyes that had always burst with a thousand brilliant ideas were now gray, flat and defeated, filled with frustration and apathy.

James could not abide the thought and motioned for another drink, but still it lingered as he slipped further and further into inebriation. Old Mackenzie. Defeated Mackenzie. Mackenzie as good as dead. Mackenzie better off dead.

James threw back the rest of his drink. He swore under

his breath as the clarity of his vision shrank to the size of a small circle. He swore again and fell heavily into a couch. Though he tried to push the thought from his mind, it would not go away.

"James!" His name, accompanied by the rough shake of his shoulder, startled him. His eyes flashed open, and he sat up.

Mackenzie stood over him. James smelled the scent of some flower waft from the other boy.

"Any luck?" James asked as Mackenzie sat down.

"It depends on what you mean by the question," Mackenzie replied.

"It depends on what you've been up to," James answered.

Mackenzie breathed a short laugh out of his nose, but his lips did not curl into a smile. His hand moved through his hair, and he scanned the crowd, noting a group of girls. James recognized some from before.

"It went well then?" he asked. He glanced at Mackenzie. James lingered on those bright eyes, remembered that there was still time, and reminded himself that Mackenzie was not a tired, defeated old man yet and would not be one.

"I always fall into a group of girls at these things," Mackenzie responded.

"I always fall into a group of myself, but it tends to not be at these things," James replied.

Mackenzie turned from the crowd to him before replying. "Any luck with that?" he asked.

James laughed but said nothing.

"I see you're indulging a little," Mackenzie continued, pointing to James' drink while his eyes moved from James to the clock. "How many?" he asked.

"Five or six." James paused to think. "Eight or nine." His eyebrows knitted in thought. "I'm ready to go home," he added.

"So soon?" Mackenzie mocked surprise.

James sighed. "Well," he bent his head back to look at the clock, "it is um, three, six, nine." James looked back at Mack and shrugged his shoulders. "Late," he said. "It's late, I think."

Mackenzie smiled. "Okay, okay." His hand reached into his pocket. "But next year." He paused to search several other pockets. "Next New Year's Eve," he amended as he smiled and pulled out a cigarette, "you need to stay with me." His fingers fiddled with the cigarette a moment until it rested in his left hand between the middle and forefinger. "Less booze, more girls. None of this drinking by yourself." Mackenzie placed the cigarette between his lips. "For now, though," he continued, "I'm dying for a smoke and some fresh air, and you'll soon be dying to have a private place to blow chunks."

"Oh, I don't feel sick," James replied as he pushed himself up from the couch.

Mackenzie threw up his hands and turned to James.

"We'll see." He placed the cigarette in his mouth. "Everyone's born. Everyone dies. Everyone hurts. Everyone wants success and love. And everyone, absolutely everyone, pukes their guts out the first time they drink that much 80-proof bourbon."

FIVE

———

"The second class (referred to as 'the mob' by Society) lives in the extreme poverty of slums."
– Amherst Rhodes, *Life in the USA* –

David counted his footfalls as a few dim, flickering lights of shanty-homes beckoned him forward. *One-two-three.*

He was small again, barely more than a toddler. His legs moved with less sure-footedness. His father was before him, a much younger version of his father, slimmer, happier. Phantom arms wrapped around him and picked him up into the air. A cake with candles. A fireplace. Nestled on a couch. Almost disappearing into the cushions.

Four-five-six. The peace lasted for a moment. He felt it in his chest, a warm looseness, but it faded as fast as purple lights in the eyes after the blindness of a flash bulb.

———

His pace quickened and did not slacken again as other memories began to dance through his mind.

The bright area of thought above his eyebrows was a kaleidoscope of memory: a pregnancy, a sister, excitement, disillusionment, boarding school, happiness, sadness, loneliness.

Seven-eight-nine. He pushed all the memories down. They no longer mattered. Some would say the past explained him, but its determination was never wanted. *Who cares who I was back then? Who cares about anything back then?* The thought slipped into his mind. *I don't even care.*

Pain in his lungs trickled into his mind, screaming at him to stop moving, but he pushed it down.

Ten-eleven-twelve.

A controlled breath in.

Thirteen-fourteen-fifteen.

A slow breath out.

Sixteen-seventeen-eighteen.

The rhythm of his feet and the sound of his lungs had already consumed his consciousness when the teeth broke through the skin of his right calf. The chaos of pain broke into the world he had ordered, the world of footfalls and breathing and movement. The pain ran hot up his leg. He tried to shake the dog off, but its teeth were latched on tight and ready to tear.

David stopped. He grabbed the dog by the neck and squeezed to the end of his might. Fear fluttered in the back of his throat. *Faster! Faster. Come on. Come on.* The words raced through his mind as he squeezed. *No time for this.* He felt tears in his eyes, tears of anger, red-hot, mindless anger.

He heard the other dogs draw near. Men's voices were not far behind, but he only swore at them. He damned them all to Hell. He would kill all the dogs; he would go down swinging, wrench the gun from one of the men's hands, and blow both of their heads off.

David's teeth clenched until his jaw hurt, and anger almost completely overpowered his conscious mind. The dog stood between himself and freedom, and at that moment, he had no desire to do anything but destroy it completely.

To kill it.

His fingers squeezed around the dog's neck until they hurt. He felt the windpipe collapse, and the dog let go. Breath wheezed from its lungs. It staggered, and David pushed it to the ground. He looked at it as its breathing whistled, its chest rose slowly, and its eyes flitted back and forth. David brought up his foot and slammed it down upon the dog's ocular ridge until he felt the bone give way beneath his heel. Even after the bone had broken, his leg came up and continued down again and again in automatic fury until its body slumped into the snow.

Another body flashed through his consciousness. Her face was branded in his mind. Her eyes, which had been alive with fear only moments before, stared over at him and into his soul. Though he had only glimpsed them, they continued to haunt him.

"It's my birthday," the cooing, quiet, gravelly voice echoed through his bones, a voice as strong as a browned leaf in the fall. "My birthday."

The dogs barked. *So close*, he thought, but for a brief second his face was heavy with sad lethargy.

"Do you think anyone cares about your birthday?" The dogs snarled as the voice barked through his mind. He heard the vicious slap across her face. Another more ruthless slap knocked her to the ground.

"You don't have a birthday anymore!" the voice growled out. "You don't exist anymore!"

David tried to stop the scene from playing in his mind, but as it faded to black, he heard her ribs crack under the force of a boot.

David's calf was still fiery with pain as he landed on the other side of the fence, and he felt blood trickle down his leg into his shoe.

He took a moment, the briefest, to pause and peer back through the links across the black expanse of nothing to see the ghetto in the moonlight. Flashlights moved like drunken searchlights over a hundred yards off, and just behind him, the other two dogs crashed into the fence yelping.

David swore under his breath, darted from the fence through a narrow alley, and burst onto a road. As his eyes adjusted to the light, his feet clopped on pavement. Blood coursed through the veins of his head. His arms pumped, and his eyes moved back and forth as he searched for an avenue of escape.

A mere house-distance away, the fence rattled. The dogs snarled, and one of the men swore, a loud, irate profanity that rang in David's ears and sent a flutter of fear into his throat.

"Bad sport, pig," the other's raspy, cigarette-tempered voice called out. "Bad sport," he grunted. "When I catch you, you'll wish you were dead." Then he laughed, a long, pure delighted, childlike, libertine laugh. His wicked smile flashed through David's mind. The man laughed again, and the world stopped. David's feet did not hit the ground. Sweat glistened on his forehead. Blood pooled in his shoe. His tattered clothing flapped out to his side like wings, and the icy wind blew through the large, torn seams. The dogs' barks blended into a single chord. Big heavy snowflakes dotted the sky. The man's laugh echoed. It sprang from the lips like a whirlwind, and it chased after David like a banshee.

The echoing memory of the woman's voice screamed through his mind. "It's my birthday," she mewled.

"You don't exist anymore!" the man growled. The thud of a boot against skin. Again. Again.

The animal-yelp of agony.

Another thud.

Cracking ribs, a snap, a crunch.

"Thud, thud, thud!" Ferocious silence. A slow exhale. And then that laugh.

The thud of the boot again.

Faster and faster David ran. Darkness ran down the windows of his mind, and everything inside turned black. His mind raced as the man's voice filled his ears. David was filled with echoes from a past of dreams, pieces of life sewn into a tatter of thought. The voices of relatives accompanied teachers, accompanied peers, parents, companions. The disjointed thought was sewn together by mindless fear.

SIX

"The third class are the slaves. Though this group is referred to as 'servants' within the United States and by law slavery is illegal, these individuals have entered into the permanent employ of Society members by way of bankruptcy and the Indentured Act, in which a person is legally bound to another for an allotted amount of time or until the debt has been paid."
– Amherst Rhodes, *Life in the USA* –

"Didju, uh, enjoy your time at the party?" Mackenzie asked. The clarity of articulation and the Societal lilt left his voice as he spoke. A cigarette bobbed in his mouth.

James shrugged. "If I enjoyed dwelling in the impossible . . ." He did not finish his thought as he stared at the big, melting snowflakes on the windshield and the last of Society's mansions.

"A thing is only impossible if you believe it to be," Mackenzie replied.

James laughed out of his nose. "Perhaps." He paused after the slow word and swallowed. "And perhaps what is possible for you may not be possible for everyone else."

Mackenzie shook his head and plucked the cigarette from his mouth to speak. "Do you want to be a slave?" he asked.

"It's all I've ever known," James answered.

"Do you enjoy it?" Mackenzie placed the cigarette in his mouth and gripped the steering wheel with both hands as they turned a corner. The drooping houses of the poor rose up along the road.

"I don't see whether it matters if I enjoy it or not," James replied.

"Well, do you ever wish?" James could hear the slight annoyance in Mackenzie's voice. He was growing irritated at the evasion of his questions.

James sighed. "I try to live the best I can within my role."

Mackenzie laughed. He glanced at James. His hand went back to his mouth to grab his cigarette, but instead of speaking, he put it out and allowed the ashtray to shut with a metallic click.

"People are where they are because that is where they are meant to be," James continued. "I'm meant to serve. Karling, to be master. Dalimore, president."

Mackenzie laughed again. "James," he glanced over at

the other boy again. "I'm going to tell you this true fact once and never again." He smiled back, waiting for James to respond, but when he saw that he would not, he continued, "*We* will soon be free."

"I just don't see how that poss—"

"You never see how anything is possible. Remember," Mackenzie rattled the words off as he swerved to miss a parked car. "Remember when I said I was going to go to a party the first time? And you swore on your mother's grave I'd get caught?"

James glanced at Mackenzie. The boy's face was alive with emotion as he spoke.

Mackenzie paused and laughed as he thought of that first party.

"Mack," James lingered on the name for a moment before continuing, "you'd be fine without anyone else to back you up, but not all of us are so self-sufficient. I've been a slave all my life. I don't know any other way of living."

The car turned another corner into even greater poverty, and James became aware of a sharp smell assaulting the tip of his nose.

Streetlamps flickered on and off. Potholes dotted the road. Parked cars were rusted shells, trash ubiquitous. Houses sagged on foundations. Windows were shattered by delinquents and replaced with anything the residents could get their hands on. Porches tilted sideways, were ripped from the houses, or were torn apart completely.

Piles of worn, blackened bricks formed badly built chimneys, and out of the chimneys flowed smoke, black and thick as tar.

"The place of my people," Mackenzie muttered under his breath.

James followed one of the dilapidated chimneys up to the column of smoke visible even at night.

The smoke was the mark of survival. The residents of the area took whatever they could find, whatever was willing to burn, and used it as fuel: rubber, cloth, wood, paper, rubbish, and corpses. Life was not a matter of dignity. Survival was the key in this jungle of houses and cars and crowds and lights and noise. And with survival the focal point of existence, their daily life was reduced to something more barbarian than civilized. But they survived; the fire of the human spirit was not snuffed, and against all adversity, against this insurmountable mountain of decaying existence, they existed.

SEVEN

"The fourth and final class are those with insanities. Seen as unfit, these individuals have been relegated to fenced-in ghettos where they are treated as little more than animals. The working class calls them 'untouchables.'"
– Amherst Rhodes, *Life in the USA* –

David heard the horn first.

He looked down at his shoes, which were stretched and broken at the seams. The soles flopped with each step, and chunks of snow slipped between the larger cracks. *Black snow.* A streetlamp fizzled and flickered above him.

The horn howled. David jumped. As he fell, the round headlights blinded him. Pain filled his hip. The pain radiated outward. It circled his pelvis, and ran down his femurs, through his leg bones, and out to every toe. It played across his ribs, stretched up his spine into his neck, and spread from bone through muscle to every appendage.

He tipped upside down. The world spun around him. It pitched. It blurred. Everything was color, shape, and finally, only blackness.

His head slammed against the ground. Pain shot through his tongue. He tasted blood. He heard tires squeal, smelled burning rubber, and passed into unconsciousness, unaware of anything except darkness, painful, hot sickness, feverish chills, and fitful, entropic agony.

~~~

The moments were long as they slid across the ice. James braced his feet against the floor of the car, and a white-knuckled hand gripped the handle above his door. His teeth bit down hard, and the figure who had darted into the roadway stared up at them with wild, tired eyes.

A boy. James saw it was a boy. Their age. Deep bags pulled under his eyes. His mouth was open as if out of breath. Sweat glistened on his face. A thicket of hair stuck to his forehead. His hands were bare, and instead of winter clothes on this frigid night, he wore a suit of rags that showed through to his skin in many places. He was dark with countless days of unwashed dirt, perhaps years of dirt.

Mackenzie stomped the brake. The car horn blared, and if it were summer, they would have stopped. If it was not for the weather, Mackenzie's actions would have not been futile, and the car would not have hit a patch of ice, and they would not have slid, and they would not have hit the boy, and James would not have seen the detail of the boy's face. He would not have been struck by the brightness of the boy's eyes behind all that dirt. (And this story would be a very different one. Indeed, history as we know it, would be very different.)

Both boys stared out the windshield in stunned silence. They gazed over at each other and shared a wide-eyed glance. James' lips parted, but his mouth was too dry to speak, and even if it were not, no words were sufficient for what he was feeling.

Mackenzie stared back in dumb reply.

The body before them was motionless. Besides the head, it appeared as a pile of rags.

Doors clicked open. Shoes crunched on the gray snow. The car doors slammed, one after the other, *dah-dun*, like a heartbeat. They walked over to the body slowly. Both boys were calm. James counted fifteen footfalls for himself and twelve for Mackenzie. Each step forward for both boys was filled with fear. Finally, after standing over the body forever, Mackenzie spoke. His words barely a whisper.

"I . . ."

James gave no reply as they stared at the body.

"I've . . ." Mackenzie breathed out a sigh. James glanced up. He had a look on his face as if he were collecting his thoughts, but James saw none of the fear in his eyes that was beginning to simmer in himself.

The two shared another glance.

"We've, um . . ." Mackenzie's hand went through each of his pockets in search of something. "I'm out of cigarettes." James was surprised at the calm in his voice.

Mackenzie let out a nervous cackle. He looked to the car, searched his pockets a second time, and then looked down to study the boy's face on the ground. He let out another laugh, amused this time. His bright blue eyes stared over at James. The slightest smile crept up the side of his mouth.

"James." The name floated in the air like a warm breath in winter.

Mackenzie looked at the body. He searched his pockets again. He grunted as his hands came out empty. "Just when you need a cigarette the most," he said as he turned from both James and the body and crunched back to the car.

A door opened. James heard shuffling. The trunk clicked open. The door thudded shut. The trunk closed with a loud whap.

James understood something significant had happened. They had hit another human with a car they had stolen. The boy on the ground was badly injured at least, likely dead. Manslaughter was murder. This was manslaughter, and that made Mackenzie a murderer in some sense.

Mackenzie returned with a large, unlit cigar in his mouth, and a thick, warm blanket under his arm. He dropped the blanket next to the body, sat on it, and stretched out his long legs. The lighter appeared from his pocket, the cigar was lit, and he stared up at James.

"Mackenzie," James said.

Mackenzie nodded toward him as smoke poured through his nose.

"Um . . ." James bit his lip and furrowed his brow. Though he did not feel the urgency of the situation, he knew he should. He knew Mackenzie should have as well. Fear and anxiety should have leapt up in each at the prospect of being convicted of a murder. But it was not present in himself. And it did not appear to be present in Mackenzie either.

"Shouldn't we hide the body?" James asked. His voice held little conviction.

Mackenzie shook his head and smiled with the cigar between his teeth.

"Why?" James continued.

Mackenzie shook his head again and pulled the cigar from his mouth. He held it between his thumb and forefinger as he brought it up to his face in inspection. "These," he motioned with the cigar to James, "are excellent." Mackenzie coughed gently. "I found a whole pack in the car. God, it's a good day."

James squinted back at him.

Mackenzie's wide-faced smile somehow grew larger. His snow-white teeth gleamed in the headlights. He looked back at the body, still with the grin on his face.

His bright-blonde hair was disheveled from the evening's activities.

"He's alright," Mackenzie said. The cigar returned to his mouth.

"Have you even checked?" James asked. "Do you even know how to check?" He followed Mackenzie's gaze to the body.

Mackenzie held up one finger as if he were a politician pushing home a point, but he did not look at James. "There are some happenings in this life that are providential," he said with a warm calmness. "And it's often the case that people don't realize the providence of those events until after they occur. But I feel a deep feeling, deep in my gut, in my heart, my soul, deep at the roots of my logical mind, that I see the future in this situation. I see the essence that goes beyond time and space, and I feel I've become a seer, a future-gazer, James."

"You're in shock. That's what you've become," James replied.

Mackenzie shook his head again, even more gently than before.

"The shock's got you batty," James continued.

Mackenzie looked up at the dirty, orange sky. He breathed out a sigh of smoke and satisfaction. "No," he said in a dreamy whisper. He glanced over at James and then back up at the starless night sky. "No shock. Sane as can be." The cigar rolled to the other side of his mouth as his eyes filled with thought.

"Remember when I was sent away to school?" Mackenzie asked.

James almost laughed at the sentiment in Mackenzie's voice.

"I like the thought of me being at boarding school, okay?" Mackenzie retorted. "Boarding school was the first—are you following me?"

James raised his eyebrows and nodded.

"Good," Mackenzie nodded back. "It was the first place I began my journey as a member of the upper class."

"Where you impersonated a Society brat?"

"I fulfilled my duties to the late Arold Karling, may he burn in a Hell of a thousand torments—thank God for leukemia—and in my copious free time, I mingled with the class two years below me."

"Two years below Arold Karling, may he burn in Hell forever," James answered impatiently.

"James Henry Anderson,"

"That's not my middle name."

"Meet David Amore, etcetera." He brushed the rest of the formalities away with a wave of his hand as if the Latin were some type of incantation.

"Mmm hmm." James stared down the dark road at the next streetlamp in the distance. "How does this have anything to do with school?" he asked.

Mackenzie looked at James. James was unsurprised to see the smile still on his face. "That's where we met."

"Nice to meet you, David," James nodded to the boy on the ground. "Too bad Mackenzie killed you."

"Oh, he's not dead, James," Mackenzie answered. "I've already told you this."

"Yeah, all the providential nonsense." James muttered a curse under his breath.

The comment sent Mackenzie breaking into loud laughter for several minutes. "You've got it," he said.

"I've got nothing," James answered, shaking his head. "I understand nothing."

Mackenzie took his time grinding the cigar out in the snow before answering. "David died in an accident four years ago. I went to his funeral, a closed casket affair. But now?" He gestured to the boy on the ground. "Back to life. Back to life," he whispered the last words to himself as if in disbelief.

"And how is this providential?" James words did not seem capable of filling the large silence that now existed. "Especially since he's dead?"

"First, he's not dead. First of the second, I know it is providential because he is back from the dead. I thought that was understood. Second of the second," Mackenzie thrust a finger toward James. "As soon as I met David, I knew you two were meant to meet, but he died. But he lives again, so now you can. The impossible happened, and only the divine could have caused it to happen."

"Why were we"—James sighed—"are we meant to meet?"

Mackenzie chuckled. "Don't you see it?" A knowing smile formed on his face.

James stared at the grimy face of the boy on the ground. "I see a dead dude," he said.

Mackenzie laughed again. "You two are the closest to twins as two unrelated people can possibly be. I'd swear you were clones. Doppelgangers." James sighed, pursed his lips, and shook his head, but Mackenzie continued. "And fate has brought you together. The fabric of reality has shifted. Like I said, I'm a prophet," he added.

~~

At first, the world was a spinning tumble. White-hot flashes of light blinded David. The flashes were overtaken by bright red until it grew darker and darker and swirled together like paint and charcoal to create a dizzying carousel of competing color. Eventually, color bled into color until he saw only a muted red desaturated by unconsciousness.

Then everything succumbed to blackness: swirling, slipping, spinning, nauseating blackness. His stomach turned, and his head throbbed. The breath came into his lungs through a parched throat. Paralyzed and helpless, he was trapped in a sea of pain he was unable to awaken to alleviate, and the panicked urge that accompanies drowning was filling him up.

Senses faded in and out. He felt as if he were floating,

and then became aware of the hard cold under his back. *Snow.* The word formed until it was torn apart by the pain.

The next to fade in was the sound of voices, two voices. *Three?* He was not sure. The voices mumbled inaudibly as if trying to communicate through water. He strained to hear but to no avail and gave up and slipped down deep, back into the sea, back into oblivious unconsciousness.

He dreamed odd, illogical dreams. Two towers stood above him. No, not towers, men, only looking like towers because of where he lay and the reflection of light. Their voices spoke like horns, trumpets of the battlefield. Though he did not understand them, he knew they were arguing. "Kill the mule or keep it?" one asked, but this one did not ask that because he did not speak English and spoke the phrase in another tongue.

"Eat it." The voices were still trumpets, but the towers were now wolves.

Now his parents.

Now the two men who were hunting him.

David felt a tug. *Two tugs,* he thought. One under his armpits and one under his knees. He was being lifted. They were moving him. The men grunted. His back scraped along the cold ground. He was set on something soft and warm.

"Do you hear dogs barking?" a voice asked. It was not the voice of either of the men chasing him. It was the voice of a boy. "Hey, James." The voice asked the question again.

David heard feet in the snow. He heard a groan. He heard a sick sigh, a retch, the sound of something pouring on the ground, and the smell of vomit wafted into his nostrils.

"Aw, James!" The voice swore loudly. "You're . . ."

David heard another retch more violent than the first.

A set of feet shuffled in the snow. Another set plodded aimlessly.

"Man," the word was a disappointed, pained cry, "you got it on my shoes!"

"Oh, um, sorry about that," James answered.

The car door slammed shut at David's feet. The reply from the first boy was as muffled as the other voices before.

Once more, before everything succumbed to the darkness, he heard a laugh.

He felt no pain when he awakened the third time. At first, he was aware of the movement beneath him. *A car.* He was sure of it. A hand rifled through a glove compartment, and the smell and taste of an old cigar overpowered the scent of the car. But these faded as well until only sound remained.

"Open a window," James said.

"Why?"

"Open your window. You're filling the car with smoke."

"Why don't you just open your window? You're the one who quit."

A sigh.

The static sound of air blowing into the car.

"Hell, it's cold," a voice said.

"Well, close the window, then," replied another.

"The smoke."

"It takes only a few minutes to smoke the things."

"It takes fifteen minutes to smoke those things!"

The other person sighed in reply.

"Are we dumping him in the river?" James asked.

"Dumping you in the river," the other voice said with an edge of annoyance.

A pause.

"Your shoes still look good," James' words were delicate.

No reply.

"So, the river then?" James asked again.

"Is he dead?"

"Looks dead to me."

Several moments of silence. The engine of the car. Shifting in seats. The opening of a window, *to throw out the cigar?* The closing of a window. Radio on. Spinning through several stations. Radio off. Silence.

"There's no doubt in my mind he's alive, James, no doubt."

"No doubt you'll be president either," James responded.

"None whatsoever," the other answered.

Part II

Holy Week

"Love conquers hate. Peace conquers war. Nonviolence triumphs over violence."
– Robert Dalimore –

EIGHT

————

"Jeremiah grew up the youngest of five boys. His father died a
few months after his eighteenth birthday."
– Esther Fleet –

"Can you turn on the TV, El?" Jeremiah turned to the mirror. His own morose eyes stared back. Nervousness coursed electric like open wires through him, and the back of his throat was a bundle of apprehension.

"You alright?" Elizabeth turned the knob after speaking, allowing the television to sing a high-pitched hum. "You ready?" she asked. The television sputtered and warbled as it displayed a static of color.

"Nervous," he responded as she reached over and adjusted the antennae to make the image clear. "I'm alright. Biggest show I've ever done." He gave her a weak smile.

————

She smiled back, and he felt a little lighter as he saw her face and forgot his own.

"Thanks, El," he said.

She shook her head, still smiling. His own face loosened, and a real smile broke out despite his nerves. "Once you start, the nerves'll be swept away," she said.

"Yeah," he replied, but the quickness of his breath was neither because of nerves nor the show. He shook his head and breathed out a laugh. He glanced at himself, then the TV, then El.

She once more became engrossed in her work.

"Another child is missing," the anchor on the television said. "A boy matching the description of Michael Lehr, a twelve-year-old, was last seen exiting a bus on Lawrey Avenue. The police haven't yet determined what has happened, though they say evidence points to a string of kidnappings."

Elizabeth grunted, and a police officer appeared on screen. Jeremiah's eyes flitted back to her concerned face as the police officer elaborated on the disappearances.

Her eyes were a soft blue. Her cheeks were slightly red with rouge. Her lips were pink and soft. A zing traveled from his belly up to his throat, her beauty overwhelming him. *It's not her beauty.* The thought continued. Something cool rested deep in his stomach. Passion crashed through his mind. Sensual snapshots flickered. Erotic animal desire was a flood. He felt the soft skin of her neck on his fingertips. Her lips brushed against his with a wave of red passion. Lips clasped lips.

No. No. He swallowed, and the fantasy shrank and was contained within the cold that rested in his stomach.

The officer finished speaking. Elizabeth let out another ambiguous vocalization. He sighed as well.

"This will be the very first Holy Week celebration without President Dalimore," the television anchor continued, "We have all missed him since his death in March. But we now have an opportunity to honor him, the greatest president in the history of the United States. Throughout this week, we will be reflecting on the life and legacy of this great and beloved leader." The anchor smiled and nodded as the camera shifted to the other.

"We are now on location for the start of the passion play, which portrays the traditional arrival of the Christian Christ into Jerusalem." A picture of Jeremiah appeared in the corner of the screen as the second anchor continued. "On the twenty-fifth anniversary of this play, we will take a special, inside look at those who have already played the god-man, and interview the actor portraying him this year to ask how he prepares for this important and difficult role."

The camera shifted back to the first anchor. "Tomorrow is the annual carnival, and Raymond Bandler Meggeran defends his title of World Heavyweight Champion on Tuesday.

"Turnout today is expected to be high," the first

anchor continued. "And this week's weather is forecasted to be beautiful and sunny with only an overcast Saturday."

Elizabeth continued her meticulous work of making up his face. Her eyes were hard and focused.

"El," he said.

El, he thought.

"Hmmm," she replied.

"How long has it been since we met?" he asked.

Eleven years. He answered his own question. *Eleven years?* He remembered that bitter cold day. Within those first moments outside, his face was numb. *A New Year's Eve party. Sledding. A conversation until three in the morning.*

"Oh, gosh." Elizabeth paused to think, sighed, and shook her head.

Never talked to someone so easily, for so long, Jeremiah thought.

"Over ten years," she said.

And still, no one else.

"Twelve years with this coming year." She continued applying the makeup to his face. "And I haven't gone sledding since I was twenty." She sighed a happy, reminiscent sigh. "I was flattered when you called me up about doing makeup for your first play."

"You mentioned makeup when we were talking," Jeremiah replied. "And I don't have any sisters. You seemed the logical choice." *And I couldn't wait to see you again.*

"The makeup wasn't very good." She smiled.

He laughed. "And now you're the best."

"Sheer practice. I could spin straw into gold if I had as long."

"The show was bad," he replied.

She chuckled now. "The worst I've ever seen. Didn't you get paid in eggs?" she asked.

"And milk. Milk and eggs," he answered.

She burst into laughter.

It's you, El, Elizabeth, his mind continued. *It's not just a physical thing. It's that you're living, breathing, moving, acting, thinking . . . It's because you're you, and you will always be you despite any changes, and I . . . and I . . .*

"It's been a long road." Her hand on his shoulder broke him away from his thoughts, and their eyes met in the mirror.

The cold once more settled in his stomach. Flickering infatuation would have sprung up in the past, but this was something different, born from time spent together, hundreds of conversations over years, pain, arguments, fights, distance, and even death. The infatuation had long faded and left them friends. Old friends.

He smiled at her and nodded. "A long road," he echoed back.

Her hand lifted off his shoulder and she moved toward the table. "All done," she said.

He looked at himself in the mirror and barely recognized the face staring back. "You've done a miracle again."

She glanced over as she packed up supplies. "I try my best."

He swallowed, the bundle of nerves still in the back of his throat.

"Sorry it took so long to finish. You only have ten or so minutes." He nodded and smiled, and she walked toward the door.

"El," he said. She stopped and turned.

"Before you leave, I just wanted to tell you . . ." He paused. A rush of words washed through his head. The apprehension gave way, and his mouth and eyes curled into a small, sad smile. "This is my last show."

She smiled back at him with deep, tender eyes. "I know," she said.

His head cocked, betraying slight surprise. "How's that?" he asked.

"Sensed it," she replied, pursing her lips.

"I just want to say thanks for everything," he said, nodding his head. "You've been a good friend. I wouldn't have made it where I am without you."

She continued to smile, shook her head, and then moved across the room to hug him.

Her eyes lit up as she pulled away. "It was my pleasure. Completely my pleasure."

An alarm went off. *Ten more minutes.*

Elizabeth nodded to it. "You should get ready."

"Yeah," he replied, and they both began to move. "Say hi to the Robs for me."

"Will do," she replied.

"El!" He did not realize he had said the word at first, but she stopped, caught off guard.

"Yeah?" she said.

"Never mind." He raised his hands. "I'll talk to you about it next week."

She smiled, nodded a goodbye, and slipped out the door.

El. The name echoed in his mind.

Yeah?

He shook his head at how stupid he was but still felt sadness filling up his eyes.

Yeah? her voice in his head asked again.

"I love you."

But she was gone. She had been gone for five years, since her wedding day.

~~~

Fireworks shot off as Jeremiah entered the crowd. Scarlet smoke billowed before him. Trumpets filled the air with triumphant song. Planes flew overhead. A boy of twelve ran out in front of him with a piece of silk fluttering behind. A trumpet blew a loud, hard, long blast, and Jeremiah halted before the path.

Every eye was fixed on him, and the world seemed to hold its breath. The only thing that could be heard was the leisurely *clop* as the donkey took a single step onto the path. A solitary firework went off above the crowd. Still, everyone remained silent. The donkey took two more steps. Two more fireworks went up into the air, each popping as weakly as the first. More fireworks flew up into the sky until their sounds overlapped like a rolling snare-drum. Another long blast sounded from a trumpet followed by another blast of the same note and another and others of different harmonizing notes until the whole neighborhood echoed with them. Finally, a single firework seemingly gone astray ascended above the others and hung in the sky for what seemed a moment too long before it gave out a tremendous *BOOM*, and the crowd erupted into a wild yell.

And El had been correct; Jeremiah's nervousness was swept away.

NINE

"Many historians believe if it were not for the infighting of the Executive Ten, they could have saved the United States from downfall and had a long, unquestioned reign."
– Samuel Judah, *American Autumn* –

David's voice filled the concrete room. A little wan light streamed through the bars at the window, and his eyes searched the half-light for a way to escape. It was cold, cold and damp and grim. The cries escaping his mouth were answered by curses and a heavy fist pounding on the door.

The dream stuttered to a room, white and blazing warm. The face of his mother was filled with smiles. His name was on her lips. *Christmas*, he thought, but as soon the thought crossed his mind, the dream stuttered again, first to a car with his father, a defeated misery on the man's face, then to a room of blinding lights and the stinging force of frigid water on skin.

"Take your clothes off," a rough voice commanded. They took away his clothes, covered him with stinging powder, and sprayed him with a hose until his skin was raw. They forced him into a cell, and he spent the night curled in a corner, filled with convulsive shivers, and wondering what had happened, wondering if he would ever be warm again.

"David." The images faded as he felt a rough hand shake him awake. The dreams blurred until they were replaced by blackness and warmth.

"David." The hand shook him harder.

David grunted in response.

"We don't want to be late," the voice whispered through the darkness.

The morning was cold, even in the house. Head still thick with sleep, he pushed himself out of bed and fumbled through the darkness until he was dressed. The servant's garb Mackenzie had given him felt as smooth as silk, and the memories that had filled his head only moments before faded to happily forgotten dreams.

Frost covered the ground when they arrived. Their breath came out like smoke, and David wrapped his thin coat more tightly about himself. A small lantern swung in Mackenzie's hand, and other small lanterns punctuated the blackness of the morning and made the whispered titters of the crowd little more than ghosts. A few had already arrived, and Mackenzie motioned them to sit at the top of a small hill; but as the blackness of morning gave way to subtle gray, every inch of the ground began to fill with people.

David was struck by the silence of the crowd. He could understand the scattered whisper and sometimes a child would cry out, but the mass of people was subdued as if they were peering at a skittish animal a stone's throw away. The cold morning air was filled with excitement. Those first gray rays of dawn, by tight anticipation.

"What time is it?" James whispered.

Mackenzie whispered back a time, and the two fell into mumbled conversation.

When he had first awakened a few months back, he was greeted by an old servant. She had told him he had been delirious for more than a week but little else. In the four long years prior, he often wondered if he had died and were suffering an eternal damnation he had never believed in, and now, caught up in this soft, warm existence, he swore this new reality could only be Heaven.

"David Amore!" He had awakened with a start at the sound of his name. As its syllables filled his ears, he wondered whether his name was spoken at all or he had merely imagined it. It had been more than four years since he had heard that name spoken on anyone's lips, and though the words sounded as if they were real, a part of him wondered if it was only a dream. *Perhaps it's all a dream.*

The thought drifted through his mind. *I'm still in chains, and it's all a dream.*

"David Amore!" the sound of his name protested. A light switch clicked, and lamplight blazed into his eyes. Slowly, the boy came into view, a thin figure, a blonde head. It towered at the foot of his bed, and said his name a final time, more quietly than before. The voice was familiar, yet he could not place it. It was a voice he knew well, one he knew he should have recognized.

"David," the boy whispered out.

David squinted as recognition dawned.

"Mackenzie?" David's voice rang with uncertainty.

Mackenzie let out a loud laugh, and David found this to be as good a confirmation as any.

"Where am I?" David asked.

"There'll be time enough for that later," Mackenzie responded. A smile filled his face.

Throughout the next days and weeks, David came to understand where he was and the full nature of his survival. Mackenzie had hit him with a car. "Providential," Mackenzie called it. He smuggled him into the Karling residence, found a doctor willing to treat him, and called in every favor he had with every servant possible to keep their mouths shut and ensure the survival of this mystery boy. Mackenzie told him none of this. Every time David would ask how he had arrived here, Mackenzie would always promise to tell him "from beginning to end" one day, but David, in the end, was forced to get the story from other servants.

David did not know why he expected anything other than avoidance. When it came to his own personal aggrandizement, Mackenzie avoided the topic. Even if a million kindnesses had been committed by the boy, no one would ever know. The most anyone ever got out of Mackenzie in the way of pride was a mouthful of dreams and the half-sarcastic, half-serious "Ladies and gentlemen, stand and meet your new king," which was sung out at any opportunity in those few short years David knew him. It was from a film, and thirteen-year-old Mackenzie, struck by the phrase, felt it a necessity to insert it into every possible situation. Four years later, the statement still graced his lips, but less frequently and at more appropriate times.

But Mackenzie isn't a king, thought David as he stood in the cold morning half-light with the tittering crowd all around. *Mackenzie's a slave.* In the past, he would have had his ears boxed by his mother for using the incorrect term, but David saw no reason to mask reality with euphemism any more. Mackenzie was a slave. It was simple. It was a fact. It was not changing any time soon.

David had made the discovery while at school. He was sick in bed when Mackenzie, who stated he was two grades above David's class, walked by with a slave ring in his ear and wearing servant's clothes. When David later pulled him aside to confront him, Mackenzie had responded with

"As sure as Dalimore is president," and not a hint of hesitation in his voice.

David was taken aback by the response, and his own came out in a chastising tone. "Why did you tell me that?" he asked harshly.

"Well, you're not going to tell," Mackenzie replied.

"You don't know that," David answered.

Mackenzie only laughed. He laughed because he was right. David would not tell because David would never tell. Mackenzie had become a friend, not merely an acquaintance, and David had no desire or will to sacrifice that friendship to Societal propriety.

Even the morning after he had met Mackenzie, when both had been invited to the birthday party of one of the boys who lived near school and, even on that day when they found one another and explored that mansion from the rafters to the cellar, he would not have said a word. In those few dark, wandering hours, he had become better friends with Mackenzie than he had with anyone else.

The boy had admitted his servitude so easily, and his words were the first snapped stitch in David's understanding of the world. David had been taught that the lower classes needed a parent, a mother, a "God our father," and without the strong hand of Society as guide, their lives would be in disarray, their neighborhoods fall into riots, their lives into ruin. But if a slave was able to function so well amidst children who were bred to rule . . .

As a child, he had thought Society's reasoning to be

solid to the core, a burly, immovable oak. *I am a member of Society. I am meant to rule. I am meant to be in control. Others are meant to serve.* Those unreasoned thoughts had served him well until that day in school almost five years ago with Mackenzie's blonde head before him and those piercing aquamarine eyes staring back.

If it were true that those of Society were born of a special lineage holding special abilities, why would youths of this caliber be so easily fooled by a slave? And why would David, a boy of Society, be sent home, and, as if he were an annoying servant girl, becast like trash into the—

David shook the thoughts out of his head. His memories always began with joy, but they ended as an ash of bitterness, a long drone of deep-seated pain. It was better to forget his past, so he did his best to forget it. He was starting a new life, and no new life could be had whilst tied to that corpse. He wanted to start over, and starting over required the world to be made anew or himself recreated.

As the first rays of red dawn slipped over the horizon, David let the memories fade from his mind. A hush went over the crowd, and he was filled with the overpowering peace of the situation. Light filled his eyes. Golden light filled the faces of those around him. This was a new start, a beginning of beginnings, and he let that thought rest on him like a heavy blanket as the trumpeter blew a long low blast on his instrument, a blast that seemed to fill up the city like the morning light. The play was beginning. It was beginning. David could feel the excitement in the air.

David was not religious, never in a real way and not in a long time, but all were familiar with the plot of the Great Play: a death, a life, a resurrection, promise of eternal life. He had been dragged to Mass as a child and been forced to sit through the droning Latin even though neither his parents nor any members of Society took the faith seriously. Their attendance was an example to the lower class. If the elites appeared to believe something, the common man would as well, and Society needed the common man to believe. A man could bear poverty and meaninglessness but not both, and Society tamped down on the rebellious inclinations of the lower class in two ways: by giving meaning to their lives or making them forget the meaninglessness; religion and hedonism. Those inclined toward rule-following became slaves to the religious order and so became tamed by their hope of one day achieving eternal life, and those inclined toward rule-breaking slipped into the slavery of whichever addiction they fancied best. The Great Play was merely a means to an end. It was true that Dalimore had instituted it in good faith twenty-five years ago, a true believer himself, but Society had only pushed it to be a national celebration because it was the perfect opioid to subdue the inclinations of both these types of poor. Religion for the pious, a party for everyone else.

David was not religious because he saw the

system—with its doctrines, its creeds, its rituals, and faith—as a tool of manipulation. He saw the logic of a divine being. He did not know how one could think one's way out of leaning toward the existence of such a being, but this god before him, this god-man on a donkey, if he were real, would have to prove himself to David.

The thing that most confused David about Mackenzie was that he bought into these beliefs. He believed without doubt and the typical burden accompanying the faithful, and David could never determine whether Mackenzie had developed such a strong belief in the divine and these religious accoutrements by dint of his personality or whether his personality had developed because of his faith.

Despite David's lack of faith, he felt an odd excitement about the play, an excitement he had not even felt as a young child. Silhouetted against the red morning sun, the man on the donkey appeared. Mackenzie smiled as the donkey clopped toward them. The crowd, which had been murmuring, sizzled to a silence filled with only the occasional percussive whisper.

David would remember that play in emotion rather than details. He remembered it being fantastical, loud, and powerful. Symbols of a faith, forgotten by all but very few, passed. He remembered there were dancers and a single dancer had been dressed more brightly than the rest in sparkling silver. She represented the morning star. What the morning star represented? He did not know or care.

Other dancers followed, each having a different symbolic meaning: one sprinkled water on the edges of the crowd. Another was dressed in an ugly costume that looked like a mummy. Another had wings and was dressed in white. Another barely danced; her face instead pointed down out of sight, and her hands, feet, and body were covered in rags. After the dancers, the actors entered. A group of priests moved around the man on the donkey and handed a man dressed in common clothes a handful of coins.

One final character walked out from behind the God-man but did not pass him. The symbolism was lost to David. The character was not dressed in period-appropriate clothing, but instead a blinding-white suit. David watched the man in the white suit as he continued to walk before the god-man until both himself and the donkey disappeared behind a bend.

David felt something bump his arm. He looked over. Mackenzie pointed far in the distance from where the God-man had come. A semi pulled an object draped with a brown cloth. The object was as wide as the truck and as tall as three houses stacked on top of one another. The vehicle pulled to the center of the crowd and stopped. A murmur filled the crowd, and a gaggle of the newscasters rushed to film the anomalous event.

"Ladies and gentlemen," a treble voice boomed over the crowd. A small man stood next to the object holding a microphone, one of the executives of the country. The crowd hushed.

"Friends." The man choked on a rising sob, controlled it, and continued, his face turning down in an uncontrollable frown. "We grieve a loss. This is the first Holy Week in twenty-five years that President Dalimore is not here with us." A moan of sadness escaped the crowd as if on cue.

Dalimore was a beloved president. During that last half-decade of the war, he had brought the nation together. He had helped the United States out of the darkness of that post-war world, and up to the point of his death, his voice rang with rebukes of the injustice perpetrated by Society.

It was a shock to the nation when he died on that cold February eve of 1976, and deep fear rose in the hearts of the people as they donned their black armbands. The second father of the nation was dead. Could the nation hope to continue? Would it not collapse without him?

"In light of the passing of the man responsible for leading us into America's second rebirth, I would like to present you, his hometown, a gift," the man continued and reached up to a rope hanging off the canvas and pulled. The canvas fell into a heap on the bed of the truck, revealing a towering, white likeness of Robert Dalimore. Both hands clasped a sword like an ancient conqueror, and, except for his head, he was clothed in exquisitely detailed and intricate armor. The crowd erupted into cheers.

Despite the sorrow of Dalimore's passing, life went back to normal for the nation within a week. Dalimore was replaced by a 'temporary' council of ten executives. His voice no longer rang out at injustices, but little else changed.

As the little man followed the rest of the parade, the crowd, a crowd that had travelled from every corner of the nation, flooded the dirt path and surrounded the statue of Dalimore, kissing his feet and setting coins and keepsakes at the base of the statue. He who had always been a voracious fighter of the abuses of Society, he who had always opposed an aristocratic oligarchy, had, in his death, become as the god-man had been in his own, a tool to control the mob and to maintain the power of the patrician class.

Thus Dalimore died, was buried, and rose again as crowd control.

TEN

———

"Revolution, they cried; revolution. We all cried revolution."
– Esther Fleet –

Early Monday morning of Holy Week, Isaiah rubbed his eyes and yawned. He had been up since five in the morning the day before and was ready for sleep, but it was his shift in the lab tonight so the only thing he could do was clench his teeth and drink pot after pot of what the scientists called coffee. With all their degrees, with even a chemist on staff, Isaiah always wondered why none of them had learned to make a decent cup of joe.

"All that intelligence wasted on science. Sheesh. Coffee is the backbone of American Society, and you PhDs think that just because you're doing ground-breaking work it doesn't matter how your coffee tastes," he would often tell them in annoyed sarcasm, and they would always find it uproariously funny.

Isaiah was not a PhD and would never be. As a lab assistant, he was assigned to the grunt work, allowing those educated to go about tasks reserved for "delicate genius." This morning the PhD on duty was pouring over puzzlements of mathematics when Isaiah walked into the room. "Dr. Stonewall," Isaiah said. "Can I get you anything, coffee, some food?"

"Alvin, call me Alvin. Okay, Isaiah?" the doctor replied.

"I'll do that, sir."

The old doctor chuckled under his breath.

"I want a cup of coffee, but I need to get up and stretch my legs, so I can take care of that myself. I can get you another cup if you'd like."

Isaiah laughed. "No, sir. I've already had enough of that ground-up, steeped Satan as it is."

Alvin laughed. "If you change your mind, just yell."

"Of course, sir. After you get back will you need my help with anything?" asked Isaiah.

"Yeah, I'd like to start up the reactor." Dr. Stonewall picked up his coffee mug and downed the final, cold contents in one gulp. Isaiah winced for him. The coffee was bad when it was warm; it was downright putrid cold.

After Dr. Stonewall left, Isaiah fell into a chair with a great, satisfied sigh. He pointed his nose to the ceiling for a moment before looking down at the papers the doctor had been poring over. He stooped farther when he saw the problem.

He sensed something wrong with the equations. Something was out of place or there was something existing that did not belong in the model. Isaiah grabbed a piece of paper, pulled out a pencil, and began to work on the problem. He had never done math of this sort in the lab before and would have been laughed at if he was seen. Suddenly, when he looked up at the papers, he noticed the inconsistency and worked even more quickly.

Fifteen minutes passed as Isaiah wrote. Twenty-five, and he continued to write feverishly. Stonewall had not come back. He had probably stopped to talk. Finally, as the thirtieth minute that Alvin had been gone was closing in, Isaiah stopped writing and, in an expression of excitement, fell backwards out of the chair.

"Dr. Stonewall!" he yelled. "Stonewall!" The man did not answer. "Alvin!" he finally yelled and forgot formality altogether.

"So, you want some coffee after all?" Stonewall called from the other end of the hall.

"No!" Isaiah yelled back.

"No coffee?" Stonewall asked, disappointed and confused.

"No coffee. You need to come here, quickly."

Stonewall did not answer, but Isaiah heard his hastened footfalls in the hall.

"What is it?" he asked as he entered. Isaiah said nothing but collected the papers Stonewall had been working on and shoved them into one hand and collected the pile he had filled out with equations and shoved them into the other. Stonewall took them to his desk and looked over his own notes before turning to what Isaiah had written. At first his face did not change, but suddenly a smile flickered over it. The smile grew. Stonewall cursed. After he finished his study of Isaiah's work, he laughed. "I would never have thought . . . So, that is what all your questions were. They should give you a PhD for this. No one's been able to make a theoretical model yet, and you . . . It's unbelievable. Isaiah, you've just made the biggest scientific discovery of the millennia. Here." The doctor started to fold up Isaiah's work. "You need to take these until we can make a public announcement and set up a time when you can speak to other physicists so there is no doubt and no arguing over who discovered it. Keep it safe. There are a lot of untrustworthy physicists on staff who wouldn't think twice about stealing credit from a lab assistant." He handed the folded papers to a nodding Isaiah, who immediately put them in his breast pocket. "Now don't let anyone see those. Credit should go to whom it is due. You'll be more famous than Einstein. Now wait here; I've got to go grab something." Stonewall left the room, and his footfalls faded down the hall. Several minutes later the doctor appeared with two mugs in his hands. He gave one to Isaiah then drew a flask out of his pocket. He filled Isaiah's mug with a little bit of liquor before filling his own. Stonewall held up his cup in a toast. Isaiah followed suit. "To you Isaiah. To cold fusion." They both downed the contents of their mugs. The liquor made Isaiah wince. *Still better than the coffee,* he thought.

ELEVEN

"*To its citizens, the decay of the United States is background noise. Their own desperation is the chief concern.*"
– Amherst Rhodes, *Life in the USA* –

It was late morning when the boys passed through the busy streets of the city under the warrior eyes of Dalimore and past the crowd of people watching as the god-man brandished a whip and sent money-changers running and tables flying.

James yawned and wiped sweat from his eyes. Palm Sunday had been a long but good day. They had found their way up to the statue of Dalimore, rubbed his foot for good luck, and attended mass, the sanctuary of the church packed to the gills. After church, the three boys made a morning of town venders, and they returned home to attend a party in the servants' quarters that lasted from midafternoon to well into evening.

James yawned again and glimpsed David, whose face held no emotion and whose eyes burned with dim, gray light. *Anger? Sadness? Who knows*, James wondered.

He could not interpret it, he could not place it, especially when juxtaposed with Mackenzie. A faint wet-newspaper-color next to a glowing forge of mirth. Happiness, joy, freedom, playfulness, drive, and determination seemed a companion of graywater.

Graywater. It was a fitting description of David. Although James knew little more than his name ("Where are you from, David?" "Around." "Where do you live?" A shadow of a smile with the reply: "Here and there."), even mysteries within the boy did not lend themselves to intrigue. He was James' height, or thereabouts. He was neither thin nor fat nor a mountain of muscle. His hair was a dark brown that seemed to be almost an odd gray in some lights. His eyes often stared off unfocused, neither happy nor sad, perfect pools of apathy. Addressed, he would turn to the speaker slowly as if he had taken the whole time to comprehend the words.

No one in the neighborhood came out to help when they had loaded David into the car in those wee hours of the year. When James picked him up, he was amazed at his lightness. His clothes decayed off his body. His face was gaunt and sunken, gray. His fingers stretched out like the extraterrestrials claimed to have been found at Roswell twenty years prior, and his limbs reminded James of brittle twigs.

III

David was delirious the first week. He was feverish, mumbling under his breath, and he awoke only to talk gibberish to phantoms.

"Starvation. His immune system's been worn down to a thread. See? Infection, all these scrapes and gashes up his leg," the doctor said. The wounds were swollen, discolored, and oozed with thick, slug-like puss. "I've set up an IV," the doctor continued. "Antibiotics. We'll see."

At first, James found him interesting. What intriguing mind lay behind the silence of the boy? But the intrigue faded until James found him as interesting as a blank piece of paper.

David's emotions were subdued, smaller vestigial versions of the real things. His movements were efficient and short. His speech was laconic, and it often seemed to James that the boy could not speak a sentence longer than five words. David's silence became tedious, and James found him annoying.

Mackenzie? Mackenzie liked him. *But Mackenzie likes everyone,* James thought as he wiped the sweat from his eyes again.

The air was thick with humidity, and a haze hung tired in the sky. The city was swallowed in heat. The only reprieve was an intermittent, fickle, fluttering wind. People used all manner of flat objects to fan themselves, and sweat stood out on foreheads and soaked through clothes.

"What time is it?" James asked. The afternoon sun

beamed in his eyes, and a film of sticky sweat covered every inch of his body. "Eh, Mack!"

Mackenzie looked up, eyes glazed with exhaustion. Sweat glistened on his forehead, and his mouth was opened and panting like a dog. He looked down at his watch as if the action sapped all his energy.

"Two thirty-five." He leaned his head back and the breeze moved his hair a half centimeter. He looked over at James with a smile. "How are you doing, James?" he asked, relishing in the misery of the other boy.

James looked back with a glare.

"David?" Mackenzie asked.

"I'm alright," David answered.

James looked at David. His skin did not glisten with sweat, and he appeared unaffected by the heat. "David?" He wiped sweat out of his eyes before continuing. "You're not sweating."

"No," the boy replied.

"Why?" James asked.

"I'm not hot."

James took a deep breath in and then blew it out. Nothing helped. Each moment seemed as if the world had grown hotter than the one before.

"You should have bribed someone," he said to Mackenzie.

"Bribe?" Mackenzie put a hand up to his chest as if to say "Me?" and continued. "How dare you. It is my duty to understand the struggle of the common man. And I will stand out in this heat until the common man has air conditioning like his betters," Mackenzie said with the puffed verbosity of the Society son he was playing today. He wore some old clothes he had stolen, and his slave ring was secreted away into one of his pockets.

"That'll be awhile," James responded.

"Well," David answered in a subdued manner, "perhaps not as long as you think."

"Why's that?" James asked.

"Cold fusion," Mackenzie answered for David. David nodded, his attention still on the crowd.

"Ah, yes." Sarcasm filled James' wide eyes. "Of course, cold fusion."

Mackenzie's head turned, and a quizzical look washed over his face.

"What about it?" James continued.

"What about it? What about it?" Mackenzie asked. James remained silent, and his eyebrows knitted in annoyance.

"You can't be serious," Mackenzie continued. "It's practically the stuff of legend." James continued to look on dumbly. "Cold fusion." Mackenzie shook his head and an uncontrollable smirk curled up the side of his mouth. "I'm sorry, James; I didn't think you were serious. I wasn't aware others weren't aware of what it was. I need"— his hand plunged into his pocket as he spoke—"a cigarette, and then I'll try my best to explain." He pulled out his cigarettes and lighter. "Did you see the news about the discovery this morning?" Mackenzie asked as he lit the cigarette.

"I caught the tail end," James replied.

Mackenzie nodded. Smoke poured from his nostrils. "Cold fusion." His brows knitted, and he brought his hand up to his chin. He bit his lip and looked at David.

"Cold fusion is essentially trying to mimic a process that occurs in the stars, but at room temperature," David answered Mackenzie's glance.

Mackenzie puffed on his cigarette as David continued.

"You're creating a power normally formed in the stars on a coffee table. Safe, small reactions."

Smoke swirled up into the air from Mackenzie's cigarette. His eyes narrowed in thought.

"It's seen as the Holy Grail of energy," David continued. "All other types would no longer be needed. If these two mathematicians *have* found a theoretical framework, in a few decades you'll see the whole earth transform. Really, it's the stuff of science fiction."

James nodded.

"The future is here," Mackenzie said. James looked up to see a big smile on his face.

David nodded. "Lots of changes," he said. "A new industrial revolution more revolutionary than before. We may not even recognize the world in fifteen years."

James' eyes were wide with interest as he imagined the future that lay before them. Buildings stretched into the stratosphere. Cars hovered past skyscraper windows.

Rockets soared through space. Men walked unaided by space helmets on new worlds.

"We're up!" Mackenzie's quick words broke him from his thoughts.

"How many?" James heard a male's voice from the ticket-booth.

"Three," Mackenzie said. The ticket master handed him three tickets, and he turned to the two other boys to hand each one.

"Cold fusion!" he said to James and clicked his tongue.

"And where does that lead?" James asked.

"Cold fusion to free energy. Free energy to a surplus of food and clean water. To every necessity fulfilled. And on and on to utopia." Mackenzie laughed. "It'll change the world."

It'll change the world. The words echoed through James' mind as they moved into the fairgrounds. Colored lights flashed on every side. A man played seven instruments off to the boys' right. Another yelled at the boys to try to play a game and win. A garish sign announced a freak show. Another sign spelled out *House of Mirrors!* "Ripley's, famous Ripley's!" a man yelled.

The fair was an odd assortment of everything, and the three boys went from one exhibit to another, one game to the next. They saw the man stick his head in the mouth of a lion. They took in a show of acrobats jumping through flaming hoops and performers juggling chainsaws and torches. A man spewed fire from his mouth. A magician made a Studebaker disappear. An archer pinned a quarter to a target at the distance of an entire football field, along with hundreds of other acts and games and exhibits to entertain. On top of this food, sophisticated to absurd, healthy to heart-stopping, delicious to disgusting, seem to spill from vendors' stalls into the streets.

The fiery sun climbed as they threw balls at a dunk tank and shot low-caliber rifles at metal milk bottles. It reached its zenith after they had watched three magic acts and two musical performances. Finally, they began to sample fair cuisine, purchasing baskets and filling them with edibles until the bottom weave threatened to break.

When the sun was just beginning to refract on the horizon, they took their food and found an open table amidst the sea of bodies. Each boy laid on part of the table with the basket on his belly, reaching up to bring a piece to his mouth. David finished first, five to ten minutes before the other two boys. James was able to clean out all but a fourth of the food, and Mackenzie left his basket having taken a bite or two from almost every food. When James commented, Mackenzie only replied, "Well, I've got to try each, or it's wasted."

By the time they had finished, the sun was red on the horizon, and shadows were thickening.

David groaned.

Mackenzie sighed.

James remained silent.

"Now what's the plan?" James asked.

"I may throw up," David said offhandedly.

Mackenzie laughed and then wheezed.

"James," Mackenzie said.

"Hmm?" James replied.

"A party?" Mackenzie asked him.

"I think you should die," James answered.

Mackenzie began to hum and then whistle a military march. He turned the march into an old show tune. The show tune morphed into a hymn and finally into a folk song. The whistle warbled and then ended in an airy, final, failed attempt. He raspberried with his tongue then broke into a chuckle. "I could use"—he sighed—"a drink."

"Well, there was a beer tent a bit back," James replied.

Mackenzie's head lolled down and shook from side to side. "Something stronger."

"From where?" James asked.

Twisting his torso as far to the left as possible, supporting his weight with his left hand, he lifted his other and pointed directly behind him. "That should do."

"Amentis Rex," James read aloud and spied a golden sign that spelled out "Members Only."

"Golden King," Mackenzie translated.

"Members only," James answered.

"Luckily, or rather, through great monetary compensation and familial prestige, the Karlings are members." He flashed a golden lapel pin he had borrowed with his clothes. "And members can bring guests."

Mackenzie slid from the table to the ground and before

he had landed, began to walk forward. A few short strides brought the boys to door and almost past the threshold.

"Staaahp!" said a rough, serious voice from a mountain of a man who impeded their progress.

"Eh, fellow," Mackenzie replied. "I'mma member." He pointed to his lapel pin.

"These two aren't," the man replied.

"These two are my guests," Mackenzie answered.

"No servants allowed in," the man boomed.

"And who's a servant?" Mackenzie's words were confident and terse.

A big meaty paw lifted and pointed at James.

"And who says so?" Mackenzie asked; his voice filled with indignation.

"How 'bout free men don't wear slave rings," the man said, motioning to the small silver loop in James' ear.

"A fashion statement," Mackenzie retorted.

"I know slave rings when I see um. He doesn't come in," the bouncer repeated.

Mackenzie sighed, folded his arms, and turned to James. "Ya mind?" He shrugged as he asked. "It'll only take a few minutes."

"I'll be fine," James answered. The boys nodded at each other, Mackenzie and David disappeared into the door, and the towering bouncer glared at him. James pursed his lips. The man continued to glare. James gave a fake sarcastic smile before turning away.

His jaw dropped absentmindedly. As he stared at the

crowd, he spied the sign and wondered how they had missed it. It was written in big, red letters that seemed to float in the air. "Welcome to the Future!" it blinked.

"Welcome!" another small, white sign said below. To the left of the second sign was a dark portal into a white tent grayed by time.

When he stepped into the tent, he saw only shapes, all brown and black, until everything came into focus. He stood for a moment and looked over at the tables of the tent. They all looked half a century old and ready to fall apart. One at the far back had a ragged young man behind it. His eyes swallowed the door greedily, hungrily but quickly darted away after seeing it was only a servant and went back to working on the contraption on the table before him.

A small man with bug eyes stood up from a chair a few steps from James. His oversized head nodded to James as he cleared his throat.

"Hello," he said. His voice croaked. He cleared his throat again and then brought his hand up to cough into a fist. After his coughing fit subsided, he nodded to James again. "Welcome to the future." He raised an arm up like a circus master announcing the next act of a show. His arm hung in the air for a moment. Finally, it fell back to his side.

A child outside yelled in delight. The only sound in the tent was the creak of the skinny boy at the back of the tent hunched over his table.

"What is this place?" James' words were half whispered.

"As I said," the small man cleared his throat again, "the future is here." He snatched a handkerchief out of his breast pocket and fell into a coughing fit. After the coughing fit, he wiped his mouth, carefully folded up his handkerchief, and stuffed it back into his breast pocket.

He smiled at James. "Do you see that?" He nodded his head to the opposite side of the tent.

James looked over and saw a table with glass on top and knobs on either end. "What is it?" he asked.

"It is a game," the man answered.

"It doesn't look like a game," James responded.

"The future of games," the man replied before once more clearing his throat.

"Looks a bit odd to me." James began to walk over to the strange table. The little man followed behind.

"Let me show you." The man passed to the other side of the table. He reached under, and James heard a sharp *snap*. The top of the table glowed like a television screen. The little man stood at the opposite side and moved some knobs. James peered into the supine television. On it he saw a thumb-length rectangle at either end and a square that moved from one side back to the other. The old man spun the knob on the other side, moving the far rectangle so that it met the moving square, which changed direction upon the meeting.

"Tennis," the little man said.

"The future of games?" James mumbled and shook his head. "What do you call it? This table TV?"

"S'called"—the man reached under the table once more, and the screen winked out—"a video game."

James gave the man a polite smile.

"You're unimpressed." The man coughed. "But go talk to everyone else. Perhaps something will stir your interest." He waved James toward the rest of the tent as he retrieved his handkerchief and fell into another coughing fit.

James considered leaving but decided against the shame it might cause the man. Without a conscious thought, his feet brought him to the thin, young man at the back of the tent. He appeared to be working on a typewriter with a small television screen. The man behind the screen punched keys on the typewriter without noticing the boy standing before of him.

James stood a few moments waiting to be noticed, but when it became clear he would not be, he gave a small cough.

The young man glanced up. He nodded to James and stopped punching keys. After giving a half-hearted, distracted smile, he spoke. "Hello," he said quietly.

James nodded back. "Uh, hi," he replied.

"Welcome to the future," the young man said before going back to work.

James bit his tongue for a moment and determined whether he should speak. "Um . . ." The vocalization elicited no response from the young man, who seemed to have become once more engrossed in his work. "How is it the future?" James asked after several moments of silent deliberation.

The man glanced up again, continuing to work. "One moment," he said, and went back to what he was working on.

Finally, after a ten-minute wait, James heard the final loud *clack* from the typewriter and the young man looked up.

"This is a computer," the man said, pointing to the contraption he had been working on. "Do you know what a computer does?"

James shook his head.

The young man nodded before continuing. "To put it simply . . ." The man scratched his head to think. "From your earrings, I see you work at a House." James almost laughed at the euphemism but instead nodded. "So, your employer gives you orders, yes?" James nodded again. The man leaned back to continue. "A computer is similar. I type a command, or an order, into this machine, and it responds to the order. That's the simplest way to put it."

"So, you punch in what you want to do?" James was unsure of what he was asking.

"It can't do everything. It can't run and get my groceries, yet. But it can do things such as, well, math." He paused to think for a moment. "So, let's say you had to complete a complex mathematical problem. I could set up a string of commands that would allow you to put the problem in, and the computer would spit out the answer. What would have taken ten to fifteen minutes, maybe a lot longer, now takes you fifteen seconds."

James looked at the machine, its black screen glowing with what appeared to be green gibberish. "So, it'll be good for mathematicians. To allow faster computations?" he asked.

"Much more than that," the man responded. "Computing and computers will revolutionize everything."

"In what way?" James answered.

"We could program computers to display time, to replace the typewriter, to cook, to clean, to drive . . . to talk." The man scratched his chin and looked straight at James. "Give it fifteen, twenty, twenty-five years, and this ugly little box"—he rapped the top of the machine with two knuckles—"will revolutionize the world. You won't even recognize it."

James pursed his lips, unsure of what to say, but soon forgot his forming thoughts as he heard a blaring horn outside. Profanity roared through the air. A woman let out a sharp, ear-splitting scream. Something thudded heavily onto metal. James heard a whimper. *A child crying?* he thought, and curiosity got the better of him. He, along with the other occupants of the tent, rushed to the flap to peer onto the street.

James saw the source of the roar: a physical laborer of

some sort. James guessed his profession by the muscle tone of his limbs and the dirt stains stuck in his clothing. In one hand, he held a ball-peen hammer. In the other, he held a bottle of booze with only a fourth left.

Across from him stood a family, a father, mother, daughter, son. Son whimpered, sitting on the ground. Daughter cowered behind mother, and mother was hunched over both children.

The father stood out in front of his family, protecting them.

The drunken worker roared out another profanity. The father winced at his monstrous tone.

The drunken man saw the wince and chuckled for a moment. "Richie, richie," the drunken man said. His eyes sobered a few shades and he lifted the hammer to point at the man. "S'your lucky day. I was gonna smash 'r head in." The hammer lowered, and he smiled a drunken smile. "I's gonna fladden it in fron' of 'r kid 'n 'r wife." He laughed. "A bit too much to drink." He hiccupped. "'ll get 'rs 'n not a momen' too zoon. We wan' justice. We'll get justice." His mouth curled into a big ugly smile. "We're coming for you." These words were sober and articulate and without a single syllable slurred. The smile was still stuck on his face when he charged the father across from him.

The events that happened after had no order. James heard a roar. *From the man with the hammer?* James thought. *The other?* There was a quick, sharp scream. Blurred bodies. Flashes of movement. Limbs tumbled. Dust was kicked into the air. The mother began to shout. Those watching stood dumbly. The hammer came down. Another roar. Another scream. "Thud, thud, thud," the hammer sang. James winced at each hammer-fall and closed his eyes. But though he closed them, he heard the impacts moreclearly. Blood poured from the body. The head caved in as the hammer met the cheek. The face exploded as the cheek bone collapsed. The mandible twisted. The body flopped down prone, and blood pooled on the concrete.

After the noise settled, James opened his eyes slowly, afraid of seeing the drunken man towering over a pulped body.

The liquor bottle was a neck of glass on the concrete. A bloody lump of flesh lay on the ground. It was barely recognizable as something that had once been living, let alone something human. Blood painted its twisted form a shocking red.

And over the body stood the father. His chest heaved. His calves shone red. Blood glistened on his face and arms. His suit was ripped. His hair appeared as if it had almost been pulled out. The hammer glistened with blood as it fell from his hand and thudded to the ground. And his family cowered behind him. His wife, shocked, stared up at him with terror in her eyes. "Come on, Jeanette. Let's go home." He held out his hand, and his wife reached up to take it. He led them away from the crimson mess as if he were taking a walk. His wife skittered this way and that, trying her best to keep her children from looking at the carnage. When they reached the end of the block, a Rolls Royce rolled up next to them, and they disappeared into the back of the limousine.

Slowly, finally, the shock lifted from James' mind, and he began to look at the others who had watched this incident. *Incident?* James thought. *What a euphemism.* He sighed as his eyes moved from one terrified face to another.

David? he thought. He was unsure whether it was the boy given the surprise pasted on his face. *David, yeah*, he repeated as he saw Mackenzie next to him.

James wanted to call out, but he could not. So, with all his strength, he willed them to look over.

Finally, they did, and Mackenzie gave a subtle nod to James. The three boys began to walk down the street until they could meet in the middle out of sight of the incident. Mackenzie and James nodded to each other with confused eyes. Neither knew what to say about what had just happened.

"Let's just go." Mackenzie began to search through his pockets and mechanically pulled out a cigarette. A police car and ambulance pushed them out of the street and wailed toward the scene of the fight.

The sounds of the hammer filled James' mind for several more hours, and he silently wondered what had just happened, but when the other boys said nothing of it either way, it faded from his mind. It had been a dispute between two men. The authorities had been on their way. The authorities would take care of it, and it would be little more than a mild inconvenience James had experienced on one blazing-hot day during Holy Week.

TWELVE

"A good many men were found hanging by their belts the next
day. All their work gone up in smoke."
– Eshter Fleet –

Ezekiel stared out the window morosely, his body hunched forward, head propped up by his arm. It had started to rain the night before and was not supposed to stop until early the next morning. The day was dreary, gray, and depressing. The warm Sunday had blown away.

There was little to be excited about as an economist these days. There was even less to be excited about if you were the economist chosen by the Executive Ten to make predictions about the future, as he was. It was neither prestigious nor a job that lasted long, for at the first hint of bad news about the economy, the Executive Ten would have their predictive economist killed. Over the past three months, five had been executed.

Because of the poor nature of the economy and because he always had to manipulate the data to fool the federal executives, Ezekiel was hardly ever in a good mood and hardly ever laughed anymore.

The whole thing concerned his wife very deeply, and she knew the change was brought on by the pressures of his new position even though he had only expressed it to her once out of anger after she had continued to inquire into why he was feeling the way he did. He had expressed to her that speaking of it outside of work only aggravated the stress to an even greater degree. He told her that home allowed him to forget some troubles of his new position, and to bring it up would lower his chances of ever having a peaceful moment. Because of this outburst, she said nothing else to him but rather responded with physical touch. It helped most of the time, but today as she stretched out her hand to place it on his back, he did not even notice.

Ezekiel had predicted an upswing in the economy this month, but Ezekiel always predicted an upswing in the economy. Though the economy rarely had an upswing, he was fortunate it varied very little (for it was always quite bad), and he had learned to manipulate graphs each month and use a certain type of language the federal executives would not understand. And another week would pass with Ezekiel's head still on his shoulders.

He had made it a great length of time as the economist, but just as he predicted with great certainty, the luck of this gambler had run out. Ezekiel had thought it would be a far less significant change that would be the signature on his death sentence, but the economy decided that both it and Ezekiel would go out with a bang.

A few weeks ago, after Ezekiel had looked at the long-term data, he predicted a national depression more devastating than the first. The stock market would go red, and no one would be able to sell anything. Jobs would be lost, inflation would skyrocket, and the Executive Ten, the cobra nest, would strangle him. He felt like a dead man already.

He had not told his wife. He did not know how. He tried several times, but his tongue would not form the words. Eventually, he gave up trying. *Why start her mourning early?* he thought, but he feared she already knew something was very wrong. She kept touching him to comfort him as she always did when she sensed something.

Her touch had once been like salve on a wound or aloe on a burn. Now it only made it burn hotter; now it only made the sting more intense. Her company, which had once been joy, had become agony. He did not want to be around her. He did not want to be around anyone.

Ezekiel was alone.

Ezekiel was alone, and he was dying. It was harder to get up in the morning. His hair was falling out. He could not keep food down. His teeth were brittle, and when he broke his fourth molar over the past two weeks, he found a place isolated from the rest of humanity and cried. Though he hid his ailments from his wife, he had been forced to tell her when he lost vision in one eye, which required her to drive him to work. *And how do I repay you, Louise? By withholding the truth? No. I repay you by dying. By leaving behind my wife and family without so much as an explanation.*

Ezekiel's mind raced every second of lunch, but he did not speak. Louise drove him back to work, and he returned her "Goodbye, I love you" with only a head nod.

He remembered his first day. "And this is the second floor. Your office will be the second one on the right." *Second office on the right*, Ezekiel thought to himself as he stepped off the elevator onto the second floor for the last time, though he did not know then it was the last time.

He entered his office, and his secretary looked up from a word processor. Her face was ashen with fear. She was the only other person who knew about the impending crash. He had tried to make sure no one else found out, but he had missed a data sheet and it caught her eye as she threw it out. She inquired. Ezekiel was devastated by the discovery and unable to lie.

"It's happened, hasn't it?" he responded to her expression.

She shook her head. "Not yet, but look at this fax."

Ezekiel walked to her desk and picked up the papers she held. It was a progression of today's financial events, more specifically, what had transpired during Ezekiel's hour-long lunch. The stock market was falling like a plane, and it was just about to crash into the—

Another fax was coming through. Ezekiel waited by the machine until it was complete and picked it up.

"Now it has," he said after glancing at the paper and dropping it in front of her.

"You should leave, sir. I've had a hotel room paid for you and your family since the beginning of the week, so they won't be able to find you when they start searching. It'll buy you a few days," she said and handed him a small tag with the hotel's name and address on it. The tag was tied to a room key. "I figured you were a bit preoccupied to do it yourself."

"Dee, if all money I had wouldn't be worthless in a couple hours, I'd give you a big bonus." He gave her a hug and quickly pulled away, went into his office, and, after a bit of racket, returned.

"Okay," he said. "What I have is more of a keepsake than anything. I tried giving it to my wife, but she said it was the ugliest thing in the world, so it has been sitting in my office drawer for more than six months and in a box in my closet before that. but it's worth some money and these next few years are going to be really tough." He pulled out a gaudy necklace. "It's silver and gold and the gemstones are diamond and opal. A gesture of thanks, Dee. Good luck on your life." He exited quickly after these final words, trying but failing to look unhurried as he made his way out of the building.

He had given Dee a necklace because it was what she had given him, a chance: a chance to save his family and a chance, though small, of saving himself. Life returned to him in a manner it had not existed for two months. This was because he now realized he'd always had something that gave him hope to continue: the ability to fight.

Ezekiel stepped out into the rain.

THIRTEEN

"The collapse of the United States was inevitable. When you take a person's voice away, the check will eventually come due."
– Moses Hehl –

The fight after the fair disappeared within an hour. The news reports said nothing concerning it.

"The quarterly economic prediction has been put out." The first news anchor momentarily glanced down at several papers in her hands as she spoke. "This upcoming July 22nd will mark twenty years of continuous economic growth. Studies conducted by the senior federal economic advisor point to no slowdown for the next fifteen years at least."

"Despite the passing of Dalimore, it is good to see his legacy will live on for years, perhaps even decades," the second anchor continued, a tinge of sadness at the edge of each syllable.

"Yes," the first anchor replied, "and those of you who want to pay your respects to the late President Dalimore can head downtown. Many have already taken the opportunity and placed flowers, coins, or other keepsakes at the foot of the Dalimore statue." She gave a gentle smile and paused for a moment of reverence.

"In other news, a date of execution has been set for the five terrorists found guilty of attempting to plant a bomb in the nation's capital building. The court has determined that the appropriate and just response is the execution of these individuals. A judge has sentenced the five to be hanged by the neck until dead this Thursday night, 6:00 pm Eastern."

"Today there is a break in the grand play, so take time to go to the fight or stay at home and prepare for the upcoming finale at the end of the week."

"We hope you all enjoy the fight. Go, Meggeran!"

The television screen winked out.

~~

A body glistening with sweat came close to losing balance and falling backward. The impact of a fist on flesh sounded like a loud slap. The fist pulled back again and rammed first into a cheek, then a jaw, then a nose. Swollen skin under the eye tore open under the power of the knuckles.

The fighter slid across the mat on the balls of his feet. His knees bent slightly, and his hands were fists protecting his face. He took a quick step forward and launched a kick into his opponent's thigh.

The winded Meggeran failed to absorb the kick, and his leg collapsed under him for a split second. While Meggeran staggered, the fighter's fist met his jaw, sending him back three steps. The fighter charged, dropped to one knee, slid in a duck-walk, and, grabbing both of Meggeran's legs behind the knees, stood up while arching his back slightly and tipped him onto the ground. Before the fighter could finish the process of submitting Meggeran, a bell clanged, saving the champion from defeat.

As the two walked back to their corners, the crowd booed at the contender. He ignored them as he sat in his corner. James saw the side of his coach's face scowl at the fighter as he spoke to him, but the movements his mouth made held no words for James. The fighter's face darkened into a scowl of its own, and he responded to his coach in what looked like argumentation. The coach spat back with a look of controlled fury. The fighter shook his head. His forehead went down into his fisted hands. Finally, he stopped shaking his head, looked at his coach, and nodded.

His coach said something back, nodded himself, and patted the fighter on the leg. The bell rang, and the fighter stood up and moved to meet Meggeran.

The contest continued differently the following rounds. The fighter slowed. Though he had dominated

Meggeran the first round, in the second he only had a small advantage. During the third, the two were evenly matched, but by the fourth, the contender's energy was on the wane and Meggeran was clearly gaining the upper hand.

Mackenzie broke out into a cheer when the bell for the fifth round rang and Meggeran began with a furious fist to the side of the head that knocked the fighter onto his back.

Mackenzie stood and cheered as Meggeran jumped forward to submit the fighter. After falling into his seat, he spoke loudly to the two other boys. "God, I love the fights!" he yelled over the crowd. He wiped the sweat that was forming on his forehead. "Thought Meggeran's streak was gone in that first round. What a way for the great to fall if that had been the case." Mackenzie took a panting breath before continuing. "Pathetic for him to fall to a man off the street." Mack wiped his forehead again. "All strategy," Mackenzie continued. "Let the fool wear himself out and then destroy him." Mackenzie smiled and his eyes gleamed as he watched the final moments of the fight. Meggeran caught the arm of the fighter and used his own arms and legs to hyperextend the fighter's elbow. Though the fighter struggled valiantly, he could not break the hold. His arm continued to bend backwards, and he gave a loud cry of pain and tapped vigorously to signal forfeiture.

The only one not on his feet and cheering was David, who sat still in his seat peering through the bodies at the fighter.

Mackenzie screamed until he was hoarse and then glanced back. When he noticed David sitting silently amidst all those standing, he collapsed into his seat.

After catching his breath, he looked towards the ring and the fighters. "Didn't you enjoy the fight?" he asked.

David glanced over, but his eyes returned to the ring and the fighters. "I did. I enjoyed the fight. But I don't have any skin in the game." As he spoke, the crowd began to sit, and the referee came to announce the winner of the contest. "They're entertaining, but I haven't seen a fight since I was young, so I don't feel an emotional connection to any fighter."

The two fighters moved to the center of the ring. The referee grabbed both at the wrist and raised Meggeran's, victorious, high into the air. The crowd cheered once more.

Mackenzie did not respond to David's comments on the fights until the fighters had exited, the final announcements had been made, and the three of them were out of the arena back on the street and heading home.

"What kind of person doesn't follow the fights?" Mackenzie asked as he began hailing cabs. When none of them would stop, he began to hail more vigorously.

"We used to when I was little, but more recently . . ." He shrugged. "For the past five years, six, maybe seven, my parents stopped watching them. So I stopped watching. And once they died . . ." David became silent.

139

"So, your parents died, ummm . . ." James tried to pick out his words delicately. "They passed away when, again?"

I never told you, David thought, but he did not allow his face to convey the slight annoyance at James' presumption. "A few years back," he answered tersely, attempting not to be abrasive but offering no additional information.

"Hmm," James answered but did not ask more, having understood the subtle hint.

"Gah!" Mackenzie yelled. The two glanced over. "What is wrong with these cabs!" he yelled. He threw up a fist and swore at another one that passed them without stopping. Frustrated, he plunged his hand into his pocket and pulled out a cigarette. Before another passed without acknowledging their existence, he had it lit and was puffing like an angry cartoon train. Two more passed, and he let out a grunt of frustration.

"I've got money to buy you, your car, and your damn house, you damn cabbie!" he yelled at the latest iteration of transportational hope. Another long curse exited his mouth.

James laughed at his antics. David showed no reaction.

Mackenzie cursed again, short and biting. "Why don't they stop?" he asked in a growl under his breath.

"They've probably got fares, Mack," James sang out.

"No," Mackenzie barked before James could finish, "not a single head in the back of any of them." He breathed out a frustrated sigh through his nose. "All of 'um empty."

He threw his cigarette down and lifted his hand to wave at another. It passed with a Doppler-wail.

David turned his focus off the stream of cabs flowing from one direction to the other. To their south, he noticed people in the far distance still pouring out of the arena. Across the street, a lonely drug store stood. Its white light streamed out. A clerk waited with a bored look behind the till, and a lone patron wandered the aisles aimlessly. Then he turned to the north and his heart leapt. "I don't think I would stop either," he said.

Mackenzie, still holding up his hand, responded, "And why's that?"

"Look," David replied.

The sounds had gone unnoticed because of the fight crowds out in the street. The boys had disregarded the noise as a brawl born from a drunken disagreement. They had not expected a riot, or whatever this was. Though it was several blocks down, and they remained in the safety of distance, all three could see the events unfold.

A building to the northeast was aflame. Fire licked up to the orange sky. Smoke billowed out. Though a fire engine had already arrived, the fire was not being attended to. Men and women blocked the road, and as cars drove down it, they would stop each vehicle, drag the driver out, and proceed to smash the car windows. Others in the crowd attacked the police who had just arrived.

"Protestors!" Mackenzie shook his head. "People protest every week in this city, nothing new." He stepped off the curb into the street. "Damn cowardly cabbies," he continued. "Just protestors. And a fire. The cops'll take care of the protestors. The firemen'll take care of the fire. Still, I'll have to force one of these cabbies to pick us up."

After he spoke he stepped in the way of the next cab. At first, it did not look as if the cab was going to stop, but at the last second, it screeched to a halt with only feet to spare.

The cabbie rolled down his window and rattled off profanities at Mackenzie.

"Get out of my way!" he yelled furiously.

"Give us a ride!" Mackenzie yelled back.

"No. Get out of my way!" the cabbie screamed.

Mackenzie stepped closer to the vehicle, so the cab could not move forward, and motioned for the other two boys to get in. David and James moved toward the closest door.

"No! No rides for you!" the cabbie yelled at the two.

"Yes!" Mackenzie yelled back.

"No!" the cabbie yelled.

James had to keep himself from laughing at the situation.

"I'll pay you double fare!" Mackenzie yelled back.

"Triple!" the cabbie answered. David and James reached the door. "Don't you get in!" the cabbie yelled. The door locks clicked shut.

"Double and I'll throw in a good tip!" Mackenzie replied.

The cabbie shook his head and threw up his hands. The door locks went up, and the three boys clambered into the car.

"Oh, smells like fish in here," Mackenzie mumbled under his breath as he entered.

"It! Does! Not!" the cabbie replied.

Mackenzie smiled at his reaction.

"Where to?" the cabbed asked with a scowl on his face.

Mackenzie relayed the information.

"Road's blocked by protestors, you see?" He pointed back toward the pandemonium.

"Well, take an alternate route then," Mackenzie replied.

"All major routes are blocked. It'll be a while before the police can clear the streets."

"And there isn't any other route?" Mackenzie asked.

The cabbie laughed. "Of course. Of course," he mumbled. "I know a way, but I want quadruple fare."

Mackenzie swore at him.

"Quadruple fare or I can drop you on the road, and you can risk the neighborhood on foot. 'S gang territory. And I'm sure a boss would love to have a few soft rich boys to entertain him."

Looks of disgust twisted onto all three boys' faces.

"Quadruple fare. I know you've got more than enough money."

"And you can't just go through the protestors?" David asked.

"I lose my car if I go near the protestors. I lose my car, I lose my livelihood."

"And going through gang turf is better?"

"Gangsters understand cash. Gangsters like cash. We've got cash. Protestors are ideologues who'll beat me and destroy my car for transporting you few bourgeoisie."

"Okay, quadruple, and let's get going a bit faster then," Mackenzie replied with a sigh. "Thief," he mumbled.

The cabbie laughed. As they sped off, James wondered how Mackenzie was going to come up with the money. *But he will*, he thought. *He always does. Somehow.*

They continued down the same avenue for several miles before veering onto a side road. Side road gave way to side road. City lights grew rarer. Buildings were in further and further stages of decomposition.

"Keep your heads down," the cabbie muttered back. "Damn. No. Keep 'em up, cuz otherwise they'll try to flag me down."

"We'll stay sitting up," Mackenzie answered.

"Good, good," the cabbie muttered to himself, but he barely heard what Mackenzie said. "We'll just get through here quickly. We'll be fine, fine, fine." His voice quivered with a fear as he spoke to himself.

The boys showed no such reservation. Instead, their eyes perked up at the sight of the ghetto, and they each looked out to study the destitute, alien landscape.

None said anything to any other. Their thoughts were like bubbles rising through the mud of a bog. So long the words struggled that they seemed aimless and empty by the time they overcame and reached the surface.

"Dresden." The cabbie glanced in his mirror as he spoke to the boys like a father commenting on a place from his past. "The place always reminded me of Dresden."

None of the boys answered, so lost were they in this echoing memory of decay.

"Shows how wicked the Soviets are. A whole city, no mercy for even women or children. All laid to waste." He swallowed as the car rolled through a stop sign. "In every paper," he said in absentminded nervousness. "Oddly similar. Eerily similar." The fear in his throat cleared, and the car reached its previous speed. "Not a pretty picture." He spoke to the boys in a mumble. "Not a pretty picture at all." The words "No, no, no" echoed through his teeth, and then briefly he went silent before fear once more got the better of his tongue.

"Enjoy the fight?" he asked back to the boys but did not wait for any to answer. "Heard it on the radio. Had to work; wish I could have gotten tickets." He paused. The blinkers clicked on and off as he focused on turning. "Good old Meggeran. Oh, he is getting old, but he's still the best. Was worried about him that first round. So close, but a champ who's been champ as long as him knows a few things about strategy." He let out a nervous chuckle. "Took 'im to school." He smiled back at the boys, and then went back to his nervous driving.

Once more the car was silent. Its engine hummed, and

its shocks squeaked as it bounced into and then out of a pothole. The cabbie shifted nervously. He sighed and mumbled under his breath as they turned another corner.

Fifteen more fretful minutes passed in silence. Then the decomposition slowly gave way. Like ice, it seemed to melt and break up. The world outside began to look newer and newer until the war-torn ghetto gave way to a modest, lower-class neighborhood, and the cabbie finally began to relax.

"Out of the gangs' turf," the cabbie called back to them. "Fifteen minutes or so." He sat back in his seat and let out a relieved sigh.

He sat in this way for a little less than five minutes, but then he suddenly perked up. "What's that?" he mumbled to himself.

And though he only spoke to himself, he caught the attention of the three boys. They directed their attention to a muffled sound from the outside of the car. A man who had just turned the corner was running down the street.

"Help!" the man screamed, and the cabbie slowed the car until it stopped.

Just as David was about to roll down the window, the four in the car saw a mob in dirty work clothes carrying all manner of makeshift weapons as if they belonged in a story of Frankenstein's monster. From inside the car they heard the clomp of boots and loud cries.

"Ayers Saunders! For Ayers Saunders!" They yelled. "Remember Saunders!"

"What's going on?" James asked. For a long few seconds, no one answered his question and only watched as the space between the fleeing man and the mob narrowed. Closer and closer they came until the mob descended on him two blocks away from the car. As his cries rose and reached out to them, the cabbie answered James' question slowly.

"Ayers Saunders," the cabbie said with no inflection in his voice.

"Who's that?" James asked as the crowd swallowed the running man.

"Society man killed him on Monday. Brutal merciless killing with a hammer," the cabbie continued. "His names been like a fire on the mouths of the working class." The cabbie let out a long sigh. "The time's come." He pressed down the clutch and shifted the car into first. It shot forward as he quickly shifted it to second, third, then fourth. "He wouldn't join them."

James shook his head and squinted his eyes in confusion. "I don't understand," he answered.

"It means people are fighting back. It means a class war. It means . . . It means I've got to get home." And after he had spoken, he would say no more but instead pressed on the gas pedal to speed the car forward, dropped them off, and sped away with a "Good luck," and forgot his pay.

FOURTEEN

---

*"After administering a survey to look at the public's view of
liberty, scientists found people desire complete autonomy that
would lead to an anarchic state, and programs which would, by
necessity, take all but a sliver of that autonomy away."*
– Esther Fleet –

The rain did not stop the next day. The drizzle that
had existed the day before turned to a downpour. Rain
blew from the side. Streetlights flickered on in the dusky
light, and a European car pulled up to the curb on the
industrial side of the city in front of a large building. The
door to the car opened, and a tall, thin man with a neatly
trimmed beard stepped out into the weather. He walked
to the building as if there were no rain. He did not bring
up his hand to shield his head, he did not move any more
quickly, and he did not even flinch or squint his eyes as the
rain pelted his face. Several individuals holding umbrellas

to the wind followed him. Though these individuals would have preferred to hurry into the building, they were forced to take on the speed of their employer lest he assume their speed as a desire to usurp his authority. Eventually, they made it inside, and all but the mustachioed man were seen shaking rain off their bodies.

Daniel looked at his workers as they moved about the factory. He was born to the lower class and knew what it was to barely makes ends meet. After he had left his parents, he had lived on the streets. One day he had seen a vendor and had decided a business was better than stealing, so he cleaned himself up and began to sell knickknacks. Being an excellent salesman, he soon had enough money to hire others to sell his wares. Eventually, his ability in business allowed him to have a respectable store and, eventually, sway over an entire company.

Daniel moved through the large, noisy building with his entourage trailing behind him. His eyes moved from this to that, machine piece to machine piece, machine to machine, machine to worker, worker to his work. He often stopped to lift a panel or peer inside the workings of a machine. Quite often, he would make a comment and his entourage would jot something down on their clipboards. He understood the machines, for the most part. When he started the company, he had not only run the company but also worked maintenance shifts in the factory. Ten years had elapsed since those long days, but just as a car from 1960 was similar in its functioning to one of 1950, so machines differed little from decade to decade.

As he continued down the rows of machines, he would also stop the random worker and ask him about the work he was doing and how satisfied he was with the conditions and pay. Though Daniel did not care in a personal sense whether his workers were satisfied and content, he cared a great deal about it from a business and financial perspective. By paying his workers well, he had kept them happy, and by keeping them happy, they had not formed a union.

Daniel did not underestimate their collective power. He had taken the advice of the Caesars and kept the people happy with his own type of bread and circuses, and he believed he was doing a better job than those ancient monarchs. So far, the company had made it through downturns in the economy without dropping the pay of its workers. Anticipating these occurrences, Daniel had put away a considerable sum of his salary each year into a fund and used the interest to pick up the slack when the company was unable to.

When he was a child, his father had created puzzle boxes that required many specific, consecutive steps to open, and Daniel had become so good at them he exceeded his father's ability to make one he could not solve. He looked at the problem of inflation as a puzzle box of a sort. If only he could pull the correct levers and turn the correct wheels in the correct order then the box would open, and he would avert financial disaster.

Early in his teenage years, he had been sitting down at the kitchen table in their home whittling a small stick into an even smaller stick when his brother pulled out a small cube about the size of four dice.

"Hey Danielle, I made a puzzle box for ya." He set the little cube down in front of Daniel. It had three levers sticking out of it, a string, two wheels, and an entire side was one large button. His brother then expressed the opinion that Daniel would not be able to find the solution. Daniel merely laughed at the comment and began working on it immediately. He worked on the small puzzle box on and off for six months after which he tossed the cube back to his brother. "You win. Now tell me the solution." His brother only smiled and shook his head. That was the final puzzle box he had attempted before he had the fight with his father and had run away from home to eventually become the business owner he was today. He did not think of that puzzle box often, but as he thought of this imminent fiscal crisis, it came back to his mind. Would this be the puzzle box he could not open?

A messenger ran into the building soaking wet from the pouring rain. Daniel did not even notice him until he tapped him on the shoulder. The man was startled from his deep thoughts but quickly regained his composure when he saw who it was. "Good or bad, Jack?" he asked the messenger as he was handed a folded piece of paper.

"I haven't read it, sir," the young man said.

Daniel grunted before he flipped the letter open and looked down. "Psh, you read the letter, but you couldn't understand it; didn't you, Jack?" The letter was company statistics, and it told him what he wished he did not know.

"No sir, swear I didn't," the messenger answered, but Daniel did not care either way. His mind was flying through combinations of numbers and variables, and he finally thought he arrived at one that worked.

"Where is the telephone?" he asked and was quickly ushered to one nearby. He dialed several numbers and, after a brief wait, was speaking to someone through the lines. He asked several questions, and after getting his answer he laughed and slammed the phone down on the receiver.

Quickly, he wrote a long note with a list of instructions on the back of the letter, folded it into a small square, as was his habit, and handed it over to the messenger. "Take this to the president of payroll," he ordered.

FIFTEEN

"The country was a golden cesspool."
– Friday Setarcos –

The rain came down like strings, holding the earth up like a cut-out-cardboard-prop piece on a stage. It sizzled and crackled like a pan of frying bacon. Above them, it drummed on the roof like nervous fingers, pinging as it slapped something metal. Once every ten minutes or so a gentle rumble could be heard from off in the distance if one listened intently, and it, along with the chattering voice of the rain, quickly passed into the background of one's thoughts.

A faint bright spot in the sky identified the sun, but the world was shrouded in gray, as if an artist drawing with a pencil had taken a finger and put a big, obscuring smudge across clarity. The warmth of the week was consumed in cold.

The newscasters made no mention of Ayers Saunders.

"Today marks the first downward trend in the economy in two decades." The words came out of the TV as thick, heavy static, as if it traveled on strands of yarn or twine and was pulled through the speakers.

"Though frightening, top economic minds state the trend is likely to be a mere aberration and will only last several weeks or a couple months at most," the first news anchor said in a voice of assurance before the second anchored continued with the report.

"The downward trend is due to an attempted terror attack on the stock exchange today by a terror cell connected to the group 'Sons of Liberty.'" The TV showed a picture of the Philadelphia Stock Exchange sitting in the sun of a warm afternoon.

On the TV, a bald man's face spoke. His head gleamed, and his eyes squinted at the sunlight. Bags hung under his eyelids, and his face was puffy from lack of sleep. Every so often, his eyes wandered off in exhaustion as he spoke, and stubble had grown dark on his face.

"Mr. Philmenor, you are a broker who works on the floor of the stock exchange." The man nodded. The field reporter, a thin man with long arms and a shirt that hung off him like a sack, continued, "Can you tell us a little of what happened from your perspective and what that may mean for the economy?"

Mr. Philmenor looked at the reporter with wide eyes, glanced at the camera, and then back at the reporter.

"Well," he said. His eyes moved from the reporter and looked at something off camera. Each eye seemed to bulge out of its socket with exhaustion. "We . . ." A hand ran over his gleaming head. He looked at the reporter again. His eyes stirred with thought, and he brought up a hand to pinch the bridge of his nose to relieve the tension. He then looked at the camera, ignoring the reporter. "Everyone started selling."

The reporter nodded along.

"Everyone started selling. It turned into a madhouse." Both hands came up and pressed into his eyes. He sighed and shook his head. "We're headed into another depression, worse than the—"

The screen cut to black for a moment and then switched back to the two news anchors in the studio.

"Sorry about that," the first anchor said. "We seem to be having some technical issues and have lost connection to our field reporter." The screen cut to the view of a building, clearly a bank. "This is Union State bank at the center of the city." The camera panned out and revealed a large crowd of people moving toward the bank and a large clump of people already waiting outside to get in. "A small number of people have run on the banks, but though this may appear to be an echo of the Great Depression and something to be worried about, all economists are saying these small runs on the banks are a minuscule part of our whole economy and will not even begin to affect it." More people crowded into the shot of the bank until it was almost completely filled with bodies, and the image winked away to nothing.

A chilly wind blew through the window. It picked up the heavy curtain, twisting it. It danced to the left and then the right, fluttering slightly like a ship's sail heading straight into the wind, and the cold wind, invisible, moved swiftly past the curtain, past a face busy with thought, and finally twisted around the head of the boy and lifted up his hair and made it dance in unison with the drape.

The window was slammed shut with a loud whack. The dance of the curtain died. It hung limply, and Mackenzie's hair rested on top of his head, slightly askew.

Mack brushed several hairs off his forehead and reached to his lap, and the crinkle of paper could be heard as he turned a page. He breathed out quietly. His face was set in neither a frown nor a smile, unreadable except the eyes, which were filled with questions. Every so often his eyes would flit away from the book he read to the window and the outside world. Here he would squint. Sometimes he would bring a hand up to touch the tip of his nose in thought. Often, he would mumble, often inaudibly. "Doesn't line up," he said to himself. His eyes remained focused on the gray world outside. He mumbled to himself again and then looked back at the book to read. His finger remained on his nose, now tapping.

"The terrorist leader responsible for this downward economic trend is a forty-seven-year-old man from a rural county in California. Police apprehended Moses Hehl at his wife's house at 8:oo am this morning." The face of a middle-aged man, clean-shaven, dressed in the button-down shirt and tie of middle management appeared on the screen. The tie was flipped over and there was a scowl on the face. In the background stood a house leaning a bit far to the left, pushed sideways by high winds that had blown through the area. "Government officials have put out a statement written by the Sons of Liberty. Moses Hehl belongs to this group, and he abides by their mission to 'overthrow the unconstitutional oppression of the American people by the executive.' Federal authorities state that many new leads have been uncovered because of his apprehension, which may lead to the final rooting out and dismemberment of the terrorist organization."

James half-listened to the fuzzy words floating from the TV to his ears. Though the rain was muted and though the room was small and quiet, his ears only heard every third word, and he comprehended even less.

The night had been a long one for all three. Images of the mob of working men as they swallowed the running man moved through their minds. The cabbie's voice clung to their ears. The name, Ayers Saunders, was an unspoken word on their lips. When each had awoken to the new day, he thought it must have merely been a dream, but overnight the name seemed to fill the mouth of every servant in the house. "Did you hear about Ayers Saunders?" "Well, he shouldn't've done what he did." "I stand with Ayers Saunders." "But can you believe it, killed so brazenly as if he didn't matter a lick." The image of the hammer coming down on the man filled the boy's minds, and all three were uneasy with the prospect of going out that day, even Mackenzie.

"Workers still protest all through the city, flocking in hundreds with their signs and banners to bring awareness to the plight of their fellow man," the reporter continued. Though James was certain he knew the reason why so many workers were turning in out in protest, not a word made mention of the name.

"Your move." David sat across from him at the table. The chess board was placed between them. When they sat down in the room, the pieces were already set up, and it had been David, absentmindedly fiddling with a pawn, who played an opening move. For five minutes, the pawn stood in the center of the board like a student in a dream at the front of class naked, exposed and solitary. James was deep in conversation with Mackenzie and only saw it when Mackenzie snatched a book of history from one of the shelves and plopped himself into a leather chair. After Mackenzie had fallen into the chair, he stopped talking, and James, left with nothing to do, found himself observing first the falling rain outside and then the empty office until his eyes stumbled on the chess board and his fingers hovered over pieces. Finally, he moved a piece. His move brought about another move by David, and a string of turns ensued.

"We're fighting for the rights of every worker. We

don't deserve to be paid like dogs, to be treated like dogs, to be killed in the streets like—" Another man, not Moses Hehl, spoke from the television screen until he was cut to black due to technical difficulties.

David castled. James moved a pawn forward to free his rook. Mackenzie sighed and turned to the window again. David made another move after a short few seconds of thought, and the TV droned once more with the voice of the lead anchor.

". . . the CEO of Lion Industries, which is responsible for a large portion of the country's electronic manufacturing. Workers have been protesting unfair pay for several years, but a recent drop in wages and an increase in layoffs and firings have led to a spike in protestor turnout."

"I guess that is what happens when a company does not treat its workers well," the other anchor piped up from his silence.

After much thought, James finally moved a piece. David bit his tongue, and then after a few moments he moved a bishop, took a knight, and nullified the gains James had made only seconds before.

James swore under his breath before moving again. After three more moves, David captured a rook.

James swore again.

"A bit berserk." Mackenzie did not even look up from his book as he said the words. "James."

James remained silent and focused on the board. Instead, the television answered Mackenzie.

"Tonight, those who belonged to the uprising of Tallahassee will be executed at 8:00 pm Eastern." A picture of the rebels' compound appeared on the screen.

James swore again.

"James," Mack said.

James glanced over to the boy but did not respond. The news began interviewing law enforcement and a politician.

James swore again.

"Try to control the center," Mackenzie continued.

James responded with silence and then another expletive before shaking his head and pushing himself away from the board.

"Aw, forget about it," he said as he leaned back into his chair. "That's it." He looked over at David as he spoke.

"Forfeit?" David asked.

"Yeah," James responded.

"We hope you have a good Friday." The news anchor chuckled after saying the words.

"And a good night," the second anchor said. Both smiled as the screen blinked to commercials.

"You've given up so quickly." Disappointment filled Mackenzie's voice.

"When you're beat . . ." James did not finish the phrase. He shrugged.

Mackenzie attempted to flip the book he was reading

onto the coffee table, but the tome bounced to the ground. David and James abandoned the board on the table. David fell into one of the comfortable chairs in the center of the room, and James dropped himself onto the couch across from Mackenzie.

"First time?" David asked James.

James leaned his head back into the chair. "Second," he responded.

"Good show," David replied.

James smiled weakly in response.

"David, you?" Mackenzie asked. "Your first time playing?"

"No," David spoke slowly, "but it feels like it might as well be."

After David answered, Mackenzie appeared as if he was about to speak, but he did not. He was cut off by a sound that sat the boys up and sent them squinting at one another.

"A scream?" David asked the question quietly as he moved toward the window.

It was a scream, a loud, piercing, bloody-murder scream. Though this realization brought James up to his feet to follow David to the window, Mackenzie continued to lounge on the chair in eyebrow-wrinkled thought.

"Police at the neighbors'," David said with no emotion in his voice.

James looked over and saw a black-and-white vehicle, but his poor vision did not allow him to determine whether it was a police car or not. "Is it?" he asked the other boy.

David nodded and squinted his eyes to try to pick out more. "Can't see much else," David said.

"Do we have binoculars or a telescope somewhere?" James turned to ask Mackenzie.

" Ope! House door just opened," David responded.

James turned his eyes back to the window and out to the neighbors' house, but his eyes could not reach across the distance to understand what was going on.

Behind the other two boys, Mackenzie pushed himself off the couch slowly.

"Mack, come look at this!" David said excitedly while waving his hand to the boy.

Mack did not go to the window, but leisurely made his way to the desk and began to rummage through the drawers.

"What's going on, David?" James asked.

"Someone's . . . no, three people are coming out of the door. Two police officers and the neighbor. It must be the neighbor."

"What are they doing?" James squinted harder, but the best he could do was make out moving blurs.

"They're beating him." It was Mackenzie's voice, and the two other boys looked back to see Mackenzie holding an old spyglass up to his face. "One is holding Mr. Henderson; the other is beating him." He took the spyglass down from his eye for a moment and shook his head.

"God, what is happening this week?" He stared over at the other house. "I can't watch this. God." He shook his head again. "Here." He thrust the telescope into David's hands, who then continued to describe the events that were transpiring with aide of the spyglass stuck to one eye.

After a time, David also shook his head and handed the spyglass to James, who, after putting it up to his face and getting the scene into focus, saw the police pick up the shockingly bloody body of Mr. Henderson, drag him to their vehicle, and toss his unconscious body into the back. A few short minutes later, the police jumped into the front of the vehicle, and the police car sped out of the driveway and down the road as if a drunk were at the wheel. James let the spyglass fall from his face; the screaming had gone on the entire time and continued to fill his ears.

Then slowly, and as one, the boys moved from the window to the chairs and couch and once more slumped down into them. A round of swearing went from one boy to the other and then bounced off each randomly like a pinball.

Mackenzie called Mr. Henderson "a saint if I've ever seen one," and at first refused to believe that he could have done anything wrong. But finally, after deliberation and discussion, they conceded that something of an illegal nature could have been going on behind the scenes, though they had no idea what because they still had the inability to imagine Mr. Henderson even hitting a fly with a swatter.

It was already past dinner when Master Karling called for James. At first, Mackenzie thought the buzz was for him, but after hearing "James Glus— I mean, Ander, uh, um, James Anderson." It was apparent he desired to speak with the other boy.

"You aren't in the middle of anything, are you?" Master Karling's tinny voice came over the intercom after James answered.

"Um, no, sir." James covered a yawn. "I'm available."

"Perfect. Perfect." There was a noise as if Master Karling was trying to find something. "Please come to my office ASAP, will you, Mr. Anderson? Dress for the weather."

"Yes, sir," James replied, but he was answered with silence.

James and Mackenzie looked at each other and then back at the intercom.

"What's so strange?" David asked.

"I'm surprised he knows my name," James said to Mackenzie.

"Karling doesn't care too much about employees. Barely cares about me, and I see him every day," Mackenzie answered.

"I guess I've got to go," James said.

Even after he had disappeared into the corridor, he continued to hear the banter between the other boys.

"What do you think it is about?" David asked.

"He did join a cult recently. Cat things, I'm assuming," Mackenzie replied.

"Um?"

James imagined David's eyes shifting back and forth and his eyebrows knotting in confusion.

"They like to eat them." Mackenzie's voice was a bit more difficult to hear now.

"Okay?" David answered.

Just a few more steps and James knew their voices would disappear altogether.

"They have a cat cooking contest; it's a big deal."

Finally, their voices became too distant and muffled to understand. James shook his head and smiled.

SIXTEEN

"If you wanted to get rid of someone in the 70s, you would pay a psychiatrist to diagnose the person with an insanity. Once they were sent to the ghetto, they no longer existed."
– Samuel Judah, *American Autumn* –

James dressed and was soon walking through the hallway near Master Karling's office when he saw the man, the vagabond, come out of the office and hustle down the hall away from him. He was a smaller man with brown hair, a scraggly beard, and tattered clothes. A thin, dark scarf, perhaps another color originally but darkened by use, was tied around his neck, and James could see pieces of a red sweater through holes in his blazer. James could only see one of the man's arms. The other seemed to be hidden in his coat or nonexistent.

Many unusual things such as this were happening in the household lately. Master Karling was not present as often as he had been before the death of Dalimore. His regular routine about the house had been broken since the end of January, and his servants had assumed that he was in his offices since then, even though there were prolonged periods in which absolutely no noise was heard from the office suite. He fired his secretary. He gave specific instructions to his chefs about meal deliveries. Different servants, never the same one twice, were called at odd times such as the middle of the night or the wee hours of the morning and were sent to do tasks, but no details could be coaxed out of them. It was all bizarre, to say the least, and rumors among the servants and even Society circulated that Master Karling must have gone some type of mad, was going through an existential crisis, or both.

James was relieved to hear sanity in the man's voice when he entered the room. "Perfect timing, James. I just got done speaking with a business associate. Great, you're dressed for the weather. I have an address. You won't find it on newer maps, but I have an older one for you. I've written down the modern names of the streets that have been changed over the years. It is about a seven- or eight-mile walk, so take the bus. It won't take you to the address, but I've marked an intersection on the map that will get you about a mile and a half away." He shoved an envelope into James' hand with the map underneath. "There is a name on the front. Give it to her." *Emily Woolf*, James read as he glanced down. "Go straight there and be careful. Then come straight back." James hesitated for more instruction from Master Karling, but when none was given, he nodded, smiled weakly, and rushed out of the room.

~~~

James gagged at the smell as he stepped off the bus into the slums. He averted his eyes from other streetwalkers. To either side rolled the same house design again and again with different colors of faded paint, different windows broken, and different toys or tools or trash lying on the lawn. Passing through a final row of houses and walking up to a chain-link fence, he looked across the barren strip of land separating "the humans over here from the animals over there"—half a mile of empty dirt. Though he tried to convince himself the stories of that place were untrue, and, though he did not intellectually assent to the danger of them, still, fear fluttered in his chest.

"Well, James," he said to himself. "Are you ready?" A sarcastic *Nope* floated through his mind as he found a gap in the fence near the ground and crawled under on his belly.

The half-mile of no man's land stretched far in its barren, treeless, grassless, and lifeless manner. Though it was only a few football fields in length, his walk across took an eternity. He crossed with little difficulty, besides fear from his own contrived evils, and arrived at the first houses. Use and time had rippled, swelled, and sunk the streets into deep troughs. During winter months, snowfall upon snowfall would pile and drift as high as houses.

The houses were no more than shacks turning to dust. The windows were shattered. All the paint had peeled off, leaving the dull, depressing-gray wood, and the doors hung off hinges. As James looked at the houses, he noticed cracks that showed all the way through to the other side. Most roofs were caved in, and many frames had rotted, given up, and become lopsided. No smoke rose from the chimneys. No people wandered the streets. The place was a ghost town, a long-forgotten graveyard filled with lifeless wind.

James consulted his map to find the first street, "Honey Dew Avenue." James found Honey Dew as bitter as anise. He had no such luck finding the rest of the street signs. Few still stood, and most had fallen and been covered with debris and mud. Despite his navigation being based on guesswork, he eventually arrived at what he was sure to be the house. A weak tendril of smoke drifted from its chimney.

Though he saw no reason the dilapidated, abandoned, garbage-filled neighborhood deserved any formality, he knocked. No inward decency compelled him to understand the lives of those in the ghetto and give them the dignity. It was simply a reaction, an unheeded, unwilled reaction. To his surprise, the door opened.

James had never met a person like this man, since he had not been alive when the untouchables lived among the regular population. He was forty, perhaps fifty (James found his face to have strange features, making it difficult to guess his age). He wore simple clothes placing function over fashion: Velcro shoes, sweatpants tucked into thick wool socks, and a big ugly sweater, and he wore them as if he had no thought to how they looked.

"I'm looking for Emily Woolf," James asked. "Is she here?" The man smiled a big smile and sauntered off, saying something to himself. James guessed the man liked this Emily, because upon hearing her name his face lit with a smile.

"I'm looking for Emily Woolf," James said again. The man turned his head as he walked away and gave another squint-eyed smile. *Am I talking to an idiot?* the boy thought. The man then walked from the porch into the house and closed the door with a hard slam, leaving James alone in the cold.

He waited a few minutes, confused and annoyed, before knocking again. As his white knuckles rapped on the door a second time, it swung open. A woman, almost sixty, stood in the doorway. The man stood behind her like a shadow.

"Who are you?" she asked warily.

"I'm James, um, Anderson. I'm looking for Emily Woolf."

"Why?" the woman asked.

"I was sent here to give her this." He held up the envelope.

"By who?" The woman did not seem in any mood for niceties.

"Iya... Jonathan Karling." He did not want to tell her because Master Karling had been so secretive about the whole thing, but the name came out without thought.

"Humph," she vocalized. "Taking an interest after all?"

After she swore at Master Karling under her breath, James was finally invited into the house. He wished he had not been. The stench was the first thing to greet him, a horrible stench, a stench he would remember his entire life. It was a mix of body odor, feces, urine, vomit, old food, burning hair, burning flesh, and death.

The living room was connected to a kitchen, and together both were filled with just over fifteen people. Some seemed distant, lost in deep thought, but James was surprised to find many conversing with one another.

James looked back to the woman. "Why are you here? There doesn't seem to be anything wrong with you." James hesitated a long moment before he asked the question.

"I'm the caretaker," she replied.

"You take care of all these people alone?" James asked.

"I'm not the only one; there are a few others," she continued, watching James as he looked around the room. The woman followed his eyes and seemed to read his mind. "Just normal people reacting to abnormal things," she responded.

James watched two men playing chess. Their conversation was about medicine. The older of the two was amidst an explanation when he stopped midsentence and his face twisted into frustration. He tried to speak, but his words came out as syntaxial nonsense. Finally, the man gave up and rested his head on top of his hands.

"Hi, I'm Emily Woolf." James looked up from the two men at a redheaded woman. Her small, freckle-covered face wore a determined look.

"Oh, hi," James said in reply to her soft voice. "I have a letter for you." He brought it up from his lap and handed it to her. She nodded, thanked him, and excused herself without comment.

Well, I guess that's that, thought James. "I should get going. It's getting late," he said.

The old woman nodded. "Say hi to Jonathan for me," she said.

James left without answering.

The smell was gone as quickly as it had come. He had done his duty as an employee. It had not been as terrible as he had expected, and the people he had seen in the ghetto were not the monsters of teenage fantasy.

As James moved north through no man's land, it was strange to him that this place had once been like any other part of the city. The houses had been lit. Smoke rose from chimneys, and the muffled voices of families were heard as one walked by. Fathers arrived home from work. The smell of food, spice, perfume, and cologne filled the houses instead of the vacant smell of the cold wind, which did not really fill a house but only possessed it.

~~~

It was a wooden object that met with James' skull. It sent a bolt of pain through his brain, and he crumpled to the ground. He felt the object strike him again, and he fell face-forward onto the cold concrete as a sharp foot was driven into his ribs. He could not cry out; he could not breathe. Several more kicks slammed into his head.

James waited face-down in the dirty street until his face became numb, then attempted to push himself onto all fours, and as the pain of exertion shot through his body, causing him to fall back, the wooden object was driven more forcefully than ever into his temple.

The world turned to black confusion when the attacker flipped him over and rifled through his pockets, cursing him for not having anything of value. James saw his blurred face through a thin slit of his eye. They were about the same age. In the end, he took James' warm clothes, shoes, and socks, leaving him exposed, face-up in the wind.

So this is how it ends, he thought as he began to slip into a half-conscious dreamlike state. *Well.* The feeling of the cold ground against his back began to fade. *At least it's warm.*

He could have died for all he knew, and this new warmth was the afterlife. It certainly was not Hell or Limbo, so he guessed it must have been Heaven, but it was such a dark place and he had always heard Heaven

173

described as being full of light. *Maybe this is the trip there,* he thought, as he was almost certain that he had become weightless and was moving through the air. He started to hear voices, voices not of joy but of grave concern. *But maybe this isn't the path to Heaven. No one mentions what the journey to Hell is like, and I don't see any white light.* Then the pain started again, worse than before, a slow groaning pain. James quickly forgot the warmth and opened his eyes. He felt a strong tug on his arm and saw the heels of a man and the ground moving beneath his face.

I guess the devil's come to drag me to Hell, was the last thing he thought before blacking out.

SEVENTEEN

"Pain was not my cage. I was. I could not escape my reality."
– James Anderson –

First the pain filled him. It was a hot pain, a pulsing pain that ran from his eye sockets around the top of his head to the base of his neck. It was a fierce pain that lingered on and on. James leaned back his head and gritted his teeth to counteract the agony, but it took no heed of his will and slowly, eventually faded of its own accord.

Next came fear. He was in a chair. He knew this. The roughness of ropes bit into his ankles and wrists. His ankles had been tied to the chair, and both hands were tied together behind his back. He strained against the ropes, but the more he tugged, the tighter they became. Despite its futility, he struggled several minutes before he sagged in the chair and realized the uselessness of his efforts. The fear that had been a mere flutter of anxiety in his chest grew into a long acid that he tasted on the back of his tongue and that stretched down through his body.

Like the pain, the fear faded as well. Eventually, only he and the room remained. Its silence filled him as he looked about. The darkness he saw seemed to stretch forever to his left, but on his right, a dirty window let in a little wan light. *An attic*, James reasoned from the slanting ceiling and the thick feel of dust and disuse about the place. But it was no attic he knew, and he began to wonder why he was here.

He had gone to the ghetto. He had delivered the letter. He had trudged back, been hit on the back of the head, brought here. *But why?* He had no memory of entering wherever he was, of being carried to the attic, of being tied to a chair.

For a moment, he wondered if this were all Mackenzie's doing. He hoped to God it was Mackenzie, but he knew this line of reasoning made no sense. Mackenzie knew he had left the estate but not where he went; and though Mackenzie enjoyed practical jokes, James did not think he was capable of one so cruel.

No. It was clear that Mackenzie had nothing to do with this. *If only*, James wished, but he could not hold such foolish hope. Reason got the better of him, and an image he had long forgotten rose in his memory. It was the face of a boy roughly his age. He was thin and had modestly long hair that covered half of his forehead before sweeping to the side of his head. A calm, content smile filled his face.

His body had turned up in a river. It had been brutalized, and he was the first. Others, always young men, continued to be found. All bore the strikingly similar wounds that made the police sure these were not separate incidents.

"The Chicagoland Killer is what we're calling him, a serial murderer," the mustachioed lawman on the television screen had explained. James had never heard the word before, but it only took a few more phrases to understand what the word meant in full.

Serial murderer. It was a term that implied the killing of multiple victims, but as the law man had stated, a serial murderer was not satisfied merely with continuous killing. "These individuals have what we call an antisocial personality, uh, sociopathic, psychopathic tendencies, and yes, they are concerned with the killing of individuals, find pleasure in it. There is almost a compulsion to kill, like an itch, but they also take pleasure in inflicting pain on their victims, as much pain as possible."

For many minutes after the thought, James felt nothing. His emotions were distant. He experienced them as the anesthetized feels pain. The room was little more than a dream. The fear stretching through his body turned to anxiety. The anxiety turned to a tingle. Again, he questioned whether he was still alive and thought it interesting one tested one's consciousness based on pain. His eyes drifted about the room. They longed toward the light coming through the window, and he breathed deeply as one adrift in the reality of a perfect summer day. The boy knew he was as good as dead, but he was no longer him. His consciousness was caught in the rapture of denial.

Things don't happen to me, James thought. *Either good or bad.* He sighed. Another had been abducted. Another tied to the chair. Another was to be brutalized. Another's body to be found. It was always another, whether good or bad. True, his mother had died. He was a slave. But the day-in and day-out existence of James was static, plotted boredom; and even in this city, tension razor-sharp, he was trapped inside the sameness of his existence and condemned to be no more than an observer of all the things happening. He was not in the midst of monumental achievement and events, he was alongside it, existing in a parallel reality. In twenty-five years he could make the claim that many proudly make, that he had experienced such-and-such an event, but he knew in his heart it did not matter. Whether he was present at such a thing mattered little to how history would play out, and he knew life would change little even for those he knew, let alone future generations, if he had never been born. *I just drift, always drift,* he thought. *Nothing ever happens to me, either good or bad,* he reiterated to himself, but the thought was a lie. He did not look on another's life, and as he came down from the high of shock, reality came rushing back in. He had been dragged through the streets. He was in this dark attic. He was tied to a chair. It was his misfortune. His captivity. His pain.

Stark truth illuminated the reality that he had a limited existence, both in the finite nature of his body and the temporality of his life, and as the image of the young, blonde boy returned to him, great empty terror and the anticipation of agony filled him up. Death was near. Death was certainly near. Black emptiness was before his eyes, but something else was on the horizon of his existence was well.

He shuddered at the thought of what was coming, and he prayed an empty prayer that he would be murdered quickly.

~~~

A shirt flew from the closet and landed on the wood floor. Mackenzie grunted, and David heard him talking to himself as several hangers shifted. Another shirt flew out of the room and landed at David's feet. Snatching one of them up, he inspected it, then stared into the gloom of the large closet, wondering how Mackenzie could see well enough to determine the color of the shirt.

"Are we, uh . . .?" David started. Mackenzie grunted again. More muttering stumbled out of the closet, and another shirt landed on the floor. "Hey Mack," David said.

More muttering and another shirt came from the closet before Mackenzie replied. "Yep," he answered with a burr of a syllable.

"Are we going as Society today?" David asked.

There was another long pause before Mackenzie emerged from the closet with an armful of clothes. "Why wouldn't we go as Society?" he asked as he dropped the clothes on the bed.

David laughed at his response. He thought the reason was obvious. Unrest had been building in the lower class. It seemed every servant he walked past had the name of Ayers Saunders on their lips. Even those who doubted anything would come of the man's death were compelled to support this new cause. The lower classes always complained. Demonstrators always existed, voicing their opinions for two, maybe three days, then fading to wherever, but in those cases, the lower classes always made Society aware of their grievance. In this case, it was ever only whispers as if everyone was keeping one big secret, and Society did not seem to know.

"We're not even going to be near the mob," Mackenzie answered as if reading his mind. "And nothing is going to happen today anyway. Easter maybe, but not until then at least." He shook his head as he continued. After he had spoken, he pointed to the pile of clothes he had collected and then to David. "Pick something out. Put it on. I've got to tell James to get over here or we'll be late."

David nodded in response and began to look through the clothes. He found a pair of pants quickly and began to put them on as Mackenzie picked up the phone and punched the call code to James' room. After a few moments ringing, Mackenzie pressed the hook and punched the code again.

"S'posed to rain today," Mackenzie said after he had waited once more, pressed the hook, and dialed James' room again.

David nodded back as he chose a shirt.

"We're getting a box," Mackenzie continued, but David could not respond because the boy followed after that with, "It's Mack over at the house. I need James." The individual on the other end replied. David heard the words as tinny noise. "Okay, thanks," Mackenzie answered tersely and dropped the phone onto the hook.

"James coming?" David asked as he finished the last few buttons of his shirt.

Mackenzie raised his eyebrows and smiled a thin sarcastic smile. "He's not over there," he replied.

"Well, he doesn't have any duties to attend to, does he?" David asked.

"Only the cook and cleaners have duties today." Mackenzie peered down at his borrowed watch and sighed.

"Hmmm," David answered as he sat down and pulled on his shoes.

Mackenzie sighed again. "James is one of the most ordinary people I know, a character trait he has no intention of changing and one I find endearing, but amidst all the normalcy of James, he has the odd habit of disappearing for about twenty-four hours. Only happens once a year or so. One day everything is normal and the next, the only evidence of him existing is his dresser and his bed. Then he returns without a word of it and goes back to his duties as if it never happened."

"Sounds annoying," David answered.

Mackenzie shook his head in reply. "No, no, it's never annoying. I think it is one of the best parts about James. I can predict his movements from a mile away, but I never can predict when he goes, where he goes, or why."

"But you're annoyed now?"

Mackenzie shook his head. He looked over at David. Another sarcastic smile crept over his face. "I've been planning this week for a month." He sighed as he looked out the window at the dreary overcast world then back at David. "You ready?" he asked.

David nodded and stood to his feet.

~~~

A sob caught in James' throat as he heard a loud creak and thuds as if someone were coming up an old staircase. The boy held his breath without thought, and a deep heaviness filled his abdomen as the sounds on the stairs filled his ears.

Thud! Like a boot. *Oooheee.* And a bleating animal. *Thud, oooheee.* Like a babbling baby. Vague emotion, a film seen through a dark, drunken fog, filled the front of his mind like dirty swamp water spilling into a porcelain tub. *Thud! Ooohee.* The noises mixed together in a menagerie of sound. The menagerie was joined by a harsh static ripple of air flowing through closed teeth.

Thud! Shhh! Oooheee. Someone's coming up the stairs. *Thud!* A cough. *Shhh!*

And then the muttering. It started as a cooing little voice. It rattled a cadence of conversation.

Another voice responded, and though James was certain it was the same voice speaking both times, it sounded as if it were from another person. The first came out like silk. It was a gentle hand on the shoulder, an uncertain, sweet, frail, little whisper. The second was rough and forceful. Energetic. It was angry like the bite of a saw into wood, a deep, menacing growl with bared teeth.

James' stomach rose in his throat, and a shudder of fear tingled down his spine.

The thuds and moaning of the steps continued. The breathing hushed in and whistled out, and James once more struggled at the rope binding him. Sweat beaded on his forehead and rolled into his eyes. It rolled down his neck and arms onto his palms. The thud on the stairs filled his mind. Each new sound was like a bass beat with all the force the percussionist could muster. The stairs no longer moaned; they wailed as if they were a banshee come to get him and drag him into death. The man's breath was the panting of a predator stalking its prey. The whistling exhale was the descent of a World War Two shell followed by the *boom* of the foot on the following step.

Straining against the rope made it bite deeper into his

wrists and ankles. Despite the pain, he continued to strain against them even as he heard the breathing pause and a door behind him that he could not see open with a long, drawling moan.

James' breath thickened as he heard the first soft steps of the boots in the room. A large shadow moved to his right. The person's breath came out in slow, asthmatic gasps. James leaned forward as far as he could, putting as much pressure on the ropes around his wrists with the hope of breaking them.

"The knots get tighter the more you pull," the figure said. His voice was gravelly.

James did not respond. The man began humming, a deep rumbling hum. He cleared his throat and coughed again. The humming continued. James heard a drawer open and several things shift within it. Something thudded onto a countertop. The man yawned.

"I hope you're comfortable." James heard a chuckle. The man yawned again. "It's been a long day. I would have been more accommodating, ah, hospitable, but . . ." He gave a single laugh. "Long days."

James did not respond.

The man laughed again.

James swallowed down fear. There was something dark in the laugh. It ran down his spine and froze his blood. It made James' heartbeats heavy in his chest.

"Do you ever think about your death?" the man asked as if he were asking a friend.

James remained silent and bit his tongue to hold back emotion.

The man stepped from behind James, but the boy could only make out the most basic features of his face in the darkness. He was a tall man, broad shouldered, and still well muscled though a paunch had grown at his midsection. He wore a suit, and it appeared as if he had just pulled off his tie. The top two buttons of his shirt were unbuttoned, and suspenders hung down either pant leg. His face was round, his nose bulbous, and the pits of darkness that were his eyes seemed to stare back at James in dead, hate-filled annoyance.

"Do you know why you're here?" the man asked. James could hear the slight edge of frustration in his voice as he spoke.

When James did not respond a third time, the man inspected the garden shears he held and clicked together several times.

"Most of you aren't talkers at first," he continued. "But I bring out the best in you. You'll talk so much for me." He let the garden shears swing to his side as his eyes inspected James then turned to look past him into the darkness.

"You're here, because you don't matter. You're all here, because you don't matter." The man let a little laugh escape his nose. His eyes returned to James and moved across the boy in slow inspection. "I've had boys from the mob. Some from Chicago's ghetto." James thought he saw a small smile form on the man's lips. "You're my third slave. You, of course, won't be my last. I've got two more in the basement now, brothers, I think. They won't be my last either, because you're all cattle. No one flinches when you slaughter a swine."

The man paused, brought the shears up in inspection once more, and began a slow leisurely walk about James as if he were a critic inspecting an art piece.

"And you don't matter because none of you do. You're all slaves. You're all owned, and you'll always be." He let another whispering sound of amusement out through his nose.

"I'm going to let you in on a little secret before I make you love me," the man whispered. His words were careful as if he were considering every inflection of what he said. "It's all manufactured," the man continued in that same gentle whisper. "We control everything." He let out a small chuckle. "Ayers Saunders? I know you've heard the name, because I know it's the only thing you have been talking about these past two days. But Society doesn't know, of course." James saw him shrug and raise his eyebrows in a knowing gesture.

"We created Ayers Saunders. We let you have him as a symbol, because it serves our purposes."

The man paused for a moment as if he were thinking of the profoundness of his own words. "How does that feel?" he asked after that long moment. "We cause even the hate within you. We giveth, we taketh. Hmmm?" The man clicked the shears together in response to his own words and let out a satisfied sigh. "It's good to be a god, let me tell you. It's good to look down at those who pass by in the streets and know I can do whatever I want to them with no repercussions."

The man stepped behind James. The boy felt a large hand on his shoulder and the warmth of the man's breath. He felt the cold metal of the shears on the tip of the littlest finger of his left hand, one blade on either side. "Can you even imagine the rush of having such power?" He chuckled again. "Complete control over another person. Can you imagine?" James could hear the broad smile in his voice. "Can you imagine someone begging you for death? Begging for anything you want besides the pain?"

James felt the blades of the shear tighten around his finger and pain shoot into his hand.

"You'll never have this power," the last words of the man before the shears closed on James' finger were barely a whisper. "And I love that."

EIGHTEEN

—————

"Dalimore initiated the play the year the war ended. Its first
show was in the same city as its last."
– Anthology of American Culture –

The breeze caressed the boys' skin. A newspaper
caught on the stone foot of Dalimore. The late president
stood without noticing. His usual stony eyes appeared soft
today, as if the occasion tugged at his heart. The grass at
his feet glowed green, and the sky was flat gray.

Friday was always the busiest day of the Great Play.

Good Friday, David thought as they entered the crowd.
Aren't three people executed on Friday? Though he knew the
answer, he smiled at the irony of the situation. *Good?* He
shook his head at the thought.

"Hot dogs're good," Mackenzie said as he motioned
with his hand full of the food. "Sure you don't want one?"

David shook his head. It was the third time Mackenzie

had asked him. In the car, the boy had made countless comments about his hunger, and when they had entered through the gates, Mackenzie's first words had been a question. "I'm hungry. Wanna hotdog?" While in line, the boy had asked him if he were sure he did not want one, and now again. Each time David told him he was not hungry, but that did not deter Mackenzie from asking.

"How did you get box seats?" David asked as they moved away from the hotdog stand and toward the area reserved for Society members.

Mackenzie glanced over with a smile. "Karling wasn't going. He wasn't doing anything with the tickets." Mackenzie shrugged. His teeth gleamed. "I needed some tickets."

"He had three?" David asked.

Mackenzie chuckled this time. "The man had six. One for him, another for his wife, four more for a 180-degree buffer."

David shook his head, and Mackenzie finished his hotdog as they entered the restricted area and were escorted to their seats like royalty.

The morning scenes of the play were a grim contrast to Sunday. The god-man was dragged before a Roman dignitary. He was questioned, whipped for no reason, clothed in a purple robe and mocked, and crowned with a thick bramble of thorns. The victorious king of Sunday was debased and bloody, and even David himself watched with an eager anticipation. Though he believed not a word

189

of the story to be true, he could not contend with his own human fascination for violence. The scenes were long ones, meant to mark time with the telling of events from the source material; but though it grew into the late morning when the first act of the day ended, the sun still hid itself behind clouds, and the world was dull and desaturated.

"What of it now?" David asked softly a few minutes after the actors had disappeared.

"Well," he shrugged, "the rest of the play."

"Sitting here?" David asked, and Mackenzie only nodded. David was filled with confusion as he looked before him and saw no adequate avenue down which one would be able to carry the cross, but his confusion was short-lived as the box lifted with all its denizens and shifted to face the other direction.

Mackenzie glanced over with a smile when the motion had stopped, but as he turned away, David thought he heard the boy let out a curse at the absent James.

~~~

The man chuckled under his breath as he left the attic. After James no longer heard the man's footfalls on the stairs, he cursed him, a loud angry profanity, and sagged into the chair in despondence. One hand cupped the other gingerly, causing blood to cover both as the liquid poured from his finger. James stared out at the darkness of the room.

"So, what now?" His voice wavered as it came out.

James sighed as pain burned through his hand, but it was only agony against the background of something greater. It had come to this. His life was over. The life of a servant was rarely enjoyable, but he wished he could live its mundane nothingness for eternity rather than this for a day.

"But then again." He did not whisper this time. Another sigh escaped him as he tried and failed to ignore the burning pain of his hand. "Then again," he continued. "Isn't my life futile in the end? All of us, futile lives, slaves, the mob, untouchables." He stared out at the blackness before him as the words of the man pressed themselves into his mind. "We live. We mill about in misery. We die. No pleasure in this life, no eternal life to come." He tried to adjust his position in the chair, but the ropes only grew tighter. "Dead here, dead there. If misery and death is my fate, why not go out with a bang, unbelievable misery and a quick death?"

Tears filled his eyes as the words left his lips. *Why, though?* he wondered as tears rolled down his face. *Why is this my life? Why do others have it easy? Why not me? Why am I always on the beating end of a stick?*

James let out a sob and then gritted his teeth. Defeat filled him for a long time. The defeat was a deep sadness. This sadness turned into frustration. The blood flowed from his hand, big tears from his eyes. The frustration turned to anger, and with a loud scream he strained at his bonds one last time with every fiber of his being, and his hands slipped up through the rope barely, just a fraction of an inch.

~~

Thunder rumbled from a great distance. The rain was a soft patter above the heads of Mackenzie and David, and David watched as small rivulets ran down the glass of the box. More distant thunder rumbled, and David looked up at the sky. Slate-gray clouds filled his vision. The world had been vibrant on Sunday, but now all life seemed to have been sucked out of it. Existence had turned into a ghost or a wavering shadow rather than the real thing.

David's eyes wandered to the others who sat in the box. It was a cool day outside, but in these seats of luxury, it was dry, comforting warmth. The members of Society near them were finishing their lunches. They ate, they drank, they conversed, and they laughed without a thought to the cold, dreary world outside. Inside was a world of paradise achieved, and what was the point of heeding anything else? Not only riches, but their place in Society had secured for them the privilege, as they saw it, of living in a world in which only their own cloistered selves existed.

David looked back to the outside world, not to the sky but the crowd this time. The lower class was a huddled mass. Hands went over heads with everything from coats to newspapers. The people wore light clothing, stained by time and patched in a dozen places. Children ran through legs without a thought to their future in this world, but an odd intensity filled the adults. He had expected a somber mood all about, but instead of sadness, they all seemed to be brooding.

Mackenzie shifted in his seat. Distant thunder broke again, and the light trickle of rain that had been falling before turned into a steady, springtime shower.

The god-man, covered in blood, appeared from behind the fountain. The crowd was filled with a murmur and then hushes before settling to silence. The bloodied man, almost naked, with a crown of thorns pressed into his head, walked in slow exhaustion stooped under the large cross.

Those who had formulated the story of Jesus certainly had done a decent job of it. Sunday, he had entered the city a king, the fulfillment of prophecies, as the story put it. Now he was walking those same streets condemned to die, a criminal with the implement of his execution on his back. There were no shouts of joy from the crowd. The man's slow procession was met with odd silence. The breath of the god-man filled David's ears, and the clatter of the cross as it fell on the ground for the first of three times seemed to echo off the buildings. He passed the fountain. Silence. Pain filled his expression. Silence. He looked up at the sky as if in miserable prayer. The silence buzzed in David's ears.

The sound amidst the silence was earsplitting. The

whole crowd shuddered in fright, and David wondered if it was a lightning strike nearby, but he had seen no lightning. The sound repeated, but this time it was followed by a piercing, seemingly endless scream.

"What was that?" he asked. The sound filled the world a third time. "What's going on?" It boomed through the city a fourth, a fifth, a sixth time. Another scream joined the first.

David's eyes flitted through the crowd and found the source of the scream. It was a young woman. A young man covered in blood was in her arms.

"Gunfire," Mackenzie said. David barely heard the word before it was swallowed up by another blast that ripped through the city, and he dove to the ground. Another report of gunfire answered it as David watched Mackenzie stand up and move toward the window.

"Mackenzie!" he cried. "Mackenzie!" he screamed the name louder. Mackenzie pressed his hand against the window, not heeding the sound of his own name.

~~~

James' body relaxed as both hands slipped up through the rope. A shock of adrenaline moved through him as he untied his legs. The exaltation of relief and the slow simmer of anxiety danced within him. One leg was freed with a long sigh. When the other was freed, James fell back into the chair in a type of euphoric, exhausted stupor. He had wished for something impossible. His wish had been granted. The emotion of freedom was intoxicating but what to do with this freedom was beyond him, so he went back to where he had been. He sat in the chair and stared into the blackness of the room.

It was the sound on the stairs that brought him to action. He broke out of his stunned silence, jumped up from the chair, and, as if it would do any good, began to stare in long and hard determination at the door. The stupor broke as the footsteps grew nearer, but though he was now aware that he should do something besides idly stand and wait for the man to come and tie him up again, he searched and searched his mind frantically but found nothing.

I could . . . I could . . . But the thoughts would not come. His mind was locked in a vice, and any plan was shoved to the side for the sake of the adrenaline which coursed through his body.

It was the door opening with a loud moan that saved him. The light appeared as a thin sliver at first. The light grew to a large wedge, and as the door revealed the man's face, James jumped forward with a mind of only fear and slammed the door shut with all his might.

The door made a sick, hollow thud as it met the man's head. It vibrated against James' hands, and chipped paint scraped against his bloody finger. As he stepped back with a cry, the man grunted. A moment of silence followed, and the man tumbled down the stairs with a loud crash.

James swore at the man through the door. A smile

filled his face. He swore at the man again and swung the door open.

The staircase was a long one, longer than he had anticipated. It was covered in dust like the attic and lit up by one sconce midway down. Far at the bottom, the man lay in an unmoving heap.

James swore in his direction again, made quick work of the stairs, and as he leapt over the man, a barb of anxiety went through chest. Though James landed safely, as he turned at the first corner of the hall, he heard an irate roar from behind.

~~~

The world did not seem real to Mackenzie as he stared from the box. It was more like something happening somewhere else than reality. He was a tourist staring at the affairs of locals, a television viewer hearing about tragedy, seeing images, but it was not his world. The city erupted with the explosion of gunfire. Fear rose on lips as screams, but he? He was just passing through, and the calamity before him was no more than curiosity to be studied.

Most of the crowd hid. Some flat on their faces, some on their knees. Many went rigid with fear, heavy tears in their eyes. One or two wailed. *How do you wail? Why do you wail?* Mackenzie wondered.

Some hid behind cars. Others the fountain, others under blankets they had brought, and some, lacking all concern for any other person but themselves, hid behind their loved ones. Many fled with the mindless fear of a coward. Several of those who fled were caught by the bite of bullets and stumbled forward. One middle-aged man remained in his seat, hotdog in one hand, the other waving off gunfire as one would a bothersome, summertime fly. A young man in his twenties roared across the crowd with a mighty voice. His arms were stretched wide, and his lips were filled with mockery of the gunman and finally silenced forever a mere five seconds into his yelling.

A final two, a man and a woman—husband and wife Mackenzie assumed—began running back and forth from safety to danger, each time with another person in tow. Mackenzie swore in surprise as they went back a fifth time, and he smiled as they saved their tenth person with no hope for their own skin. It was they who brought him back to reality. After helping an old man to safety, they returned to the fray, running hand in hand. The wife spotted someone cowering behind a body, and as the two ran to retrieve the person, the wife tumbled backward, and her blouse blossomed red. Before the husband could react, he was hit as well and tumbled to the ground with his wife. Mackenzie watched as they leaned against one another in their final moments, and whatever apathy that had filled him before was replaced by sadness. They had saved so many. It did not seem right that they die.

Mackenzie heard muffled yelling off to his left and turned. He saw a face. *Whose face?* he thought. He saw eyes. *Whose eyes?* They stared back wide. The mouth opened in a yell. *My name?* Mackenzie thought.

He turned to face the crowd. His image reflected off the window. A teenage boy stared back with wondering eyes. His blonde hair was white. He did not feel a smile on his face, but it was there.

Then the glass shattered into a million pieces. The wind and the noise of the bullet zoomed past his head, and something bit deep into his shoulder. He felt pain, like animal jaws clamping down on his bones, like the kick of a horse.

~~~

"Mackenzie!" David screamed. Others' screams echoed back to him. "Mackenzie!" The boy looked at the crowd as if he were studying a work of art. "Mackenzie!" The screamed name was sandpaper through David's throat.

Mackenzie glanced at him but did not move. Their eyes met, but Mackenzie was distant, as if he were looking at a stranger.

He screamed the name again, but it was lost in the boom of a gunshot. The glass of the box exploded. A bullet thudded into the wall, and the ricochet of the bullets pressed David's face to the floor.

~~~

The man's feet thudded closely behind James. His

breath wheezed out like a donkey's braying. "Back in the chair!" he barked at the boy, and a shiver of fear ran up James' spine.

As James turned another corner and frantically searched for an exit, he caught another glimpse of the man's bloated face. James gave no thought to how fast he ran. His breath rushed in and out, and it felt as if someone had cracked open his chest, taken a pliers, grabbed the bottom edge of his lungs, and begun to tear them out. The sound of the man's feet grew louder and closer, and the tearing at James' chest forced him to slow.

The man barked another curse and laughed.

A large, winding, wooden staircase appeared at his feet as the man laughed, and he flung himself forward so fast that he was unable to keep his footing and slid the entire way down.

After James had tumbled to the final step, he picked himself off the ground and took off running as fast as his legs could carry him. Turning the corner, he sighed in relief as he saw that the man had only reached the top of the stairs, but as James turned to look where he was going, he swore. His own profanity rang in his ears as he searched and searched but found no way forward.

He cursed again.

The man laughed.

A dead end.

~~

Mackenzie's face stung with hot pain. A deep ache ran through his chest. He groaned, and he heard a voice as if through water. The voice yelled something, the same thing again and again.

The gunfire boomed like distant thunder. The screams from the crowd were like artillery shells.

The voice yelled again.

Mackenzie's eyes were filled with red. Though his face continued to sting with pain, the great ache in his shoulder became numb as if anesthetized.

And that voice again, he thought as he gritted his teeth at the pain in his face. *What is it saying?* he asked himself, but no matter how hard he tried, he could not pick apart the sounds.

NINETEEN

"Let a man never think of himself incapable of his forefather's
evil, lest he fall into the same evil himself."
– Alexander Viccor –

God, David thought after the gunfire ended. He heard a man pick up his voice in a wail. The man cried out for several long minutes until his cry turned into a soft, pathetic whimper. The voice yelled through David's mind. The man fought against reality itself. *Good luck.* David turned from the crowd to the back of the box.

He looked over at Mackenzie, and he felt . . . he was unsure. It was something like heartbreak, but it was far worse, a far more permanent and devastating emotion. David put his hand up to his face and let out a long, loud sigh, hoping he would wake up from a dream, wishing away what he saw like a small child making ever-changing deals with God to change some undesired aspect of his life.

"Mackenzie," he whispered, though he knew it was no good.

"Mackenzie," he whispered again with only a thread of hope.

"Mackenzie."

Mackenzie swore he heard the name. The world had been euphoric, and he was sure either it was a dream, or those memories of pain were a dream. He could not decide which.

"Mackenzie," he heard again and felt the deep bite through his shoulder. Only a moment later, his face burned hot with pain.

Mackenzie gritted his teeth at the pain and opened his eyes. Cold, gentle rain fell on his face. The glass roof of the box had been shattered, and raindrops filled his vision as they plummeted to earth.

"Mackenzie." He heard his name a third time, a different emotion in the voice. Before the voice had been filled by the vacuity of loss, now it held the spark of hope.

The rain fell from the ugly, gray sky. It caught on a flag that fluttered above him. High above the flag thunderheads appeared.

Relief swept through David as Mackenzie groaned in pain.

"Mack," David said. He was answered by another groan. "Mack," he repeated.

"It's going to storm," Mackenzie croaked. He looked over at David and their eyes met. Mackenzie smiled. David pursed his lips.

"It's already storming," David replied.

Mackenzie laughed, but he was caught mid-laugh as pain shot from his shoulder to his chest. A short gasp escaped him, but he recovered his composure in a moment.

"David," he croaked again.

"Yeah," David answered.

"Help me up."

"Okay," David responded, moving quickly to Mackenzie's side; and with much wincing and many cries, the other boy was able to sit, then stand to his feet.

"You're a mess, Mack," David said as they both sat down in their original seats. David inspected Mackenzie's bloodied face, then his bloodied torso, then his blood-stained hair.

"Well, I've been shot. Twice!" Mackenzie answered. "Shoulder, -shoulder," he continued with a stutter through the pain. "A graze across my jawline, as you can see, and up past my temple. And a bullet through my shoulder." He breathed out a sigh, and a look of pain crossed his face.

"We need to get you to a doctor," David said.

Mackenzie did not answer. He stared across the crowd. Each face showed the same shock he felt. Some in the crowd sat motionless. Many were grasping their loved ones in long, relieved embraces. Others, too many others, were stooped over motionless bodies with sobs in their throats and tears in their eyes.

"What a show we have this year," Mackenzie's words were filled with humorless, grim sarcasm. He swore under his breath, and a dark look filled his face.

"We should get to a doctor," David repeated.

Mackenzie nodded. "We'll go," he said. "Let me, ah, a cigarette. I need a cigarette. I just . . . and then we'll go."

David nodded. Each of them found a dry cigarette.

"What happened, as you were standing there?" David asked after they had lit them.

Mackenzie shook his head and shrugged. "People dying," he answered. "A shooter, in a window, on a roof? They hung those terrorists yesterday. Maybe this is . . ." He shook his head and shrugged again.

~~~

James took a deep breath and swore as he stared at the blank wall at the end of the hallway. A brief curiosity of why it ended abruptly when it should have continued floated through his mind, but he forced his thoughts away from the wall and to any possible solution for his current situation.

The man laughed.

To tell me he knows I'm trapped. James shook his head as he turned back the way he had come, and the man's silhouette appeared at the far end of the hall.

James took a deep breath of hesitation as he realized there was only one viable avenue of escape, and a scream filled the air, his own. It came unbeckoned and without thought. It was a scream of fear, yes, but more than that. A scream of overwhelming fear, but a scream borne from a world in which the object of the fear was unavoidable. The man was before him, a dead-end behind. He could have frozen with fear. James could have kept his distance, and his emotions would have approved. The part of him that burned with fear told him to stop. It tugged at his chest, but he knew the only way he would escape would be running back the way he came. So, he ran as fast as he could possibly hope.

His finger burned with pain. His hand was still filled with the blood that had saved him. The feeling of the ropes around his ankles, wrists, and chest flashed through his mind. The man stood before him once more as a monster in the shadows, and James was once more at his every whim. Though James' heart was rigid with fear, he approached the man at a gallop. The fear of meeting that man in the doorway met the fear of defeat, and those incompatible fears burned inside him. Though every fiber of his body pulled him away from the man, he flung himself forward. He knew any other option was ultimate defeat.

With a thread of bravery, he ran. With a thread of bravery, he knocked the man back just enough to slip through the doorway. As a hand grabbed his forearm, it was that thread of bravery that allowed him to fight tooth and nail until he was free and running back down the hallway. Finally, as he burst from the hallway into a bright foyer, this thread of bravery was replaced by blind panic, and all courageous thoughts were replaced by a red door with an ugly face carved into his body: freedom.

But even as James ran those last yards, he felt exposed amidst the vastness of the room. He felt as small as the man had said, as small as the man had treated him. The man was correct, ultimately. Others held power, and he was subservient. Even freed from his service at the House Karling, he knew this to be the case. Society would still exist. He would never be a part of Society. If Society chose something for him, he did not see how he could resist. They were giants, and what was he?

~~~

David's eyes drifted from the dazed crowd to the box behind him. No windows were left, and glass covered the floor in small, gleaming shards. Though the Society members seemed as dazed as anyone else, no one in the box besides Mackenzie appeared to be injured. Now wet with rain, all stood to their feet with little emotion, assessed the crowd with a glance, and walked out of the box in a dignified, though brisk, manner.

When the final member of Society had left and the boys were in the box alone, David glanced over at Mackenzie. A cigarette stuck out of the boy's face, and smoke curled around his head despite the rain. Though precipitation had washed most of the blood from his face, his shirt was still a deep red, and his hair continued to maintain its pink hue.

The fire that always burned bright in Mackenzie's eyes was now only a fitful ember, and his face, always so animated, seemed as rigid as stone with the look of gloom it now held.

Mackenzie grunted.

"Hmmm?" David replied.

"Someone's climbing Dalimore, or something," Mackenzie answered with a half-distracted comment.

~~~

James stumbled from the house to a cobbled path. To his right was a small yard. To his left a garden, still dormant from the winter. Before him he saw a huge iron gate, a brick wall, and a tall city building looming up beyond that. Though most of them had already been demolished or moved to more spacious locations, either by the lakefront or to outskirts of the city, enough Society homes still existed near the city center for James to be aware of them. As he ran through the foyer, he worried escaping would only lead to another chase through the vast acreage that accompanied the Society mansions of a more modern era. James supposed the urban location made for easier abductions when the man behind had a yen for killing.

James approached the wall at a gallop, jumped up, grabbed the edge, and scrambled to the top. He smiled as he stared down the street and thanked Mackenzie for the countless unneeded times he had forced him to climb the tree outside the servants' quarters. His smile grew larger as he saw the statue of Dalimore several blocks to the west.

Mackenzie and David, he thought as he dropped from the wall and ran. Mackenzie had talked to him about how he had obtained tickets for box seats. James could not begin to guess how he had acquired them, but at this moment he was more concerned with keeping alive. He ran a block. Another. James glanced back and saw nothing of the man. He looked forward, and saw the crowd looming up before him. James quickened his pace, but he did not get far before looking up to see a man with dark hair and square glasses standing on the large concrete base of the president's statue.

~~

"Working men and women." Gene had written the speech beforehand, and though he had labored for the right words to begin, he never found them, and greeting the people of the city felt lame on his tongue. To his surprise, those standing nearby looked to him. Even with that uninspiring greeting in that uninspiring voice, with his uninspiring anxiety evident, the people looked to him as if he had the answers to the all questions that filled their hearts.

And that is why we needed a gunman, Gene. Utter tragedy to soften them up. Gene's anxiety faded as he continued.

"You think this is a common terror attack?" More began to turn their eyes to him and the statue of Dalimore. "Do terrorists kill so many of us when they attack?" he continued. "Look around. Terrorists kill Society, but I see only us dead. This isn't the work of a terrorist. It's an attack on the common people. This is clear. And Society has spared themselves." Many of those in the crowd began to nod as Gene continued.

"For twenty years we've been poor." He paused. That is what he had written, but he knew the words would not satisfy this crowd and he had the words that would. "No. We've been poor since the beginning of time. And the rich have always taken everything from us. Money, food, our children, our lives. Just as they took everything from Ayers Saunders." A murmur of agreement rose from the crowd, and Gene suppressed a smile of delight at how well the speech was working. "Just like they'll take everything from your children." This brought a shout of anger from the crowd, and Gene had to pause until it died back to a murmur. "They've amassed wealth, and we are poor. They have power; we have none." Another murmur of disapproval arose from the crowd. Gene paused to look out at the lower class, the mob as Society called them, and met eyes with many of those who nodded in agreement.

"But now is the time for things to change. For Ayers Saunders, for ourselves. For our children." The entire crowd was in his grasp at those words. Just as Roy had explained, once he had tugged at their heartstrings, he needed only to say the word and they would obey him like the good little soldiers they hated so much.

"We must be the change!" His chest swelled as he prepared for his final words.

~~~

"We must rise up!" The man yelled over the crowd and thrust his hand up into the air as David watched. David expected the crowd to shout with deafening assent, but before they could, a lightning bolt struck the statue of Dalimore and the whole city shook with a sound that was far greater than that of the gunfire. The little rain that had been falling on them now turned into a downpour, and another crack of thunder filled the city center.

For a moment, the people were silent. Some had covered their heads at the sound, but they slowly turned their faces to look, not at the man who had spoken, but Dalimore. David heard an inaudible yell from the far end of the crowd. It was answered by another and another until all David could hear was the sound of voices.

"Mackenzie!" he shouted into the other boy's ear. Mackenzie turned with a quizzical look on his face. "Mack!" he yelled again. "We need to go!" He now understood why all the members of Society had left so quickly, and he wished he had the same foresight as they did.

"Why?" Mackenzie asked, shaking his head.

"They're after Society, Mack!" he yelled at the top of his lungs. "And we're Society today!"

~~~

The crowd flowed like water. It moved with determination as if it had its own supreme goals apart from the individuals within it. Its emotion was electric in James' chest. All he could hear were the cries of the people, but those words of the man seemed to echo off the buildings and fill every inch of the city. James cried out. The speech had stirred something deep inside him. At first, he had remained silent, but with so many around screaming for this same desire, the cry burst from him.

We're doing something, he thought. *The common people are doing something.* Mackenzie had been right to hope. Mackenzie was right all along, and he had been living as a miserable fool.

"You're all slaves. You're all owned," the man said in the house. "And you'll always be."

James laughed at the man's words as he passed the statue of Dalimore and looked at the ordinariness of those around himself.

~~~

David scanned the crowd. Lips parted. Together the people yelled out a chant. "Crucify!" they shouted as he walked at a brisk pace toward the short barrier that separated those of Society from the mob. Mackenzie walked ahead of him, cradling his injured side. "Crucify!" the crowd continued to chant.

David shook his head. That story long ago had told of a death that offered freedom. The word echoed from the crowd's lips. They believed another type of death would be life for them. Society would be a plummeting star, and they would be restored. Restored to what? They had no idea, but they moved toward it despite of their ignorance. They believed this riot would open a portal into a world of light.

David knew the riot was inevitable. Every day since the new year, he had sensed a subtle tension. The people were unhappy, angry, and all they needed was a spark. "Which you got today," David mumbled.

You think you're moving toward freedom? He shook his head and remembered how his parents had talked of the lower classes as if they were little children deserving punishment. "They want a sacrifice, and Society will give them death," he said the words aloud. He could barely hear himself over their chants. Frustration filled his voice at the utter stupidity of the situation.

Mackenzie gripped his hand and pulled him forward. David looked at the other boy. "What?" he asked.

Mackenzie swore.

"What?" David asked again.

Mackenzie pointed toward the center of the crowd. David looked to see the crowd surrounding the actor. The cross was on his back, and large stones collided with his body. David let out a loud curse. He had expected looting, flipped cars, broken windows.

He swore again as he watched another bloodied man dropped next to the actor with the cross and sent flying forward with a vicious kick.

"Crucify!" The word came out in a ferocious shout.

"Two more," Mackenzie said as he pulled David forward more quickly. "Four crucified today," he continued as they turned from those condemned to die and searched for the edge of the crowd.

~~~

James moved at a brisk walk with the crowd. The air was filled with excited shouts from those around him. They were moving towards something monumental, a touchstone in the history of the world. James knew. He did not know how he knew, but he knew. Everything was changing for the better.

Perhaps one man could do very little, but millions upon millions of people? How could they be stopped? The assumption he had always made was that power was in the hands of Society. It was just as the man in the house had said before he cut off James' finger: he would always be a slave. He would live a slave. He would die a slave. That was his story, and his story would never change.

Mackenzie understood the world differently. Mackenzie had hope, and even more, a faith that he would not remain a slave. And for brief moments at the start of this bicentennial, James had felt that same hope. But the hope had disappeared as fast as it had arrived, like water through his hands, like vapor in the air, like the passing pleasure of a cigarette. Perhaps Mackenzie could have such high hopes for the future, but James needed proof. He could not live off words alone. The boy needed to see, to hear, to smell, touch, and taste the world being changed before he would believe it.

He needed this body of people moving swiftly, moving with purpose, moving as one, collecting their strength toward one common goal. Mackenzie's words were theoretical principles, but these men and women, their faces, their shouts, their bodies, were the nail holes in the palms, the wound in the side.

James' hope was short-lived within that crowd. His own thoughts of hope were their own vapor on the wind, their own quick cigarette-satisfaction. In one moment, he was filled with a sense of being a part of something larger than himself, something important. In the next, his stomach knotted in fear as he saw something he never imagined he would see.

When he heard the word 'crucify' he thought nothing of it. It seemed appropriate for the situation. In the old story, someone had been put to death so people could rise from the ashes. Today, something was put to death to make way for the new.

The word 'crucify' filled his ears again and again, but

until he saw the five bloodied men, he had never considered taking it literally. He stopped, not knowing what to do, not knowing what to think. Though he had gleaned that there had been one from the man's speech, he had not experienced the shooting. All others around had, and the unreasonable pain brought forth their unreasoned anger, and now it was bringing forth unreasonable, pointless, cruel death.

~~~

"Society!"

Mackenzie almost laughed at the word as he saw the man lift a long, spindly finger and pointed it at David and himself. *Hardly,* he thought as he glanced at David. The two nodded to each other, and they darted away from the man who yelled.

"Society!" the man yelled again, causing those near to look around and spy them as well. A small, sad laugh escaped Mackenzie at the irony. Only living in the ghetto would have made them something further from Society, but they were as much members of Society to the crowd as he had been to the youths of Society for those several years prior.

All comes back around, Mackenzie thought as he pushed past another person and saw it was only a yard or two before they were out of the crowd. Mackenzie took in a deep breath and let it out in relief. Even before he could take in another, he felt a deep pain move through his body as a strong hand closed around his bad shoulder. Mackenzie cried out, more in fear than pain, as several more hands grabbed and pulled him back into the crowd. He cried again as the last hope of freedom slipped away. but before it was gone, he heard a cry from David. Those who held him shifted, their hands loosened, and he went stumbling from their grip until he fell onto his stomach just outside the crowd.

~~~

A voice roared behind James as he stood staring dumbly at the top of the cross in the distance. The voice roared again. "Move!" it shouted.

James glanced back to attend to the voice, but as he did, he felt two large hands on his back giving him a strong shove. The boy stumbled forward into the person in front of him. This person stumbled forward into another who turned back to yell and connect his fist to the other's face.

James stumbled into several others before he regained his balance and moved toward the edge of the crowd, but the damage was already done. Another fist met another face. Other hands pushed. Feet kicked. Fingers clawed. Anger and frustration was met with anger and frustration until the forward movement of the crowd decayed into a brawl.

~~~

Mackenzie laughed as he rushed away from the crowd.

"We're out, Davey!" he called back as he ran. He let out another laugh. "We made it!" he yelled back to David again as he spied the open door of the shop and slipped into it. A large smile spread over his face. He ran to the back and dropped to the ground with his eyes riveted to the window at the front.

His lungs burned. His breath came out in a pant, but relief swept through him. They had made it. They had made it out, barely, but they had.

"David," he breathed out a tired sigh. "Thought we were done, but we"—he turned to where he swore he had heard the other boy sit down, but he was alone—"made it." The final words tumbled out of his mouth, and profanity followed them.

The window at the front of the shop shattered. Some of the mob entered, only to leave with arms full of wares, but Mackenzie sat stunned. David was still in the crowd that was streaming before his eyes.

~~~

David's mind raced. *Mackenzie!* The name flashed through his mind. He prayed that him barrelling into the men had made some difference, that the boy had made it out, but David never saw whether he did or not.

Someone near swore at him. Another yelled, "What the Hell are you doing?" Two men, one short and thick, the other tall and thin, shoved him backward. He landed face down, the palms of his hands scraping off on the concrete.

Within a moment, David's face was pressed into the ground. The cement scraped at the flesh of his cheek, and a foot stepped onto the back of his head, compressing his ocular ridge.

TWENTY

—————

"With the roar of the crowd in our ears, my mother, my brother,
and I waited hours for my father to return to the car. Of course,
he never did."
– Esther Fleet –

"Sir." Daniel's driver had one hand still on the wheel as he spoke. "The roads are blocked off here, too. It looks like the show had a bigger turnout than expected."

"Drive through them; they'll move," Daniel said, not bothering to open his eyes to look.

He thought he had adequately diverted money to save his company, but the economic crash had placed him in a position of inevitable insolvency.

"Sir, they aren't moving," his driver said as he tried to navigate through the people.

"Well, goddamnit, drive over them, Aaron!" His words were a terse angry sigh.

"Yes, sir."

Immediately he regretted his outburst. "I'm sorry," he continued. "A lot is at stake right now."

"No offense taken, sir," Aaron replied graciously.

"You have any advice on what I should do? I've asked everyone else, and I haven't been able to find anything helpful."

"Well, being a regular person, making a regular wage, it isn't the worst thing that could happen."

"I built this company ground up. It took years," Daniel replied. "And now I'm going to lose it in less than three days."

"Every dog has its day, sir."

"So, I've heard," Daniel replied.

A stone slightly smaller than a baseball hit the windshield, shattering it. Daniel heard a pounding on the car, and the vehicle sagged forward and to the left as if someone had just slashed a tire. The car rocked back and forth, and someone with a stone the size of a fist began to beat on one of the back windows. Aaron quickly locked the doors, but he and his employer soon found the car tilted onto its side and then over onto its roof.

~~~

Isaiah regretted missing the show. Sunday, he had planned the entire day around the production but was caught in an overnight shift when his relief had not shown. He had worked the entire eight-hour shift because everyone had obligations they could not miss. At first, the rejection had made him steam, but he then realized he would have done the same thing.

Isaiah was happy he could see at least part of the show. He had never seen his brother act before. As a young man, he had laughed when Jeremiah told the family of his professional acting goals because he thought it was a joke, but after realizing his brother was serious, he thought, *why not?* He understood what it was like to hear the criticism of older brothers and sympathized. *If he really wants to do it, why not?*

Jeremiah had succeeded. Today was the first time Isaiah would ever see his brother act, and he was impressed and quickly decided he would follow along the route, from the trial before Pilate to Jeremiah being taken down from the cross, rather than simply sitting and taking in the show as if it were a parade.

It was only moments after the shouts of revolution reached his ears that Jeremiah was seized.

The newly famous "scientist" and "colleague of the famous Dr. Stonewall" was struck with terror upon hearing his own name and seeing multiple members of the mob pointing at him.

"Isaiah, Dr. Isaiah," one of them said. "Rich doctor Isaiah, Pee-Aich-Dee." The word "rich" scared him. He knew rich was synonymous with evil.

As Isaiah turned on his heel and tried to run, one of the members of the group that had been pointing at him dove, caught his foot, tripped him, and sent him tumbling him to the ground.

~~~

The weight of the cross was the world on Jeremiah's back. Blood ran from his forehead into his eyes, blinding him with red pain. Rocks bounced off his body and left burning welts, and his legs moved forward in a run as fast as he was physically able to move. "Faster!" a voice screamed behind him. "Faster!" Another rock struck his back.

Jeremiah's lungs burned; his heart felt about to burst.

"Faster!" the voice roared.

Jeremiah was aware of little else other than two figures out of the corner of his eyes who were violently pushed forward along with him, the ground before him, and his own pain.

"Jeremiah." He shook his head, swearing he had heard his name. "Jeremiah," he heard again, but guessed it was only hallucinations brought on by the trauma to his head.

~~~

Hosea caught a glimpse of the three men isolated in the center of the crowd and knew something was terribly wrong when a brick came crashing through his window and almost hit him in the face.

He had never liked shows of any sort and had ever given this as his reason for being absent at each—including this one, despite a free ticket and its prestige.

Before, when he was a drug addict, he had been too busy getting high to do anything else. Now reformed, he was too busy with priestly duties.

He had planned his days to avoid this week's shows, but, unfortunately, he had forgotten something at his parish and the parish was located a few buildings up the road from the newly erected statue of Robert Dalimore.

Later he planned on returning to have a service for the few scattered individuals who were not out partying, but each year it was a service attended by fewer and fewer, and, to Hosea, each year it seemed a little more worthless.

He could not find his book in the parish and cursed when he heard the crowd outside.

"Crucify him! Crucify him!" was yelled with such honesty, an itch of curiosity made him peek out of his office window. It was the fact that three people appeared as if they were being led to execution and two of these were not costumed that led him to the conclusion that something was amiss. It was the brick flying through his window that made him rush down the church steps and out onto the street yelling.

"What are you doing?! Stop!" he screamed. "Stop! You can't do this to innocent peo—!" The crowd must have assumed something about him because several individuals sneaked up from behind, and one of them came down upon his head with something hard and heavy.

223

~~

Ezekiel could not help himself when he saw what was happening. His position as the presidential economist, and more specifically his failure at predicting the stock market crash, called for discretion, but he had not been raised to be quiet with evil before him. Though he knew it foolishness to vocalize his distaste, in the estimation of the crowd it was an indiscretion that warranted a death. As soon as Ezekiel began to speak out against what was going on, ten to fifteen men grabbed him and carried him off toward the other four men, three conscious, one unconscious.

Ezekiel did not know what to say, let alone think, when he was dropped into the circle.

"Zeke," Daniel yelled out to his brother in good humor, though Ezekiel could see pain in his eyes as he always did and always would. *Although perhaps not for very long,* he thought. "You should be out of the country right now, brother, with the government after you," Daniel continued.

Ezekiel yelled back to his brother, "No such luck with the transportation workers' boycott."

"Lazy pieces of . . . You should have been the one to make it out if any of the Fleets did, having a wife and family. All of us were happy you weren't here with us. Though I'm happy to see you, I'm not happy to see you." He paused and faked a smile. "I thought losing all my money and my company would be the biggest problem I'd be facing all year." He let out a pant. They had beat him some and even walking was exhausting.

"If any of the Fleets go down, all go down." Ezekiel smiled, but the tear rolling down his cheek betrayed his emotions. He grabbed his brother's arm.

"Go cry on Jeremiah. They beat him badly and have him carrying a cross. He needs a bit of help, for what help is worth right now."

Ezekiel nodded his head and moved over by his brother, who was gasping for air as he struggled to keep the cross up. Ezekiel ducked under one of the beams and stood up to his full height, an action that took all the weight of the cross off Jeremiah's back. Jeremiah sighed in relief.

"You didn't come to my show," Jeremiah yelled over to him.

"Ah, sorry, Jerry, but the economy is kind of going to Hell, and for the past three weeks I've been slowly dying."

"Welcome to the club," Jeremiah said jokingly.

Ezekiel laughed under his breath.

"Just like a Fleet you are, little brother," Ezekiel said.

"Shut up with that 'little' crap. And up until they dropped Daniel and Isaiah into the lions' den with me, I was cussing and crying like a baby," Jeremiah answered.

"What? I thought you three never got along," Ezekiel replied.

"I guess you come to an understanding when you are

going to be dying together. Seems that blood is thicker than water after all." He paused to take a deep, labored breath in before continuing with the hint of a smile on his face. "They say everyone dies alone, Zeke. Guess that's not true about the Fleet brothers."

"Could it be any other way?" Ezekiel looked at Jeremiah, always his little brother by both age and stature, and he saw no fear in his eyes. He looked back at Daniel and Isaiah, with Hosea's unconscious body between them, and saw sadness but not fear. He looked inside himself and saw a fearlessness there as well.

Isaiah met his eyes, and both shared a smile.

"Did Jerry tell you that he thinks you're a bastard for not coming to his show?" Isaiah said.

"What is he talking about? I'm at his show. I'm even *in* his show. Hell, I'm carrying the bloody cross for God's sake." Ezekiel answered.

Jeremiah burst into pain-filled laughter.

"Iz, I heard you developed cold fusion." Ezekiel called out to his other brother.

"Not exactly. I did some mathematics that show a specific theoretical model for cold fusion is possible and probably practical. Actually," Isaiah held onto Hosea with only one arm to reach into his breast pocket and draw out a folded piece of paper with the other, "this is the mathematical model here." He put the paper back in his pocket.

"You're not going to give it to someone?" Ezekiel said.

"Can't anymore. But I figure someone will find it while digging through my corpse,"

"And what if they don't?" Ezekiel asked.

"Well, I guess the world isn't ready for cold fusion," Isaiah said. "This piece of crap we're carrying should wake up. I want to say goodbye to him."

"No need to say goodbye," Daniel yelled from behind the two. "All five Fleet brothers will be passing into eternal glory only minutes apart."

"Well, wake him up anyway. He should be conscious for this. It wouldn't be right if he wasn't. Slap him in the face a bit."

TWENTY ONE

"April gave way to riots in most major cities."
– Samuel Judah, *American Autumn* –

Mackenzie lifted himself off the ground after the last of the crowd had passed. As he moved through the shop, glass popped beneath his feet, and looking down toward the crowd, he saw only a few shop windows remained whole. Though it was unlikely any members of the crowd would see him, and those who were looting did not care whether he existed, Mackenzie moved with caution.

The whole avenue had been destroyed, several cars flipped. Anything able to be broken had been, and the bodies of those who were not fast enough for the mob filled the street. Mackenzie wondered if some were dead. *Others to add to the four they're killing already, I suppose.* Mackenzie looked at the crowd as it moved away. Its pace seemed to have quickened.

He looked away from the crowd and to the statue of Dalimore. The man who had given the speech on the base of the statue was gone. Only the president was left, but in the excitement of the riot, Mackenzie had not noticed the new feature of the man. Though still easily recognized as Dalimore, the lightning had marred him by chipping the clean features of his face away, leaving only bits and pieces of paint here and there, and sending a long, ugly, electrical smudge down his chest. Though one could still tell he was Dalimore, the head of the statue appeared to have aged decades, though it had only been up less than a week.

~~~

James broke from the crowd and ran until he found cover behind a car. Behind was a storm of people pouring towards Golgotha; in front, the rain had collected into a deluge. Thick streams flooded the gutters of the streets. Smoke trickled from dozens of cars. Trash and the bodies of those trampled littered the avenue. Windows were no more than razor panes, and wet glass glinted on the pavement like a thousand shining stars.

His eyes moved from side to side warily, and at each small sound he would stop to listen, then turn in full circles to make certain no one had stopped along with him. Several times he did this before he saw the person.

The individual was male, and he was staring toward the statue. James determined that this person was probably from the mob and most likely dangerous. He decided the best course of action against an individual of violence was violence, and was soon sprinting so quickly forward that he stumbled forward in a lean which would place him flat on his face if he were to stop.

~~~

Mackenzie fell through the air. Pain branched from his shoulder through his body like electricity, and as he landed on his forehead, he was surprised that he did not hear the cracking of bones when his head bounced off the concrete.

Arms wrapped around his throat, and without thinking, Mackenzie bit the attacker's arm, which brought a cry of pain. He thought the bite would be a sufficient deterrent to his attacker, but to be safe he followed it with a knee to the tailbone and knocked the attacker to his stomach. This action separated Mackenzie enough from his attacker to attempt a grab at his ankle and so have at least some control in the fight, however small that may have been, but his attacker was too quick and spun along with him, easily evading Mackenzie's grasp.

~~~

As James spun, he instinctively hooked an arm around his opponent's neck and locked it in place with his other hand. He was careful to put the hold in under the mouth this time. He did not want to be bitten again.

His opponent tried to tear the arms away from his neck

but must have realized the futility of the action because it was not long before he gave up.

I will knock him out and run like Hell, he said to himself, and looked up at the crowd to the east. As he saw a cross lifting up above the crowd like some type of unholy religious ceremony, his arms loosened in surprise.

~~~

The arms around Mackenzie's throat tightened, pressing his Adam's apple back into his windpipe. His breath became a weak wheeze, and his vision blurred and began to grow dark.

Then the grip around his neck loosened, and with barely a thought Mackenzie slipped the arms off his neck, and pushed his hips backward and up so his opponent had no firm connection to the ground. He grabbed the limp arm of his opponent with his good arm and turned his body sideways, causing his opponent to flip onto his back.

Mackenzie jumped on top and placed his legs across the man's belly. He sat on his attacker's waist, found the neck with his fingers, closed his eyes, and squeezed as hard as possible until the breath of his opponent came out in whistling gasps. His arm coursed with almost unbearable pain as he felt the soft skin of the neck beneath his hands, and he wondered how long he would be able to go on. *Only a moment longer*, he thought. *But is that enough?*

He let out a deep sigh and opened his eyes. The crowd roared behind him. Each heartbeat made his arm throb with pain, and he glanced down at his squirming opponent.

~~

The world that had begun to grow darker and darker to James slowly filled with light, and he opened his eyes to see and feel the large raindrops as they fell from heaven. Mackenzie's face poked into his vision inquisitively, and he heard a "hmmm" from the other boy as if he were trying to figure something out.

Mackenzie's head poked into James' vision again, but this time it was accompanied by a very hard slap to across his face and sudden pain.

"Hey, James." Mackenzie's face was still in the center of his vision. "Hey, Jamie!" Mackenzie slapped James again. James moaned. "Ah, there you go, Jamie. Back to the world of the living." Mackenzie's face still loomed in James' vision a mere half foot away from his nose.

"Get out of my face," James said hoarsely as he pushed him away. James rolled to his side and sat up slowly. Mackenzie slapped him again, harder than before.

"Aaaah! Stop slapping me!" James yelled.

"You deserved it," Mackenzie replied.

"How the . . .Why do I deserve to be slapped three times?!" James said. His voice threatened to crack.

"Well, you attacked me. Then you tried to kill me. Then once I realized who you were, I noticed your hand covered in blood. So, I slapped you for almost getting killed and, oh yeah." He slapped James again.

"You son of—"

"And that was for disappearing off the face of the Earth again."

"Thanks," James said sarcastically as he rubbed his cheek.

"Welcome back."

"Good to see you, too," James replied.

"Where have you been?" Mackenzie asked.

James raised his eyebrows. He smiled, but his smile was filled with a grimace of pain. "Ahh." He brought his right arm up quickly to his left side.

"You alright?" Mackenzie asked.

James looked at him through hooded eyes. He swallowed pain in before answering. "I, ah . . ." A wince passed over his face. "I think I've broken a rib." Every syllable sent shooting pain through his side.

Mackenzie looked to the crowd in the distance. "They've stopped," he said in a half-articulate mumble.

James, still holding his side, glanced over at the crowd that seemed to stand still just five hundred yards away. Another cross had risen above the mob. He could still hear the people chant but could not make out what they were saying.

"David's somewhere in there," Mackenzie continued. "Somewhere." James looked over at the boy's face. The chest and right sleeve of his shirt were drenched in blood.

233

"He and I were near each other during the gunfire. Bullet grazed my face. Got one in the shoulder." James' eyes moved from Mackenzie's blood-soaked shirt up to the blood that flowed from the gash across his temple. Where there had always been a slight, mischievous smirk curling up one side of the mouth, there was a gloomy, cold stone seriousness. The fire in his eyes had turned to ash. Everything was gray.

"Or David's on the ground," James replied, focusing his attention on the crowd and trying to make out the unintelligible words they chanted.

"Or on the ground," Mackenzie repeated, as if he had not thought of the possibility. The gloomy eyes met with James'. The boy ran his hand through his pink hair, and his eyes moved from the crowd to the scattered bodies, victims of countless eager feet.

The voice of the crowd was still loud in Mackenzie's ears. Though he knew they still called for crucifixion, the voices were just out of his reach, and the sound of a pain-filled moan made him jump as it filled his ears.

The sound had made James jump as well, which had sent a flash of pain through his side. "God," James said in pain-filled, almost angry annoyance.

Mackenzie took no notice of the words or pain of James or himself. As soon as he heard the moan, his eyes moved from body to body of those trampled by the crowd. He searched for movement, for any signs of life. His eyes searched back and forth, back and forth, and began to count bodies. Twenty-five, he counted, but none moved. His eyes passed carefully over a second time. His eyes passed a third time. On the fourth time, he was about to give up when he saw a hand move up to a face.

~~~

David heard his name. His eyes were filled with raindrops and he tilted his head to allow the water to trickle off his face. The voice had come from somewhere off to his left. The sound of the crowd was behind him.

"David!" The voice was like the happy bark of a dog. Feet scuffled.

"David!" He felt a tug at his arm and opened his eyes to see the face of Mackenzie filling his vision.

Mackenzie's face turned off to David's left. "Hey, James, come over here. I'm gonna need some help!"

They had David on his feet in moments. All three boys winced at the exertion. Each had his own wounds still fresh in his body, and the effect of these wounds played across their faces.

"We're always finding you on your back in bad weather, aren't we?" Mackenzie said. A little lightheartedness returned to his voice.

David laughed. The laugh was followed by a grimace. "Your fault both times," he replied, and Mackenzie burst into laughter for a moment before drawing in a deep wincing breath and cradling his arm.

"Five up," James said.

The other boys glanced at him. They followed his gaze toward the crowd, and all three let their eyes linger as the final two crosses were raised to make five.

"Where did they get the other two?" David asked.

The other boys glanced at him with confused looks.

"The story only has three crosses," he continued.

"Where there's a will . . ." James' voice trailed off as their eyes returned to the crucified. "You know."

David grunted. Mackenzie laughed under his breath, another short humorless laugh.

"Let's go." Mackenzie's words were almost a whisper. "Let's be done with it."

The other two nodded, and they left.

TWENTY TWO

"What a fascinating case study, Society juxtaposed against decay."
– The Gray Ghost –

The news of Friday had spread. The silence of Saturday passed. The nation prayed on Sunday.

Those who had been able to sleep woke early; those who had not rose even earlier. A short collective breath of guilt was taken, and the people of the city filtered off to church whether they believed in God or not.

They sat in pews of churches across the city. Preachers opened their scriptures with sobriety and spoke their good news somberly. "At least it was over," someone whispered loud enough for most in the church to hear. Yes, at least it was over, but it had happened. The morning was bittersweet sacrament. It had happened, but "at least it is over." Even those who had made up the mob spoke those words. That part of them that stood by as five men were crucified was already forgotten.

As Mackenzie, David, and James walked out of the church, bells across the city rang and mingled with each other's sounds. Five rings for the five men. Almost as soon as the ringing started, it stopped. The same silence as Saturday pressed down on the crowd.

As soon as the memory of the bells faded into nonexistence, the Humvees rolled up, and soldiers poured from them. They directed the barrels of their guns toward civilians, and David heard the nasally voice of a tall, thin colonel ordering everyone to the city center. "Anyone who does not comply will be shot," the colonel yelled over the crowd.

The crowd sauntered west to the city center. David looked around at the other civilians, at the soldiers, at the colonel.

"You know what is happening?" The question came in a hushed tone from James at his left.

David shook his head in reply. *No one but that colonel knows*, he thought.

It took a mere fifteen minutes to arrive at the city center. As David surveyed the area, he saw some civilians were being prodded out of trucks. More and more arrived on foot and were pushed into the crowd. David watched as several soldiers set up a machine gun on a tripod and trained it on the crowd. Several others took sledge hammers and broke the fountain down so those on the opposite side would be able to see the makeshift stage that had been set up. More and more civilians were brought to the city center and pressed together until steam rose off the crowd, and people began fainting from the heat.

The crowd was filled with a murmur, quiet, subdued, a knot in every single stomach. David caught bits and pieces of conversation, questions: "What's going on?" "Why are we here?"

Finally, after several hours and too many crowds combined to count, the colonel stepped up onto the small platform.

David looked up through the space between an arm and an abdomen and watched the man as he stared at the crowd. Several soldiers pushed through the crowd and led person after person up to the front around the platform and fountain. David heard the sobbing of wives and the screaming of husbands as their spouses were grabbed by the soldiers and forced to the stage. Every age of adult seemed to be represented at the center.

David watched as a soldier broke through the barrier of the crowd and started to move directly toward him. As the soldier reached his hand toward him, David bit his teeth down until his jaw hurt.

The man grabbed him by the shoulder, turned him, and walked past the boy, releasing his shoulder as he did. David was not to be chosen. His body relaxed, and he let out a long, relieved sigh.

~~~

The arm was a vice gripping James' shoulder. The fingers curled under his clavicle as he was dragged sideways. He heard a yelp of surprise and pain of some sort from Mackenzie as the soldier dragged him to the front. Arriving at the center of the crowd, the soldier threw James at the feet of those who had already been chosen. James felt a sharp kick to his ribs but barely noticed. A fear of something far worse filled him, and he was barely able to stand up among the others.

He felt big tears well up in his eyes. They rolled down his face. A sob caught in his throat. He tried to run out through the crowd, but a soldier struck James sharply in the forehead with the butt of his rifle. After he had fallen to the ground, the soldier kicked him in the head until he stopped struggling.

James tried to curl up in the fetal position, but the soldier grabbed his hair and dragged him back to his feet. He tried to collapse several more times but was stopped each time by the soldier dragging him back up by his hair. Finally, the boy stood on his own.

The little courage that had existed on Friday was not enough to sustain him. James felt like a coward, and he was going to die that way.

The colonel's voice droned through a megaphone.

"Citizens," he said. "Citizens. Citizens. Citizens." He repeated the words in condescending sarcasm. "Happy

Easter Sunday to you." James could hear the smile in his voice although he could not see him. "It has been a good Holy Week, hasn't it?" No one answered.

"I enjoyed the week myself. I enjoyed five crucified instead of three. It was an interesting change in the format. The problem is"—James heard the man sigh—"the Executive Ten did not appreciate it. So, I've been sent to teach you a lesson. This is how you are to be taught. A hundred individuals have been selected. They have been brought to the front, as you see." James heard a click and then the cocking of a gun. There was the sound of footfalls on the rickety platform, and then the yell of an individual from the crowd. James turned to see the crowd part, and a single man emerge.

"Let them go," the man yelled to the colonel.

The footsteps on the platform stopped. The colonel laughed. The man sauntered to the stage.

"Who do you think you are?" The colonel was indignant and offended. "Why would I let all these people go because of the whim of a single man?"

"At least let one go. Let me take the place of one of them," The man answered back, and James realized he was the man who had spoken at the foot of Dalimore only two days before.

"What is the difference to me?" the colonel replied. "Okay, pick one." His voice was impatient.

James saw the man point in his direction, and the soldier who had brought him up grabbed him by the shoulder and James tumbled through the crowd onto his head. He watched what occurred sideways through the legs of another member of the crowd, too scared and too shocked to move.

"Sir, come up by me," said the colonel to the man who had taken his place. James was almost certain the colonel was drunk. He must have been drinking the entire time the civilians were assembling.

James watched as the man made his way onto the platform. The colonel swaggered over to the man and placed his hand on the man's shoulder and studied his face.

"Why did you come up here?" James barely heard the question.

The man replied with a loud voice, "I'm responsible for the riot."

"Hmmm." The soft, slurred reply of the colonel was odd compared to the man's strong voice. "You're a bit old as a replacement; I don't think you'll do." James saw the man grit his teeth as the colonel sauntered to the edge of the platform. The crowd held its breath as he spoke.

"I gave back a child, but after considering the man's offer, it doesn't seem appropriate to replace a child with an adult. So, citizens, I'm asking for a replacement for the one I gave back to you. That, or give up the one I gave to you." A paralyzing fear again filled James as he waited for one of those around to point him out. He silently thanked them when they did not.

A long moment passed. The colonel waited, eyebrows raised looking out at the crowd. The five on the crosses had not yet been taken down, and James saw them far in the distance on the hill behind the man's head. Then a boy ran out into the space between the crowd and those chosen.

He was perhaps five or six years old. He had dropped a small rubber ball which, as if it had been possessed by a most horrific, evil demon, had chosen this time of all times to run away from him.

James heard a laugh, a snort really, from the colonel. If the boy had been able to step out of his situation, if he had been able to stop time, rewind, and replay the snort over and over again until he had forgotten the context and his anger and the hatred he had built up toward this colonel, he would have understood it. He would have heard the nuance of a sniffle in the snort, an overpowering agony tied up in the laugh but hidden by the stupor brought on by the liquor the man had been consuming. James heard the snort as a laugh, but the laugh was no laugh at all. Humans, those amazing creatures able to express amusement and never once be amused. The snort was a sob, an expression of emotion showing the colonel was only a hairsbreadth away from dissolving into tears.

Ah, but he did not. Instead, he brought the pistol he had been playing with up, sighted, and fired. He did not kill the boy with that one shot. Instead, he hit his shoulder and knocked him off his feet. The colonel then moved on the platform to get a clear view of the boy, aimed again and shot truer this time. He hit him in the chest, moved again to the center of the platform, and brought the megaphone back to his mouth.

"Now that the replacement is taken care of, let us begin." His voice was colder now, irate. He was irate not at the people standing before him but himself. He hated himself the instant he started to speak. He had learned to loathe himself when he pulled the trigger, yet these were his orders and he knew that he may yet learn to truly laugh at atrocity.

James watched as the colonel placed his gun back in his holster and grabbed one of the rifles from a soldier. He inspected the gun; the action opened then closed, and the colonel nodded his head. He brought the rifle up to his shoulder and made his way off the stage. James watched as he brought the gun up and pressed the first individual onto his knees. The others who were chosen moved away as quickly as possible. James barely heard the colonel as he mumbled something along the lines of "a bullet a man." Then, in one swift motion, he swung the barrel of the rifle from the ground to the man's head and fired. The rifle blast filled the city center for a moment then was swallowed by silence. The old man remained on his knees for a moment before thudding to the concrete. The colonel had already moved to the next of the condemned, a woman, middle-aged. She was on the ground trying to scurry away, but the colonel was too quick with the shot and she sprawled backward, hitting the back of her skull with a crack. James closed his eyes to block out what he was seeing, but he was unable to block out the rhythmic composition now occurring. *Kaboom, thud, kaboom, thud, kaboom, thud.* The rhythm seemed to go on forever. James thought these noises would go on until the last person had been shot, but suddenly the rhythm was broken. Instead of a *kaboom, thud, kaboom,* the rhythm was *kaboom, thud, kaboom, thud, dink.*

James opened his eyes in that moment of silence and looked over at the officer. The colonel released the magazine from the rifle and motioned for another as he allowed the first to clatter on the ground. Out of the side of James' vision, a new magazine came flying, and the colonel caught it, clicked it into the bottom of the weapon, and cocked the gun to chamber a round. Without looking down at the man he was shooting, he pulled the trigger. The gun spat out another *kaboom.* The rhythm began again. James tried to close his eyes but could not. Body after body fell to the ground. The rifle continued to yell as the bullets ripped out of the barrel and tore into the victims. The colonel, despite his intoxicated state, moved quickly and shot accurately. Another body thudded. Two more times the rhythm paused to allow an ammo magazine to be ejected and another clicked into its place.

Each of the victim's deaths was as varied as their looks. Some, both men and women, went out screaming for their lives. Others sat on their haunches staring at the face of the colonel. Some bared their teeth. Some prayed silently, some out loud. Some fought. Some tried to flee. Many broke down in tears and had to be held up by the soldiers who accompanied the colonel on his walk about the city center. Some passed with dignity, others like animals. Despite the way in which their earthly existence ended, they all became no more than piled corpses, no longer human, mere abominations.

James turned his head away from the pile of bodies after the last one had fallen to the ground. He could hear sobbing rising from the crowd, weeping, screaming. The crowd wailed. In his peripheral vision, he saw a woman run up to the little boy's body, grab him, and run back into the crowd with her face buried in the little shirt.

The crowd rushed over to those who had been shot to collect their loved ones. The firing of a pistol into the air halted their movement, and all looked up at the center of the platform where the colonel had again taken his place. For a final time, the man lifted the megaphone up to his mouth and spoke.

"Bury them," was all he said before he allowed the megaphone to clatter onto the platform and was led through the crowd by a group of soldiers with their rifles pointed out.

Part III

The Fall

"Some are lights in the world. God forbid they are ever snuffed."
– David Amore –

TWENTY THREE

"Dalimore was the thin sinew of sanity holding the nation together. We'd been born-again into his name, but he was dead, and the United States along with him."
– Samuel Judah, *American Autumn* –

The hope of the city fled Easter Sunday. That day of celebration and life was only destruction and death. Pickaxes and shovels were distributed to the crowd. "Dig here," the soldiers commanded, and a hole was dug through concrete and dirt. The bodies were thrown in, and rubble rising a foot above the roadway was the only memorial to the dead.

James stared at that mound in the darkness. It was where the fountain once stood. He looked to Dalimore. Though the president had been lit each night during Holy Week, he no longer was. Everything seemed to be darkness in this new world.

A few scattered military patrols roamed the streets the Wednesday after Easter. Martial law was enacted a Sunday later. Soldiers flooded into the city, checkpoints were set up, and all, save Society, were required to have an almost-impossibly-acquired permit to move about freely.

"For the safety of our city," the mayor had said, but even an idiot understood what it was.

Martial law. A collar and leash for the neck of the city.

Rumors leaked out of the ghettos. Some said the people were being consolidated into an internment camp out west. Some said those with insanities were being sent to work camps. More extreme commentators thought they were being tortured or experimented on, and one, a prominent figure in the news, accused the government of exterminating them. "This is only another example of that evil called eugenics," Mr. Wiley wrote. Three days later Mr. Wiley suffered a fatal fall from his third-floor apartment in Chicago. A suicide note was found. Mr. Wiley would speak and write no more, and his words, barely proliferated, were soon forgotten. Only extremists gave any credence to his viewpoint. "No country would kill its own people," one radio personality commentated. "It would be like, uh, like, like a mother killing her child; it simply isn't done."

Rumors circulated of unrest throughout the country. Word of riots, but none could be sure what was true or false. Was it an honest report or the anxious fantasy of some slave distorted by the passage through a thousand tongues? Either way, it did not matter. Despite rumors of possible uprisings, it did not change the fact that the city was alone in its suffering. All of them were alone.

There was day, bright and hope-filled. Then the night came, cold and black. The little hope James had for anything resembling a comfortable future was gone, and, even more so, Mackenzie no longer spoke of his own hopes. Gone were his wild flights of fancy. Gone was his bright, gleaming smile. The fire in his eyes never recovered from that weak, wan flicker of Easter. Jokes on his lips were said with humorless inflection. Gone was the over-used "Stand and meet your new king." Gone were all things about Mackenzie except that small, frail smirk that lingered on his face when amused.

Subdued, James thought, but he knew the word was not accurate. Subdued connoted some restriction on him, like ropes on the wrist or a yoke on his back that need only be broken. Mackenzie had changed. Easter Sunday had changed him. A heavy thought had been laid on his mind that pulled all other thoughts into its orbit.

~~~

"Just a little farther," David whispered to Mackenzie.

"Better than the last place?" Mackenzie whispered back.

"Best place you've ever been," David replied to Mackenzie.

Mackenzie nodded as David turned and peeked out

from the car they hid behind. James crouched to his right silently. A thought sparked in Mackenzie's mind, and he had a sudden urge to whisper a joke to James. But the thought was like smoke, and the little lingering humor left as fast as it had arrived.

Though only two months had passed since those days of laughter, the past felt no more than a dream. Everything before was the sweet memory of youthful summers amid this bitter cold winter of old age. Those months felt like years, perhaps decades, and Mackenzie doubted those days of humor and laughter would ever return. Darkness was the new norm, and he supposed he ought to get used to it.

Darkness, the boy thought as he looked at the fence topped with barbed wire that stretched far into the night. Two soldiers patrolled lazily near a gap in the fence at the foot of Dalimore. This was the taste of the Executive Ten's martial law: movement restricted to all but Society and even a curfew restricting the aristocracy from sundown to sunup.

It was David, not Mackenzie, who had suggested going out. Tension filled the House. Anxiety thickened the air. Conversations between servants were whispered, but even these whispered conversations never mentioned Holy Week. It was as if those eight days had never existed. Mackenzie decided he would pay them no heed either, suffering silently and honorably, as he saw it, but David paced like a caged animal. Complaint after complaint was loud in the boy's mouth until they made James itch with annoyance, and an animosity grow between the two.

"Can you shut up?" James yelled at the boy after a particularly long and hot day in the House.

"We could go out at night." David continued with an echoing whisper every night thereafter, and eventually, after a "Couldn't hurt to try, could it?" from David, Mackenzie began to ask the question himself.

Soon the three found themselves disappearing into the shadows of the city, searching, always searching. Mackenzie was not sure what they were looking for, but he knew they were looking for something. They talked as if they were. As they inspected each place they visited, they talked both of its benefits and detractions. They went back and forth, each pointing out a different aspect of the place, and each time so far, they all shook their heads in agreement that they would not be coming back.

God, I wish I could smoke, he thought as he peeked through the window or the car and saw one of the patrolling soldiers with a cigarette stuck in his mouth. The heavy thought of Easter loomed into his mind, and he needed something to calm his nerves. *One little cigarette,* but he knew it was stupid, dangerous. It was far after curfew, and one sighting or whiff of smoke would have the soldiers on them within moments. Besides, he knew a cigarette would only temporarily and partially ease the burden. No quick fix existed for such painful, dark, existential meandering. It was a weight he had to carry.

"Do something." Mackenzie was in the shop again. The window shattered. David was not beside him. "Do something." The soldier again grabbed James by the collar pulling him toward the stage. "Do something," a little voice inside his head had whispered as he stared at the lazy stream of lettering on that shop window of Good Friday. The voice said the same thing as the colonel's voice drawled out on Easter.

"Do something."

But Mackenzie did not. Filled with fear, he could not even bring himself to the beginning of action.

Do something.

But, I, but . . .

And Mackenzie could not overcome that fear. Mackenzie was a coward, and Mackenzie could not contend with that fact. He had spent countless hour upon countless hour building himself up, and in the briefest of moments, everything burned up. The countless hours spent were worthless.

Mackenzie leaned his back against the cold car. *What I would do for a cigarette,* he thought, but he knew it was not a cigarette he desired in the end. A cigarette was a momentary distraction from his thoughts, like any pleasure would be. He was not who he thought he was, not who he wished to be. Something was wrong with him, and there was something all three of them hoped for that he could not fully understand, something laying just beyond the horizon of his mind, which could fix him, make him who he was meant to be.

But what this thing was, he did not know.

~~

David watched as the patrol meandered back and forth near the foot of Dalimore. Mackenzie rested silently beside him, and James shifted uneasily beside Mackenzie. David enjoyed going out at night. It was dangerous, risky, required skill, and there was a chance he would not be going home. He had not had so much fun doing something in, well, he could not remember. Maybe sometime when he was a small child. But he did not like taking James. James did not hear patrols. He walked loudly. He talked loudly. He talked too often and at the worst times. Though David was thrilled by the risk of being out, he had no desire to die because of the mistake of another.

"He's going to get us killed," David whispered to Mackenzie after James had tripped and a soldier almost stepped on him. It scared James. David saw it in his eyes and heard it in his voice after James had crawled back from the middle of the street. David did not risk chastising words at the time and could just barely restrain the back of his hand from hitting the other boy harshly across the face. *For his own good*, David thought.

After James had almost been caught, David did not want to bring him again and only agreed to after Mackenzie's continual pestering. Though David still had reservations, James was doing significantly better than before, and David considered that he may yet learn discretion.

David glanced at the two other boys again then back at the gap in the fence before letting out a quiet sigh, and annoyance bit into him. Some higher-up in the military had probably given an order to take every precaution to thwart another riot in the city. This probable order was probably mulled over by a lower-ranking officer who had made a conclusion which was an infinite annoyance to David. The lower ranking officer who probably mulled over this probable executive command probably came to a decision that the probability of a riot occurring was improbable if the population was unable to form a mob. This idiot officer had decided a chain link fence with only one opening at the city center was the best solution. Because of this idiot officer and his idiot fence, David either had the choice to lead the other boys around it, which would add another five miles to their journey, or to lead them through the short break in the fence that would reduce their travel time by hours.

At first, they were going to take the long route around the fence, but after assessing James' ability to move quietly, he decided the time saved outweighed the risk. Of course, this all would be fully determined after the deed had been done.

Or undone, he thought.

Mackenzie and James followed David across the street

to a pile of trash for cover. James turned to look into the oblivion of the night, and as he did he felt a hand like a vice around his collar. Before he could react, David had flipped him around and pulled him close. James attempted to bring his hands up to his face and push David away, but David had anticipated this action. As David brought James' face close to his own, his other arm came down to block the boy's hands.

James felt David's hot breath on his ear and neck.

"Shh. Shh. Stop. Listen up," David whispered into his ear. "Twenty yards down this street and another ten to the left is an opening in that big, stupid fence. There are two guards, only two. They patrol, wander, or something like that." David took his hand off James' collar, wiped the sweat from his forehead, and grabbed the collar again before continuing. "Now these two guys have a sloppy patrol back and forth twenty yards each, got it?" David felt James' head nod. "Now, when they get to the end of an area, they pause for fifteen, twenty, maybe thirty seconds. That is our window of opportunity. It's a little risky but you can make it through just fine because the guards, well, they're lazy. But if we're spotted they will alert their whole little guard house that has six other guards sleeping in it, and then everything'll hit the fan. Mess up, we're all dead. All you need to do is copy exactly what I do. Got it?" James nodded again. Finally, David released his collar and pushed him away with one swift motion. Then David grabbed Mackenzie, said a quick few words to him, and faced the street with a pivot. He paused to listen for a moment before darting down the street.

James lagged several steps behind the other two. He could see an even greater edge of caution in both. Each of their steps was picked out with delicate care. Their arms were up with palms facing out, relaxed but ready for any action needed.

When the guards were preoccupied, David led them first to an old Chevy a few feet away, and finally, when they had another opportunity, through the gate. David let out a long, relieved sigh when they reached cover on the other side.

The rest of the journey was now left to a short matter of stop-listen-go, and they arrived at the heavy oak doors of a tall, gothic church. Upon entering it they were enveloped in a deep, heavy silence.

"Hey, Davey," Mackenzie said. "I thought you didn't like church." He laughed as they walked up to the front.

David pulled out a pack of cigarettes without answering and stuck one in his mouth. He lit it and pulled it back out of his mouth to speak, but James spoke first.

"It's too dark in here to see anything," he said.

Mackenzie grunted in agreement.

"You like candles?" David asked as he stood off to the side of the room in the darkness. Suddenly, a single candle flame revealed a whole wall of them. David lit another with the cherry of his cigarette.

"Smoke a cigarette. Use a candle already lit. There are

about three hundred on either side. Another three hundred up front."

The sanctuary was cold and vast. Its arching ceiling stretched up in delicate elegance into a deep, oblivious blackness above their heads. The marble floor gleamed like a giant, flawless pearl, and each wall was filled with stained-glass windows made from hundreds of pieces of colored glass. The sanctuary was one that inspired a sense of spiritual awe in those that entered it, a transcendence that confronted even the most hard-hearted unbeliever with a perspicuous taste of divine serendipity. Though the philistine hearts of the three boys remained empty of awe as they stared into the depths of the church, as they talked throughout the night, they were sure of one thing: they would return to this place.

TWENTY FOUR

"What ended the United States? Every problem imaginable."
— Moses Hehl —

The boys were only able to go to the church once more before the end of June. Their plan had been to sneak out several times in the final two weeks, but on the first of those final weeks, all servants were given the evening task of preparing for a party that was to be thrown on the Fourth of July. Though Mackenzie and James voiced their intention of skipping the work in those days leading up to the holiday, Janice, as if she could read their minds, would calmly remind them each day that she would be taking note of their attendance in the evening, and long sweltering summer days of duties led to evenings filled with the tedious preparations which led to exhaustion which led to bed.

"Oh, of course she knows," Mackenzie replied to James

as they worked one of those long nights. He shook his head and a little wan smile appeared on his face. "She knows everything. Probably thinks she's keeping us alive."

Finally, the party came, the cleanup went, and the boys were able to find time and energy to once more sneak into the city. Little had changed in the weeks they had missed. Several patrols had shifted, but besides this, nothing impeded them until David sidled alongside a building, peeked around the corner toward the church and immediately waved the other two back in the direction they had come.

"A guard plopped himself right outside the church door. I almost walked out in plain sight of him before I noticed," he said after he had found a place secluded in some obscure alley far away from any military patrol. "He's in the shadows of that little entryway. Probably waiting around for people like us to stumble across his path." The next word David spoke was so quiet it was inaudible, a curse. "Guess we won't be going there anymore."

"Well, wait a second, David," Mackenzie spoke quietly but clearly. "You don't suppose that church has a back, maybe side door?" David's eyes lit up at the possibility. "Cause if there is . . ." Mackenzie cocked his head slightly. The statement was one neither asking for nor requiring an answer.

David nodded and immediately moved back the way they had come. He led them up from the alley to the street. From here the church was close to two hundred yards to the west. After pausing to look and listen in his canine-like manner and seeing that the road held little to no risks, he darted across and led them through twisted streets and a disorienting maze of alleys until they arrived at the side of the church ten minutes later.

Finding no door on the south side, they crept slowly through the bushes and moved to the back. There they found a door, much smaller than the front ones but made of the same wood and carved in the same ornate fashion.

David mumbled curses after he tried the door.

Mackenzie sidled up alongside him as David fished through the pockets of his coat and trousers. "What's up?" Mackenzie asked in the same articulate, whispery voice in which he had spoken before.

"Door's locked." David spoke in an unhindered, harsh whisper. James moved closer to hear the other boys as they continued their conversation.

"Well, what are we going to do?" Mackenzie asked.

David gave a sigh before continuing. "Can try to pick it, but it's a bet." He found what he was looking for as he spoke and pulled out two oddly bent paperclips. "Lock picks," he explained.

"You think you can pick this one?" Mackenzie interrupted.

"I'll try." David took a sharp breath in. "Get in those shadows there." He started to position the paperclips in his hand as James and Mackenzie reached the shadow. David gave them a nod, reached back to scratch his head, and turned toward the door. *Here goes nothing*, he thought as he crouched and fumbled his lock picking set into the keyhole. *Okay, fit this in the top . . . no, no, the bottom of the keyhole? No, it's the top. Okay.* One of the paper clips snagged in the keyhole. David grunted. *Stupid thing. Just fit.* He took in another sharp breath, and as he gave a frustrated growl, it slid in smoothly. He sighed in relief. *Now turn this clockwise? Pick in. Okay. I think I've got a pin.* He let the paper clip loosen and heard the small click of a pin falling back into place. *Good.* He put tension back on the paperclip and began to move the other in a fulcrum-like motion.

Five minutes passed, and he had already set several of the pins and checked his progress the only way he knew how: he released the paper clip and listened for pins to drop. He heard three small clicks as confirmation. *Well, I'm doing something right*, he thought. Another ten minutes passed as he continued setting pins and releasing the paper clip to hear them fall back down again.

As sweat started to make it difficult to hold the paper clips, David let out a frustrated sigh. *One more time. One more time, and then I'm giving up*, he said to himself as he looked back at the dark keyhole. *Okay, I've got one pin up, I think. Um, I don't know.* David held his breath and gritted his teeth. *I don't feel any more.* David continued to fiddle with his lock pick until his picking of the lock consisted of a thoughtless wriggling of the bent paperclip.

"Got it," he almost yelled out to Mackenzie and James. He could not help the smile from spreading across his face.

The frustration that had twisted his mind into knots turned to unraveled satisfaction as he pulled the heavy door open, and the three boys sneaked into the quiet church. James shut the door quietly behind them, and the three of them were enveloped in complete darkness.

"Hey, hey. Where are you guys?" James asked.

"No need to whisper," David said from across the room. The flash of a lighter illuminated his face. The large cigar between his lips glowed red under the flame. The flame of the lighter disappeared, and the solitary cherry of the cigar floated around the room as David moved.

"Where did you get that?" James asked as the flame of the lighter lit up Mackenzie's face.

"Found 'em," Mackenzie said. Smoke obscured his cigar's ember for a moment. James did not inquire further about where he had "found them." He was not sure he wanted to know.

"Let's go to the sanctuary." The ember of David's cigar disappeared as he turned.

Mackenzie gave the affirmative and the ember of his cigar also disappeared. James was the last to leave the smoke-filled room out into the gloomy hallway. A glowing red sign marked the exit, and a soft grayness reached from the sanctuary toward them. When they reached the end of the hall, David stopped abruptly, causing the other two to bump into him and almost knock him over. As soon as David regained his balance, he crouched down, pulled the cigar out of his mouth, and ground it out on the hallway

264

carpet. He then stood fully erect, groped in the dark of the hallway, and, after finding Mackenzie's shoulder, drew him close to whisper in his ear.

"Better put out your cigar. I think I hear some voices up ahead. I'm going to check it out." Mackenzie heard David's clothes rustling as he turned and disappeared down the hall.

"What did he say?" James' whispered over Mackenzie's left shoulder.

Mackenzie turned to him and answered, "Said he heard voices up ahead." James cursed under his breath. "It'll probably be fine, James. We just won't be here tonight."

"Yeah, I understand this, but I'm not in the mood to go all the way back to the house when we just got here."

"Let's just wait before we decide what to do," Mackenzie answered.

James and Mackenzie waited five minutes before David returned. "Guys, you've got to come and see this," he said after he appeared as a silhouette at the end of the hall. James thought he saw David motion them forward with his arm. "But quiet. Can't say a word." David moved out to the hall, obscured by the shape of Mackenzie following him. James followed in quick steps, careful not lose the other two.

As they entered the sanctuary, James saw nothing from which the sound of a human voice could come. Curiosity overwhelmed him, and he had an aggravating desire to ask

David what he had found. *What were those voices that David heard?* The question festered in his mind like irritated skin that had grown into a painful itch.

~~~

As they passed through the sanctuary and made their way down a flight of steps to a hallway, Mackenzie braced himself for a practical joke meant to send himself and James running back up to the sanctuary in terror. *Sorry, James,* he thought to himself, wanting to tell the other boy to prepare but unable to in case David's claims were legitimate. *And if they aren't, well, James and I will get him back when he comes upstairs to find us.* Mackenzie planned the revenge as he moved down the hallway, which was only dimly and eerily lit red by an exit sign. A hand on Mackenzie's shoulder halted his thoughts, and he looked up to see David's deeply shadowed face and the boy's hand resting on a doorknob. Mackenzie felt James step on his ankles. David looked up to him, pointed to the door, then looked back at Mackenzie. He slowly opened it so as not to allow it even the slightest satisfaction of the hinge moaning, and disappeared into the blackness beyond. Mackenzie followed. This new room was complete oblivion, and he was certain it was a trick.

"One more room. If you listen, you can hear them." David moved on to tell James the same thing.

Hear them? I don't hear anything. This has got to be a— Then Mackenzie did hear it, some sort of voice, male, muffled. For an odd reason, he wanted to smack David. In almost any other situation, this would have resulted in a prank, but today? Mackenzie felt as if a prank of some sort had still been pulled on him and him alone. *How dare he not trick me when I expect him to?* The small hint of amusement curled on Mackenzie's face as he followed David into the room.

~~~

When James first entered the room, he thought it was a joke. *Yes, this must be a joke*, he decided. *These things do not happen in real life. The very reason that fantastical stories such as myths, legends, fairytales, and religion are so widely spread is because these things don't happen, and that is the very reason people find them intriguing.*

Although he felt certain of his reasoning, doubt rested within him. Though he did not yet understand the phenomenon as doubt, he often experienced it. When the day was slow, when the night came, and he had no duties, after he had grown tired of reading, when nothing else was left to do in the day but it was still too early for bed, bare truth was all that would remain in his thoughts. The sea of existence with all its waves of activities and things to occupy would suddenly grow very calm. Peering down into it from his dinghy of a life, he suddenly would realize that the existence he had seen as beautiful on its surface was unknowable depths. *Is there a bottom? Is there a firm foothold? Is there any meaning? Is there anything?*

The corpse of doubt made its way up to the surface to speak, not in words, but in an inhuman, overwhelming dread. Each time it surfaced it attacked a belief, and he felt as if he were being torn to pieces. At first, he would simply find some heavy objection, tie it to a leg or an arm of the corpse, and he would plunk the corpse back into the water, sighing in relief both because it had disappeared and because the waves had begun to roll again.

But it would be back. The corpse came back and not alone. Somehow it spawned in its decay, and, at the right time in life, it along with its children rose to the surface again to speak that same terrible dread as before. The older James grew, the more corpses appeared during these quiet periods. He at first saw this denial of doubt to a watery grave the best possible solution. Eventually, he took to the habit of eating the corpse.

Though he sank the corpse that night, uncertainty arose about the nature of secret societies, of masked men, and clandestine doings.

David made a motion to the other boys for silence, and soon all three of them lay on their bellies peering just over the edge to see the seven masked people that sat at that small, old, chipped table.

One wore an extremely expensive suit, possibly a politician, and sat next to a man who wore a suit that might as well have been rags in contrast. There was the robe of professorship (for at that time it again was in fashion for collegiate professionals to wear their honorary robe designating their level of scholarship). James was almost certain that the design of this individual's robe placed her as a Ph.D. Another was in the uniform of a low-ranking military officer. One had on the white coat of a scientist or medical professional. The first of the final two was certainly a cleric, and the last, who the boys assumed to be the leader for he sat at the head of the table, wore the casual dress of a blue-collar worker.

This confused James. At first, he doubted his initial thought that this man was their leader, but after hearing the conversation, he was certain it was true. He had a commanding tone and a way of speaking that placed him far above the understanding of James. He certainly was not merely of the working class but a man who must have been rigorously schooled since coming out of the womb. James recognized the words the man spoke as English, but they were words that he had rarely heard and he understood little of what was being spoken. *It certainly must be a code of some sort,* James thought as he listened. *Either a code or the most bizarre sort of checklist for packing to go on some trip that I have ever heard. This seems to be the final check before the car is loaded and the odd bunch is chauffeured to the train station.*

Similar thoughts spun through the minds of the other two boys.

Mackenzie found the leader to be asking questions similar to a checklist but thought it was less like these individuals were going on a trip and more like they were talking about a machine. "Does this piece check out?" the leader seemed to ask. "And what of this piece? And that piece? And how is this functioning? And what is the work output or how are the fluid levels?"

They seem to be planning an attack of some sort, David thought to himself early on, though the idea seemed to spring up in his mind rather than come from the depths of any serious thought. *Yes, if I were planning an attack that is how I would go about it. Attack when the enemy least expects it. Use the weather to one's advantage. Stay hidden even after striking the first blow. Confuse the enemy. Strike quickly and hard and draw back before they even understand what is going on. Drive a wedge between them. Divide and conquer. They seem to have ten targets, ten chinks in the armor. Yes, certainly a battle plan.*

David was the only one of the three satisfied with his assessment, and he was the only one of the three who had a smile rather than confused frustration on his face when they came to their final line of dialogue.

"Ten then?" the leader asked.

"Ten," the man in the cheap suit answered.

"Good," the leader replied before he turned to speak to another. "And the hands?"

"With teeth and feet and eyes sir, sharp eyes, sharp teeth, fleet feet."

"Good." He addressed the whole crowd, "And with these hands, it is uncreated."

The others repeated what the leader had said in the unison of a liturgy, "With these hands, it is uncreated."

The seven stood and filed out of the room into the darkness of the hallway. The meeting was over. None took off their masks. The leader quickly picked up an assortment of papers and retrieved a briefcase that had been hidden from the boys' view under the table and filed the papers into it. Finally, he stepped through the doorway, and, as a final thought, reached back into the room to shut off the light.

The boys did not speak until a half hour of silence passed. David cursed. James laughed a little. Mackenzie was the first to speak intelligently.

"Well, that was a bit odd."

"I would say," James added.

"What just happened?" David said. James and Mackenzie turned after David had spoken and saw him standing at the ugly table below them.

TWENTY FIVE

―――――――――

"America is divided in a thousand ways. State attacks state. Leaders are self-serving. The most powerful is victor, and millions are trampled underfoot."
– Amherst Rhodes, *Life in the USA* –

The next night they again journeyed out to the church. Again, David picked the lock to the back door, and they sneaked their way through the sanctuary to their spot above the heads of "the council," as they soon called the seven out of convenience. Again, the council spoke in riddles which were less a discussion and more an odd checklist. Again, they filed out. Again, the boys discussed it until morning, and again they got no further in their understanding. This happened almost every night until the end of July.

Although the boys did not fully understand what the council was talking about, they did come to certain conclusions about the individuals. Though he did not remember where his mind had collected the information, Mackenzie was able to place the origin of the masks as Native American. The professor down below was certainly a Ph.D., and they all agreed David's interpretation of what was said was the most comprehensive and intelligent of them all. Soon even James adopted it. This was all the information they could tease out of the council, but the true intentions of the seven were as hidden as their faces behind the masks. Even David's hypothesis that they spoke of war plans began to fray at the ends and unravel as it failed to account for key details in the conversation.

July 31st was the last night of the council. The boys returned August 1st, but no one showed. The boys came the 2nd, the 3rd, the 4th, the 5th, but they did not even see the slightest sign of the council whose riddles they had listened to in vain. After the 5th, they returned on and off until mid-August, but still no signs were to be seen that anyone had been in the room. Finally, as August ended, along with its summer weather, they gave up any hope of ever seeing the council again.

September 25th arrived, and an event that is seldom remembered today by those outside academic historians occurred.

A fight had broken out on the border of Pennsylvania and New Jersey between two police officers resulting in one shooting the other. The New Jersey officer, who killed the other, swore that the officer of the law from Pennsylvania had attacked him and he had only fought out of self-defense. "Only to save my own skin," his whiny voice said through tinny televisions across the United States.

The Pennsylvania police force, led by a hot head, saw the tale as an unjust blemish on their honor. Within twenty-four hours of the death, the police of Philadelphia stormed into the tiny New Jersey precinct and slaughtered every one of the officers. The government was unable to keep a lid on the boiling pot, and within hours of the attack the news bubbled over and spread across the entire nation. Some sided with the Philadelphia officers, some with those from New Jersey, and state governments began to prepare for the second civil war.

It should have arrived. It should have sprung out of the tension of that spring of a nation wound tight. Lines should have been set up. One side should have expressed its discontent at the way the nation was governed, and the United States should have lashed back with all the might it had in preservation of the Union. Countrymen should have stood against countrymen, father against son, brother against brother. The fuse that had been lit should have resulted in the organized tactics of soldiers quickly executed to bring about pain, death, and destruction to their newfound fraternal enemy.

But hidden minds were at work, and hidden wills brought on unexpected events.

Was what happened their intention? The answer is lost to history. Whoever these movers were, their faces were never known.

TWENTY SIX

———

"We do not know who orchestrated the October 1st
executions, and I doubt we ever will."
– Will Whitman, *A Fading Past* –

He had taken a nickname again, George Washington. Back in the Navy, it had been given to him as a good-natured joke by his Seal team. It was a rather idiotic instance that brought about the designation. Titus had told some of the others about the time he had fallen off the roof of a three-story building and had only gotten a scratch to show for it. No one believed him, but he continued to insist that the story was true for an entire month. Finally, midway through the fifth week, they sat on a rumbling plane only minutes before they were about to go plummeting toward the earth when Titus gave a holler with those all too familiar words, "I am not lying!"

"Shut up, George Washington!" an annoyed voice screamed after him.

Titus eventually gave up trying to convince them of the truth, but to his dismay, the name stuck.

Now, he imagined the first president, powdered wig and all, dressed in the black of an assassin, a pistol cradled in his hand with the long cylindrical suppressor pointing skyward. He missed hearing the founding father's name barked out in his direction. After seven years of not hearing it, those guttural syllables meant to express identification had become pure, elegant music.

Titus leaned his weight against the lavender wall and peered through the cracked door from which light streamed out onto the maroon carpeting. A gentle alto voice droned with that soothing, fire-like crackle of a phonograph, and Titus, no more than a shadow, slipped through the door. The figure of an ancient, wrinkled man lay on the bed, apparently asleep. He wore a purple monogrammed robe and slippers which were currently sticking half-on, half-off his feet at a cockeyed angle.

Titus stood erect, walked over to the bed, grabbed the bedpost, and lowered himself until he was level with the old man's face, a position which allowed him to see every wrinkle, pockmark, and pore.

He took a black flower out of a small jacket pocket and placed it on the bed stand, a chrysanthemum. It was part of the contract. The messenger gave him the flower and told him it was to be placed next to the job. *The job?* he thought as he looked down and remembered what the messenger said. He shrugged as he brought the gun up to the back of the man's head. *I suppose using euphemisms is one of the ways that my employers keep a clear conscience. Whatever.*

A great, sad, emotional intensity grew in the tenor of the alto's song. Titus squeezed down on the trigger. The song crescendoed until the woman was stretched to her vocal limits.

Titus let out a slow breath.

The man adjusted his head.

The record began to skip.

TWENTY SEVEN

"The world was on fire? Ain't it always?"
– Friday Setarcos –

Gentle snores filled the room as James opened the window, and a cold breeze wrapped around him as he stared into that October night. Those all-to-familiar branches twisted up outside the window. "Getting to be that time of year again," he mumbled to himself.

"Hey, James, you coming?" Mackenzie called from below.

No New Year's Eve parties this year, I guess, he thought. Mackenzie had not risked impersonation since Easter, and James doubted he would with the coming year either. *Soon, there'll be snow on the ground.* He sighed. *Christmas. Maybe I should bring a coat tonight.*

"James," Mackenzie called up again in a sing-song voice.

James shook away his distracting thoughts and looked back at the tree, preparing himself for another climb. Here goes literally nothing. He laughed to himself as he stuck his body out of the window and grabbed the first branch. The bark was cold and rough against his skin, but James barely noticed. They had been down this tree hundreds of times. The bark never changed, and the tree never changed, as far as he knew. It never seemed to grow taller, never looked older. It stood as strong as ever. Though he did not like his station, it was just as the tree, immovable, ever the same. It was everything he had ever known. Existence was an unchanging monolith, and he never had the faintest inkling that it would ever be anything else.

He had climbed the same tree hundreds of time, and everything followed the pattern of the tree. Same House. Same estate. Same city. Same life.

But now things had changed. It was difficult for him to wrap his mind around this fact. He stretched to comprehend the fullness of the situation. It was the same tree. It was the same house. It was the same estate. Same city, etc. It was all the same, but everything had changed. All the physical entities of the city remained unaltered except in minor, seemingly insignificant ways, but the world was completely different. James felt as if he had entered a portal to another dimension that mirrored his own. The pieces that made up reality looked the same. No, the pieces *were* the same, but the sum of those pieces was vastly different. The world outside himself was one he no longer knew, no longer understood. It was not his world.

James was greeted with a nod and a smile from Mackenzie as he dropped from the last limb to the ground.

"Jimbob," David greeted him softly. Since their animosity about going out at night, David had begun to use diminutive forms of his name. To annoy him, James assumed.

Both boys had a cigarette in their mouth, and James was at least thankful David was around for that, so Mackenzie would stop bugging him about smoking. *For once*, he thought.

James nodded to Mackenzie but did not respond to David.

"It'll eventually have to end," Mackenzie said in reply to something James had not heard.

David answered with a shrug, "I suppose, eventually. I just wouldn't count on it being too soon. Society plays a long game. This might be the city for a long time. Maybe the whole country, if the rumors are true and more cities are rioting."

Mackenzie sighed. The smirk he had greeted James with was replaced by dour disappointment.

James supposed this change of existence affected Mackenzie most of all. Though he was not sure of the details of the other boy's thoughts, he thought he could do a decent job guessing. What could become of hopes? What could become of his dreams in a world so dark, in a future so bleak? Even for Mackenzie, James guessed it was hard to stand up under it.

As they moved past the first checkpoint and away from the Society neighborhoods, Mackenzie became silent, and the three boys passed through the city to its dividing fence without incident, without even a sign of soldiers. They continued to hear and see nothing as they moved toward the gap along the fence, and upon arriving at the gap, they saw no soldiers there either.

Mackenzie let out a long, loud sigh.

"What's wrong?" James asked as they stared toward the empty opening.

Mackenzie shook his head and pursed his lips. He gave a shrug. "Feels wrong," he said.

"Feels like a jackpot to me," David answered.

"It feels like a trap," Mackenzie continued.

David glanced back. "A trap for who, Mack? Us?"

Mackenzie shrugged and pursed his lips again but did not answer.

"I say we take advantage of our good fortune and get through before they come back," James replied to both.

David let a breath of a laugh out through his nose. "For once in our existence, we agree, Jimmy."

James rolled his eyes at the misuse of his name but did not respond.

"I just have a bad feeling," Mackenzie responded. "Just, just . . ." He brought a deep breath in. "Can we search the area?" he asked. "Each of us or all of us or one of us. Search around and see, for something, anything?"

David shrugged. "I don't see why not," he said. "I can go," he continued. "No point in all of us going."

The other two nodded, and David left them. He made a wide circle around the area and was greeted by emptiness. He crossed the old, dirt path of Holy Week several times as he searched. He walked along the wide boulevard and saw the park where the fair had been set up on the far end. The tents and barricades had been taken down, but the trash that had accumulated, seemingly lifetimes ago, still rolled down the street like desert tumbleweeds.

The box where they had sat during the play was still shattered. Glass glittered on the ground in the moonlight. The fountain was a mound of rubble. In the distance, he knew the five men still hung on the crosses, but he did not look up to see. Dalimore still stood strong as ever, and out of curiosity, David walked to the foot of the late—the last—president and looked up to study his charred features. As he did, he waved the other two over to the gap.

"I still have a bad feeling," Mackenzie whispered to James when they saw David walk up to the statue and wave them over.

"David's thorough," James responded. "He'd catch something if there was something to catch."

"You trust him," Mackenzie said with the slight edge of sarcasm.

"Only in this," James answered.

Mackenzie breathed out a laugh and nodded, and David waved for them to come more quickly.

"Empty," he said when they reached the foot of the statue. "Never seen the city so empty."

James grunted and glanced at the statue and then at the gap.

"Still worried?" David asked Mackenzie.

Mackenzie shrugged. "I . . ." He shook his head. "The weather, maybe. Could be ghosts." He stared through the fence at the darkness beyond. "I was shot here, you know. Maybe that has something to do with it." He pursed his lips and shrugged once more.

"Well," James replied, "probably not the best to go on hanging out here all night."

Mackenzie breathed out another laugh and nodded.

"What's so funny?" James asked.

A small smile spread up the side of Mackenzie's mouth, and he pointed at James. "When we started going out, you couldn't sneak past an opium addict."

A short chuckle escaped David.

"And now, look at you." Mackenzie said the words like a proud father. He let out a long, satisfied sigh.

"Well, we should get going," James answered.

"Never been prouder of you," Mackenzie continued. Though no inflection of pride sounded in his voice, the other half of his mouth curled up to complete his smile, the first James had seen since darkness had descended on them.

Mackenzie turned from him to look at the gap in the fence, and the smile faded from his face as fast as it had arrived.

"I wasn't that bad," James answered.

Mackenzie sighed. All amusement had left his voice. The same weight seemed to return to him as he began to turn and walk toward the fence. "You couldn't sneak up on a marching band," Mackenzie answered. His voice was once more filled with that same flat, unamused sarcasm.

James shook his head as he and David followed, side by side, but Mackenzie did not notice. "Really?" Incredulity filled his face at the revelation.

"No," David said to his side. No inflection filled the boy's voice, and James could tell he was taking delicate care not to offend him. "He's right." David began to nod. "You were the worst."

James shook his head as they passed through the gap, but he soon forgot the comments as they entered into the trash-strewn streets of a slum. The acrid smell of black smoke filled their nostrils. They no longer spoke as they had in the city center or while walking through the estates, and even their whispered conversations were reduced to only what was absolutely needed. This was not due to discretion. Rather, the depression of the slums always seemed to press them into silence. It was an ugly place.

They did not want to acknowledge its existence. They had experienced the death of the five. They had experienced the death of the hundred. They lived in this new world of darkness, and none of them wanted any more of it. When no words were spoken, the slums remained a passing memory, maybe even an unpleasant dream, but speaking? Each of them knew it gave the place full life.

Despite their silence, Mackenzie seemed to cheer some, and when they passed out of the slums and resumed their conversations, he no longer spoke of any uneasiness. His knitted eyebrows of concern were undone, and even that full, though small, smile was seen on his face once more.

Time is all it'll take before Mackenzie is back to normal, before everything is back to normal, James thought as they turned and spied a steeple through the darkness.

He allowed his mind to wander as they walked down the side of the street, but gunfire broke him out of his thoughts as the strong arm of David sent him to the ground.

Mackenzie swore as a bullet zoomed overhead. More gunfire answered the first, and bullets thudded into a car sickeningly close. Then the rattle of machine-gun fire from the opposite direction pressed the boys to the ground. Their lips filled with profanity and prayers.

"Got to get out of here!" David called to the others. "Gotta move!" he yelled.

~~~

James nodded, but out of the corner of his eye he saw Mackenzie shake his head. David met James' eyes, and he motioned with his head toward the far side of the road to an alley. "This isn't our fight," he said. "They're not shooting at us. Careful."

James nodded, and moved toward the far side of the street. Though he began as quickly as he could, his movement brought a rain of bullets down on his position, and, after swearing, he waited for them to stop before continuing at a crawl.

Not shooting at us? he thought as he inched his way forward. *Who the Hell are they shooting at, then?* The zoom of bullets filling the space above his head silenced his thoughts, and he reached the alley with little more than scraped hands. After crawling halfway into the alley, he finally pushed himself up until he was seated and looked back. Mackenzie and David only had two or three feet left, and James watched in those long moments as they moved forward side by side. David would move, wait, and then reach back to pull Mackenzie along. He moved, waited, and tugged at Mackenzie's shirt several times before they reached the alley. Finally, David stood up, he and James dragged Mackenzie to his feet, and they took off running.

Though they heard no gunfire from up ahead, the noise of the firefight still filled their ears, and the three boys were careful to investigate every oddly shaped shadow they saw as they continued to the church. Eventually, after the longest, most careful journey through the city they had ever taken, they arrived at the church and entered through the front door, which they found unlocked and unguarded.

They at first sat or lay on the pews, but eventually they grew bored and climbed up to the pulpit. David was the first to go up. He ran and jumped, catching a ledge too far to reach on tip toes, and was pushed farther up by Mackenzie until he could use the divots in the wall to scale the rest. James went up after David in the same manner, and finally it was Mackenzie's turn. Running as quickly as he possibly could, he jumped up, pushed off the wall, and grabbed a ledge just above the one David and James were able to reach. He caught it with only two sets of knuckles and had to kick and kick and scrape his feet against the wall until he was able to build up enough momentum to reach up to a wooden pole carved into the side of the pulpit. From that point on, he climbed to the top with ease.

David clicked his tongue and shook his head, clearly impressed.

David and Mackenzie sat on either side of the pulpit's walls, allowing their legs to dangle in empty air. The open room seemed to make the distance from the ground to the pulpit even greater. Mackenzie thought nothing of it, often stretching his body far over the edge, but David's vision spun with vertigo and his hand clenched the edge of the pulpit like a vice. James stood between them in the place of the priest, hanging his arms over the edge and allowing them to sway like the pendulum of a clock.

The gunfire lasted half an hour after they climbed the pulpit and then sputtered into pop-shots which crackled like the fireworks of an enthusiastic patriot the few weeks preceding the Fourth of July. A cold wind whistled through the buildings. Rain pattered the stained-glass windows. All of October had been like this, windy and cold, rain falling on and off endlessly. Autumn was bitter and dreary, overcast, dull, and entirely gray. The only color punctuating the gray boredom was the fiery red of the leaves, but even these were turning brown, falling, and being tread into the mud underfoot. In a few easily counted days, the final frail leaf would cling its last to the stem and be blown to the ground, drifting and darting pathetically in an unwilling roll.

Each of the boys sat in their silent worlds, sat in their own thoughts, and the thoughts of each were snarled like a nasty head of hair, disordered like a city after a great flood or hurricane or tornado, rotting like a compost pile filled with once-living animals, twisted together like the foul pustule of a rat's nest. And in their rats' nests, they sat in loneliness, loneliness never being possessed by each although each at some point had wrongly assumed sole possession but rather a something being held (perhaps together) by the whole.

They sat in this company of isolation, consumed by

their thoughts, for an hour, perhaps a little longer. Finally, Mackenzie became bored, climbed down, and dropped gently to the floor. He walked to a candle that had melted into a puddle onto the floor and kicked at it with his toe.

"We should leave." He said it to himself, though his voice called through the room.

"I'm fine with that." James voice was little more than a whisper.

"Not yet. Not yet," David disagreed. "I've got this bad feeling that something is going to h—"

The loud *kaboom* of rifle fire tore through the church.

"And I was right." Another gun fired in reply; another firefight had begun.

Mackenzie swore. "It's getting light out there," he said. "I would rather not be in here when the sun comes up."

"Better than being shot," David replied.

"David is right, Mack," James said. "Staying in here is better than getting shot."

"We aren't going to get shot," Mackenzie called back.

As if in answer to Mackenzie, a bullet thudded into the heavy wooden door. He nodded in response, a look of understanding forming on his face. "Okay, we'll stay here." The words fell out of his mouth.

Another bullet thudded into the door, making him flinch. Another shattered a large pane of stained glass, scattered it on the concrete floor, and thudded into the far wall. More bullets tore through the glass and zoomed overhead. Mackenzie dove to the floor, and David ducked into the pulpit. Whoever had been shooting at the church lowered their aim, and bullets zoomed through the stained glass at head level.

James watched Mackenzie as he lay on the ground. Mackenzie scrunched up into the fetal position and pushed his fingers into his ears. James would have watched longer, but a bullet hit the pulpit just below his neck, sending him shooting down to safety.

TWENTY EIGHT

"Death is not romantic. Death is not glorious. And there is no peace to be found in it."
– Alexander Viccor –

I'm going to die! The words screamed through Mackenzie's mind. *I don't want to die,* he thought. He clutched his knees and brought his legs up more tightly to his body. His every muscle tensed. His head shook. He shut his eyes tight. The world dulled around him, and he seemed to split open and look outwards toward another reality, a reality of blackness. The blackness grew until it consumed his whole vision. He felt bitter cold, sapped of all energy.

He did not hear the bullets whizzing overhead anymore. Everything around dulled as he waited, waited,

waited, waited for the fast, hot feeling of a bullet biting into him, that quick panic flowing through his brain, and the cold creeping on as the warm blood abandoned his body. Time dilated as if to give him intimate knowledge of what true fear was, but he did not have the mind to attend to the opportunity. The fear had consumed him and become him, and in doing so, grown too great to understand. The darkness became a monster—enormous—and in the darkness, nothing was to be understood.

So, he waited. He waited even after the short bursts of gunfire had ended. He waited even as James and David screamed for him to stand. He waited even after James jumped down and dragged him to his feet. The dull world did not sharpen even as they stumbled to the spot under the pulpit, even as the other boys fumbled until they were able to hoist him up. The terror and darkness did not lessen even as James grabbed him by the shoulders, shook him, and yelled, "Mackenzie! Mackenzie, you alright? Mackenzie!?"

The memory of being shot in April flashed through his mind, the memory of shattering glass, of tumbling back, of hot pain as the bullet tore through his flesh, of David's cries. He had been in shock when it happened, in some type of peace. It had taken a week for the emotions to catch up; they came in quick snatches of terror. Now, they overwhelmed him, but no pain accompanied the terror. Mackenzie looked around wondering if he had been hit, wondering if this painlessness he experienced was only a brief spectral period before he would pass on into another existence. He saw the faces of David and James, but he heard their voices muffled as ones speaking through water.

Are they looking at me? he asked himself. *Or just in my direction?* The voices had an urgency to them. *How did I get up here? Am I shot? Was I shot, so they dragged me up here? But where is the pain?*

Am I dying? he asked himself in disbelief. The faces of David and James still yelled. Mackenzie did not see the hand of James as he brought it out with its palm spread wide. He was not aware of it moving quickly through the air. *Am I—* He was not able to finish the thought before a sharp slap hit his face and brought him back to full reality.

His whole body winced in pain and surprise. He cried out, looked around, and suddenly realized what the other boys were saying.

"Mackenzie, you okay?!"

"Snap out of it!"

Their voices faded as he looked at each. Both faces looked back at him in expectation.

"Am I alive?" he asked, looking to James for an answer.

The other two both replied together with a strong "Yes!"

Mackenzie fell back in relieved exhaustion. "I thought I was dead," he said.

"We thought you were dead, too," David said.

"It was a nightmare," Mackenzie continued as he

leaned his head against the side of the pulpit and let out a relieved sigh. He was safe. He heard the other two boys slump down and sigh as well. They all were safe.

~~~

Mackenzie was glad to merely sit for some time. Having been awake the entire night previous, he would slip into sleep during the lulls in the battle, only to be plunged into a waking reality of terror. Soon he would fall back to sleep only to be jerked awake again by more gunfire. The other boys had no such trouble.

The gunfire stopped when the sun rose and lit up the church with a pale, overcast light, and in mid-morning silence all three fell into deep, dream-filled sleep.

Mackenzie was the first to awaken in the early afternoon, 2:34 to be exact. He rubbed his sleepy eyes and looked across the small area of the pulpit at the other two still deep in slumber. Mackenzie yawned. The breathing of James and David was heavy and dissonant. Mackenzie adjusted his feet and peered over the edge of the pulpit. Most of the stained glass on either side of the church had been shot out, and much of it lay scattered on the ground, its color robbed of light.

Sunlight streamed through the empty window panes. Somewhere to his left, he heard the subdued voice of a man. Mackenzie ducked back down behind the pulpit and crossed his arms over his chest for warmth. The cool air of autumn had crept through the broken windows and filled the church.

He heard more subdued voices from outside, ever subdued, never clear. He considered waking the other boys, gave it some thought, but every time he went to wake them he would be distracted by something else. It was when he stood up again and looked out the window to the north, supposing a type of peace existed there, that David woke.

"What time is it?" David asked.

Mackenzie looked down at his watch. "5:46," he said after he looked back out the window. "It's been quiet for a while now."

"How long has it been?" David asked.

Mackenzie looked down at his watch. He thought for a moment. "Three hours-ish. Maybe longer."

"Should I wake James? We could get out of here," David answered.

"Let him sleep for now. I hear voices outside still. I mean, the north seems clear but . . . I don't know; I've been hearing shots from everywhere, you know."

"I think we should wake James," David answered.

"No, no, just let him sleep, David."

"Why? This is our chance to get out of here and back—"

"Shhh!" The sound bit into the silence.

"What? I just thi—"

"Hush! Shh! Shut up! I hear something."

"I don't h—" Mackenzie clamped a hand over David's mouth. David made a noise but stopped. His eyes grew wide. The heavy wooden door to the church was moaning open. Mackenzie released David, and in unison they peeked into the sanctuary.

The *womp* of heavy boots on the marble floor. The voices of men speaking in another language. Both boys guessed Russian. The boys heard more boots, and eventually a middle-aged man walked slowly into the sanctuary and began peering around to survey the chapel. David and Mackenzie quickly ducked back into the pulpit.

The man began to speak more quickly. His speech was not the meandering speech of a person speaking to himself but the clear, articulate, rhythmic speech of a man giving orders. The boys heard his footfalls as he moved about the room until he stopped under the pulpit. The two boys held their breath. The man spoke again, clearer this time, but his speech pattern had changed from one of decisive, intentional rhythm to one with many pauses between thoughts as if he were stopping to consider what was to be done about the pulpit. The boys gave looks of relief to one another when he finally walked away.

Mackenzie jerked his head up and forward using his chin to motion towards James. David looked at the other boy, who was still fast asleep. He shook his head. Mackenzie smiled.

"We should get him up now," Mackenzie whispered.

David shook his head vigorously. "He'd make too

much noise. He's a terrible sneak, and we can't get out. This is the most discrete I've ever seen him."

Mackenzie gave a nod of disappointed understanding before mouthing, "Okay."

Mackenzie slumped down next to James. He wanted to wake him up with a poke and inform him, "You are a lot uglier when you sleep," but he stayed his hand and bit his tongue. Comedy would have to wait until a later date. Now was not the time. *Now is the time to be serious,* he thought, and his humorous thoughts began to turn sour, turn towards darker things that he feared, like the shattering glass, the yell of David, the bite of the bullet, and death—his own death and that of the other two. He tried to push the thoughts out of his head, but they refused to budge even an inch. The light, cheery moments before became sullen and morose. The smile on his face turned into a slight, almost unnoticeable frown as anxiety crept its way into his heart. The last thing he wanted was death, for himself or anyone else.

He imagined the death of those back at the estate. As he saw it, even the most protected place in the house, the basement, offered little protection against tearing bullets. *Tearing bullets?* he thought. *What about grenades or bombs from planes?* Mackenzie looked over at James. A shudder filled him as he imagined the other boy as a corpse. He forced the thought out of his head and looked over to David as David peered over the edge of the pulpit to survey the rest of the sanctuary. David seemed relaxed; he seemed to know what he was doing.

"Forty men in the church right now," David whispered as he dropped next to Mackenzie. "Probably filled the whole place, basement, back offices."

"Why do you think that?" Mackenzie whispered.

"It's what I'd do," David answered.

"So, don't wake James?"

David shook his head.

Mackenzie looked at James who slept peacefully; the image of his corpse did not return. *Lucky bastard*, he joked to get his mind off the situation. *You know you're a bastard? Your parents were never actually married. Your father's last name isn't Anderson. I don't know what it is, but it isn't Anderson. I think your mother planned to tell you herself, but, well, you know.* Mackenzie shrugged as if he were not merely forming a conversation in his mind.

"What are you shrugging for?" David asked.

"Nothing, nothing. Cold, that's all." He shook his head as he spoke. He smiled at his own thoughts.

"I don't think it'll be too cold much longer. Saw some guys boarding up the windows, lighting fires around the room," David said.

"Good," Mackenzie answered.

I'm a bastard? Hmmm, interesting, the conjured voice of James replied in Mackenzie's mind, and Mackenzie attended to it as if it were the boy actually speaking.

Yep, you're a bastard, James. George and Janice talk about it all the time. I figure since we're practically family, it's my duty to tell you.

Bastard, eh? the imaginary voice of James asked.

Yeah, I'm sorry to have to be the one to tell you, but you deserve to know the truth.

The voice of James in Mackenzie's head laughed. *I may be a bastard, but at least I'm a lucky bastard.*

Despite this joke being from himself, Mackenzie's brow furrowed as if he were offended by the response. "Bastard," he whispered, still believing he was thinking the words.

"Lucky bastard." David's voice startled Mackenzie who was unaware he had spoken aloud.

"Yeah." Mackenzie's body slumped. He had returned from his brief mental hiatus, and nothing had changed. "How long do you think we'll be here?" he asked David.

David's shoulders shrugged. A string of apathetic expletives ran through Mackenzie's mind like a train.

The boys talked no longer. Though Mackenzie had a great deal to say, he was worn out by his own thoughts, and he knew if they were heard, they would be caught. If they were caught, they would be dead.

Fists against guns? he thought. *Can't outrun a bullet.*

~~~

The setting of the sun took a lifetime. Minutes were hours, and hours, days. It was only at the point when the sun was low in the sky, blazing red like a hot coal, that they realized it was setting. The remaining colored glass of the western window no longer beamed, but only glowed dully. The light of the room was that of twilight.

Eventually, all light from the sun was gone and the only light that remained in the room was the soft glow of small fires piercing the darkness as little points, until a man went around the room and these lights disappeared as well.

David and Mackenzie refused to sleep out of a fear that one of them would snore and be heard by the men below. At quarter to three, smelling the soldiers lighting up cigarettes, the two pulled out their own and had soon filled up the area of the pulpit with a haze of smoke. Neither had smoked since before they left the Karling's, and scratching the addiction's itch was sweet, relaxing euphoria.

"I needed this," Mackenzie whispered. A cloud of smoke floated out of his mouth, lit only by a cigarette's ember.

"Why's it so dark?" the whispered voice of James replied.

The boy's sudden intrusion made Mackenzie want to laugh, but out of discretion, he refrained. "Welcome back to the world of the living," he whispered over to James.

"Middle of the night," David replied.

"What time is it?" James asked.

Mackenzie drew on the cigarette and brought his watch to his face. "3:02, no, 3:03 AM. Now 3:03."

"Why are you whispering?" James asked.

"Soldiers here in the church," David said quickly, quietly.

"Why didn't you wake me up?" James whispered.

"David thought you should sleep," Mackenzie answered.

James yawned and leaned his head against the side of the pulpit.

At five there was another changing of the guard, and with six came the first announcement of the sun in the east. The soldiers relit their fires and the smell of cooking food wafted up to the pulpit. The boys salivated like hungry dogs at the scent. Stomachs rumbled, and each felt the pain of hunger pierce his side.

The voices of the soldiers seemed to betray a better mood than the night before. Their breakfasting lasted a little over a half an hour, but the smell of food stuck in the air until nightfall. The hunger at first came and went in waves. They would feel the sharp bite of hunger, but after a period had passed, their bodies would adjust, and the hunger would subside. Eventually, the relief left completely and only hunger remained. The hunger twisted their stomachs into knots, and the boys struggled to keep themselves silent. It was in this posture that another night arrived.

Mackenzie was the first to fall asleep. They had been silent for a long time, and suddenly his head fell sideways onto David's shoulder. David pushed him away, and he flopped onto his side.

James looked over at Mackenzie and shook his head in disbelief. "How the heck is he asleep?" The question was meant to stay in his mind.

David shook his head in response.

"What time is it?" James asked. Though he did not prefer David's company, he was too tired and hungry to act on it.

David reached across the sleeping boy's body and grabbed his wrist, but this startled the other boy awake.

"Wha-what?" he asked.

"What time is it, Mack?" David whispered to Mackenzie.

Sleepily, Mackenzie sat up and dramatically brought the watch up to his face. "6:47," he answered and stretched his arms high into the air with a yawn.

"Thanks, that's all I wanted to know," James answered.

"Yeah, thanks for waking me," Mackenzie's voice was thick with sleep as he replied. "Can I go back to sleep now? I was having such a good dream."

"Yeah, sure. What was your dream?" David asked.

Mackenzie smiled. "It was summer, sunny, nice and warm. I was sitting on the edge of the porch of my country house when out from the field two lions came bounding and playing, really peaceful."

"Country house?" James replied.

"And the lions didn't eat you?" David asked.

Mackenzie yawned. "Yeah, my country house. And of course they didn't eat me. They were my friends." James stifled a laugh. "It was a dream, James; I can have whatever friends I want, even if they are lions. Better friends than you two."

"Better?" There was a sound of a smile in James' voice.

"Oh, shut up. The lions were totally cool with each other, sniffing each other's butts, sharing their food, wrestling."

"Lions sniff each other's butts?" James asked.

"They're my lion friends in my dream; they can sniff anyone's butts I want them to." Mackenzie was too tired to joke. He said every word with complete seriousness as if he were defending some basic right of his in question.

"Not my butt," James said under his breath.

Mackenzie sat up and looked straight at James. "If you are in my dream, my lion friends can sniff anywhere they damn well please."

"Whoa. Whoa. Don't bite my head off. Whatever you want. Whatever you want," James answered.

"I'm still stuck on the fact that you want the lions sniffing others' butts," David joked. An odd smile of unexpected amusement curled up on James' mouth at David's response.

"Hey!" Mackenzie whispered in a voice a bit too loud for comfort.

"Okay, sorry," David said. "Tell us more."

"No. I'm going back to sleep and to the best dream I've

304

ever had." He yawned and slumped against the wall, arms crossed, eyes closed, head tilted.

"Best dream you've ever had, huh?" James asked.

"Shut up, James," Mackenzie said, not even bothering to move or open his eyes.

"Night, Mack," David said.

"Shut your sissy mouth, too, David." After he spoke Mackenzie opened a chastising eye and looked first at David then James. Despite trying to control themselves, little quiet laughs escaped after this absurd gesture.

"Godforsaken," Mackenzie whispered in annoyance. The two quieted. Another five minutes passed, and they heard the heavy breathing of Mackenzie.

David and James sat in silence. They were in a good mood but not good enough to share conversation with each other. David was the first to fall asleep. James lay awake a few hours more and fell asleep in the early morning. His last thought was that there had been no fighting in the area since the soldiers had taken up their base in the church.

TWENTY NINE

"I'm amazed at how profoundly and often my life has been influenced by the cigarette addiction of another."
– James Anderson –

Mackenzie woke with David's hand clamped around his shoulder. The gunfire was near, the rifles singing. Sweat covered his entire body and relief washed over him. He quickly gave David a big hug.

The other boy drew back. "What are you doing?" he asked.

Mackenzie laughed. "I was having a terrible dream and you saved me," he said. "I was—"

"No time! No time!" David cried. "This is our chance to move. The soldiers are busy fighting. We've got to go!"

Mackenzie looked at the boy. Urgency filled his voice. His face was wrinkled in concentration. His fingers bit deep into Mackenzie's arm and tugged him to his feet. The boy blurred, and Mackenzie shook his head to clear his mind. A deep darkness was to his left. *A trick of the light?* he wondered, but as he turned toward it, he was confronted with the gaping black maw of a doorway. Steps were barely visible in the gloom beyond. *Steps for the priest to go up to the pulpit.* Mackenzie shook his head as the doorway, the stairwell, and its stairs became depthless.

"Mackenzie." The hand tugged at him again.

"James," Mackenzie responded as his hands went into his pockets. "Where's James?" He retrieved a cigarette and had it lit in a moment. *Clear my head. I need to clear my head.* Smoke entered his lungs, and he felt calm wash over him as the addiction was satisfied.

"He's at the bottom of the stairs," David replied.

Mackenzie stared back into the darkness. The doorway was still a depthless abyss. "The door's open?" Mackenzie commented and then sucked in another lungful of smoke.

David shook his head. "Now, Mackenzie." His voice bit down in frustration. Another tug, stronger than the others, jerked Mackenzie toward the door, and for a moment, he lost his balance.

"Okay, okay," he said as he grabbed the side of the pulpit. "Okay." He took one final drag of smoke into his lungs and tossed the cigarette behind himself and out of the pulpit. "Let's go." His head began to clear as David turned from him and released his arm, and he followed the other boy down the stairs. The stairs led to a small corridor where they found James, sitting on his haunches and framed in the half-light of the gray church.

"What do you see?" David asked the other boy.

"Still fighting," James rasped out. "Can't go out the front," he continued. "Best chance is the back." The boy glanced across the rest of the church. "Only real chance is the back."

David sighed. Mackenzie wondered what the church looked like from the floor. They had spied on the soldiers from above. Above was safe. That had been shown by the pulpit stopping bullets, but they would soon be exposed, and who knows whether they would be seen. All it would take would be one error, one glimpse from a soldier.

Mackenzie sighed to himself. James swore, and David sidled up alongside the boy in the doorway to determine the lay of the land. The two whispered to each other, but Mackenzie heard none of it. His ears were filled with the sound of gunfire, his stomach with butterflies. His mind raced. He could almost hear the zoom of the bullets over his head as he stood in the protection of the hall.

The sting of that bullet from Good Friday never seemed to leave his shoulder or chest. David called for him to move. James dragged him to his feet and helped him up to the pulpit. Both had saved him from this stupidity, from his cowardice, but he could not let them now. He feared the rushing pain of the bullet. He feared his own blood flowing out, his lungs filled with a pant, his life ebbing away. He did not want to die. Of course he did not want to die. He was only seventeen years old, and there were deep dreams in his mind yet to be realized, but this desire butted up against another. This fear was buffeted by another fear, and the two fears could not coexist. He could not act upon both if the situation called for either. He did not want to die, and he did not want either James or David to die.

But if gunfire tore through the air. . . But if bullets threatened them with death . . .

The fears had already done battle. David had been swept up in the crowd of Friday. James had been dragged to the Easter stage. Neither survived because of his actions. Nothing Mackenzie did saved either from their brushes with Grim. Rather, his inaction had likely brought them closer to the edge of death. He feared his friends' deaths. He feared being robbed of them forever. But he feared his own death far worse.

The fears stood face to face. Fraternity had not overcome cowardice, and he could see no reason why it ever would when experience had evidenced this so clearly. This he feared most of all.

"Damnit!" David's loud profanity broke him from his thoughts, and he looked toward the doorway.

"What?" he asked.

"Been spotted. Got to go. ASAP," David replied.

"Got to go, now. His back is turned," James said the words as quickly as he was able, and the boy disappeared out the door before Mackenzie heard what he said.

David disappeared after, and Mackenzie followed a moment later when understanding dawned on him.

The gunfire was louder here in the sanctuary than it had been in the hall. Little light flowed through the boarded windows. The glass from the windows no longer glittered. The high ceiling of the place seemed to stretch to the stars, and calm peace was replaced by war.

The three boys traversed the sanctuary to the hallway in a few quick bounds, but as they flung open the door and entered the hallway and its safe darkness, Mackenzie heard a loud yell, "Ambush!" and looked back to see a soldier with cigarette smoke curling up from one hand and the other hand pointing directly at him. Another call of "Ambush!" left the man's lips, and Mackenzie slammed the door and did not stop running until he had slipped into the deep darkness of the office and locked the man out.

"They're coming!" he almost shouted to the other boys. David grunted. James swore.

"What took you so long to wake up?" James asked, not worrying about whispering. As James asked the question, David opened the door to the outside carefully and peeked out.

"Dreaming," Mackenzie answered out with a pant.

"Lions, again?" James replied. "Good dream?"

"Terrible dream," Mackenzie answered.

"Yeah?" James said.

"Not now," David interrupted. "We've got to figure a

way out of here. They're guarding outside." He peeked again tentatively. James sat on a chair, Mackenzie on a small table in the middle of the room. They watched as David paused. His eyes barely peeked through the door and scanned the darkness. He turned to the room, swearing under his breath, and turned to the other two boys. "They've set sandbags in a ring around the door, a really little ring." David shook his head. "I don't know." He stuck his knuckles into his tired eyes. He swore again, this time loud enough for the other boys to hear clearly.

The hallway door slammed after David's voice had faded into the darkness. James and David began to discuss how they would escape the church. "Stand behind the door. We'll all jump him." "Grab something heavy." But Mackenzie knew it would not work. Their exit was that thin sliver of light streaming through the back door. That was where they would escape, and it would do no good attempting to attack one soldier when more had been alerted and more would come.

We're going out. Mackenzie's mind filled with the words unwilled. *We're going out,* he thought. "And we're not coming back," he muttered to himself. *But to crawl, to run, to what?*

What? The word was no more than a shape on his lips. The footsteps were louder in the hall. The man slammed open another door of another room, and Mackenzie heard a loud curse.

But it was all pointless. If they left through this door,

they would certainly be seen. Soldiers crouched behind sandbags just outside. It was not as if they could merely crawl past their ankles without one of the soldiers looking down. Someone would see them. It would never work. At least in this room, they had the cover of darkness, but out there they would be throwing themselves at the feet of death himself.

Then Mackenzie understood. The realization struck him like a bright, branching flash of lightning.

"David! James!" he shouted. His shout halted their conversation, and they turned to attend to his summons.

"Follow me. Give it three seconds. Hide behind the first thing you see. We'll make it. We'll make it. I promise."

Mackenzie filled with fear as he grabbed the door handle. He was jumping off a cliff into dark waters, though perhaps a bit more dangerous. The dark waters of night certainly had sharp hidden rocks, ready to deal death like an ambushing enemy of war, but each of these "rocks" outside had a mind, and each had their own fear, and each held a wooden and metal stick easily capable of tearing devastation through the body.

Mackenzie hesitated for the briefest moment. Any sane person would have hesitated in a similar manner. Only one completely disconnected from reality or one too naïve would be so reckless to thrust himself into a firefight and think that he would survive the event. Even those with a death wish would hesitate. That primal self-preservation welled up inside Mackenzie, and fear froze him in his tracks. He did not want to die. But he knew he must go forward. Finally, he allowed his body to relax, took a deep breath, held it for a long moment, and blew it out slowly. He pursed his lips, bit the lower one, and set his teeth together. *You've got to go, Mack*, he told himself. *They won't be able to wait forever.* He shook his head, bolted out the door, and flopped heavily onto the cold ground, hitting his elbow so hard he cried out. He stifled his cry by biting his hand and hid his face in the grass, too scared to breathe. He felt no pain; he heard no voices yelling in his direction. Mackenzie looked up. The soldiers were far too close for sanity's sake, but they had not seen him. They were occupied with the bullets flying over their own heads.

Mackenzie took a deep, fear-filled breath, wondering if he would be able to do it, whether he could go through with the plan. But he knew the decision had already been made. Someone had to die, either willingly or unwillingly. Fate demanded a sacrifice.

And why not? Why not me? He took another terror-filled breath in. He breathed out determination. This was his duty to the other two. To himself. Those long-past days of Holy Week had robbed him of something, stolen it away, and he had feared such deep, deep fears. Piercing fears. And those fears still existed. Those fears still burned within him. They still circled his mind. They still threatened panic, but they did not overcome him. They were great, but they did not control him. He kept them in check. Barely. But he kept them in check.

"Ladies and gentlemen!"

He screamed the words at the top of his voice as he jumped to his feet and took off running behind the soldiers. He saw them turn. He saw the surprise in their faces. A yell leapt from their mouths. Gun muzzles greeted him.

More cries left the soldiers' mouths. Rifle fire entered his ears, but he felt no pain. He turned to corner of the church. He led them from the door. The bullets zoomed past his head. Terror, deep terror filled him, but it did not matter. He had done it. He had lured them away. He had dodged the bullets. He, James Mackenzie Jacobe, had been trapped in the straight-jacket of terror, a claustrophobic frozen in a narrow crawlspace, and had willed himself to act even in the face of almost certain death.

~~~

David and James ran without thought. The soldiers were gone. Only one remained, but he was too distracted by a barrage of bullets as they passed. Gunfire and the cries of men came from behind the church, but they neither saw nor heard any sign of Mackenzie. They were too distracted, too adrenaline-filled. Their heartbeats filled their ears even after the gunfire from the back of the church faded and the soldiers once more took up their places behind the sandbags.

"Mackenzie," David whispered, and James thought the same thing. Both hoped Mackenzie was not a shadow laying on the ground; maybe, just maybe he was alive. Though no more was said than those three syllables of his name, wishes, wishes, wishes filled the minds of David and James. The wishes were a circle of thought. As soon as one would end, another would begin.

James sighed as he looked at the church, at the door that had been their exit. He had escaped. David had escaped. *Mackenzie?* The word circled his mind as he wished for the impossible to be.

"Good."

James turned to the panting voice.

"Good." The speaker was shrouded in shadow. "Thought you'd run off," Mackenzie said. "I sure would've. Good."

"Mackenzie," James whispered.

"David." Mackenzie paused. "James." He took in a long, tired breath. "Let's get the Hell out of here." A large, toothy smile spread across his face.

THIRTY

———

"Mackenzie knew who he was; he was the only one of us who did."
– David Amore –

Warmth. The gentle comforting breeze of morning, like the breath of a lover, blew up over James' neck and onto his eyelids like a kiss. He stretched his limbs and rolled from his stomach onto his back, and the light of the morning shone through his eyelids and filled his vision up with a peaceful, rosy red.

Warmth. The birds chirped outside. They warbled and tweeted. They whistled and cooed. Something scurried through the brush, and the sound of a woodpecker knocking on a tree echoed through the air. James sighed and smiled as he opened his eyes. The light reflected off the rustic wooden surfaces of the cabin and seemed to make the entire room give off a faint but inviting glow.

———

Yawning, he pushed the soft quilt off himself and rotated until his feet touched the smooth warmth of the floor. He stood slowly. Sunbeams streamed through the cabin dust, and James moved from the bed across the cabin to the door. As he moved to the porch, the gentle browns of the cabin faded into the light-blue sky, and a patchwork valley of greens cascaded below him like the rapids of a gorge until they were met by the quick, sharp swells of bald mountain faces in the distance. James stood awed, and the door continued its creaking swing until it thudded into the side of the cabin.

James heard a tired groan and looked over to see Mackenzie in a rocking chair reaching up to rub his sleepy eyes. He shook his head, looked out at the mountains and finally over to James. "James." He stretched his arms above his head and gave out another, longer groan. As he stretched his neck from side to side, he looked at his watch. "You finally up? It's already eleven." Mackenzie yawned. "I've been up for hours waiting for you." His eyes returned to the mountains.

"By up do you mean sleeping on the porch?" James asked.

"Resting my eyes," Mackenzie replied with a smile.

James looked over at the other boy and back at the valley before finally plopping himself down on the step of the porch. "Where are we?" he asked.

"Don't you see for yourself?" Mackenzie answered.

"Mountains?"

"Mountains. The most beautiful place in the world." Mackenzie continued to stare off into the distance. He smiled.

"Okay," James squinted in confusion, but the importance of where they were seemed to fade. "Why are we here?" he asked instead.

Mackenzie stared over at him before replying. "We won, James," he said.

"We won?" James asked.

Mackenzie nodded back slowly. "We won. We won everything."

"Everything?" James settled back against a beam of the porch and allowed his body to sag into relaxation.

"Everything, and now everything is ours. This is it from now on. This and everything else we want. Mountains in the summer. Coastlines in the winter. This is it, James." Mackenzie sighed, stretched his arms high, and placed his hands behind his head. "This is the feeling of victory." Mackenzie closed his eyes. He leaned back, and let out a loud laugh.

"Ladies and gentlemen . . ."

James woke to cold darkness, and though he tried to hold onto the rich calmness of that dream, it quickly faded as he stared into the cold, dead darkness of the house and left only the finale of that weak lingering phrase.

He and David left the church. Hot lead zoomed through the air. The firefight continued. Bullets thudded into the ground, and they ran until the sound of the weapons were distant. They passed through the gap in the fence with little discretion. They passed the statue of Dalimore. They passed the god-man, the shattered box, the fairgrounds. Dark streaks of the city streamed by like a river, and when they reached the gate of the Karling estate, David nodded and continued.

When he entered, James found the estate abandoned. He reasoned the Karlings had evacuated and the servants fled when they heard the gunfire, but in the end, he had no certainty and did not care. He knew he would find little comfort whether he had a comforter or not.

At first, he tried to sleep. The darkness was deep. The exhaustion of the last several days pressed him into bed, but rest eluded him. Eventually, he began to wander the estate, seeking to dull the bitter emotion inside, but each place was only another reminder of the pain. He passed the kitchen and watched Mackenzie, several years younger, stealing donuts from the counter. He passed the great hall. Mackenzie was being shooed out of the room by Janice, who brandished a large broom. The boy's cries filled the garden. Mackenzie's young voice filled the woods. He explained to James how they were going to build "the best fort in the world." His golden tie still fluttered as James passed the fountain. A smile curled on James' face as he watched Mackenzie hide behind the servants' quarters and under one of the large trees as the boy lit his first cigarette. Everywhere he went, he saw

Mackenzie's smile. Everywhere he went, his laugh echoed through the world.

"Down the tree, Mack?" James heard his own voice. It had been many years before.

"Is there any other way?" Mackenzie replied.

James stared at the tree. He saw it in every season. It gleamed with springtime rain. Summer foliage hid its limbs. It burst with the colors of fall, was dead with winter snow. James listened for Mackenzie's voice, telling him to hurry as he always did, but only the wind replied.

Mackenzie's room was small, spartan. James opened the closet. Servant's clothes stared back at him. The first three drawers of the dresser contained the same. Only the last had anything of note. Beneath all the clothes was a small box that contained the few possessions Mackenzie had to his name: a picture of his mother (the same blonde hair and piercing eyes as his), a necklace, a key, a purple heart, and finally Mackenzie's slave ring.

James picked up the slave ring and set the rest of the box on the dresser. He sighed as he stared at the small earing in his palm. *This is it,* he thought. *All I have left of him. A slave ring and memories. That's all.*

James reached up. He felt the soft metal ring in his own ear. Gently, slowly, he pulled it off and looked down at both, one in each hand. His gleamed back a warm bronze, Mackenzie's a cold silver. James let out a sigh. He allowed his own to fall to the ground and brought Mackenzie's up to his ear. *All I have left,* he thought. *Everything else, gone.*

This was reality.

Two left the church.

This was reality.

He was alone.

James slumped onto the bed without thought and fell asleep as he stared at the door. He slept long and deep and awoke in darkness.

"Ladies and gentlemen," he whispered to himself as the images and warmth of that sunny dream slipped away and were replaced by the creeping cold of October. He could not finish the phrase. He did not want to. He did not think he should. "Ladies and gentlemen," his voice trailed off from exhaustion, and he stared into the darkness.

"I had a home a long time ago," he said to himself after many silent hours. "I thought this was home," he told an absent Mackenzie. "But I don't think it ever could b—"

Something hard clunked against the side of the house, interrupting James' words. Startled, he jumped. He heard the sound again. Something was hitting the window. *Rocks?* he thought. *That would make sense.* He heard another shower of them. His brow knitted in annoyance. James lifted his head off the pillow and looked across the room. He sat up as more stones sounded against the house.

~~~

The last time they had seen each other, they had departed in silence. He had left James at the gate, and the boy had entered without a word. David had walked until the night became old, until the night became dead and his mind heavy with apathy. For hours, he wandered this way and that, careful to avoid the sound of gunfire. He found nowhere to stop. Sometimes he would loiter for several minutes, never sitting, always acting busy as if he were trying to fool an audience of onlookers that did not exist, and always he would wander away from each of these places and move to another. Each place stirred some restless spirit within him that eventually forced him back to the Karling estate. When he did not find James in the servants' quarters, he sensed the boy would be in Mackenzie's room.

David tossed the stone he held over his shoulder. It clattered on the footpath before falling with a hush into some nearby grass.

"Go away, David," James yelled through the window.

"Wanna hang out?" David called back to the boy.

James wanted to laugh but could not find the will.

"Jimmy?" David continued. His voice was desperate. It was lonely.

"Why?" James answered.

"I . . ." David's voice trailed off after the sound, but James did not need an answer. He already understood on some base level, and he lifted the window and nodded his head.

"Sure," he said, before David could continue.

~~~

"Why did you come back?" James asked as they sneaked first through this alley then that. There was no need to whisper. There had been no fighting in the city for the past week. "Why did you find me?" he amended.

David laughed. A smirk grew on his face and did not fade even as he spoke. "Because I'm alone. Because you're alone. Because life is a Hell-hole you can't climb out of."

The words betrayed an odd amusement. Either the amusement was merely a thin veil pathetically attempting to cover hopelessness, or it was true amusement springing from somewhere deep inside David as he became aware of the absurdity of the situation, the absurdity of human life. It was a laugh recognizing the futility of not only his situation but also of the futile, vaporous struggle he saw as the whole of existence. And the morbidity of the thought demanded a laugh.

James continued to follow David as they snaked their way east through the city. Finally, they climbed through a broken window and up flight after flight of stairs until they reached the top of the tallest building in town.

David plopped himself on the edge and peered down below. He fished in his pocket and pulled out a pack of cigarettes. He offered none to James and tried to forget reality as he looked across the city, now almost completely black. A few cars moved about the below. Almost everyone had vacated the city, and those who did not were asleep in their beds . . . or what they called their beds.

All those human struggles were put to rest with the night, and from this vista, the city was not a place of short, brutish injustice. It was a patchwork of lights, a beautiful panorama stretching out before David. The individual struggles of each person had faded into the background, but eventually, the clarity disappeared. The cigarette gave no satisfaction, and this place he thought might give him some peace was as dead as the rest of the world.

"It's not the right place?" he asked James as they stood to their feet to leave.

"We never found the right place," James answered.

David let a breath of a laugh out through his nose. "I suppose not," he said as they started down the stairs.

"It's going to be a long winter," James said behind him.

David wrapped his arms tightly around his body. The air was cold, too cold for this time of year. The weather was a month ahead of itself. He gave James a distracted nod.

THIRTY ONE

———

"He's the best friend I've ever had, hands down."
— James Anderson —

The final weeks of October melded together into one amorphous period. Days and nights passed by without differentiation. The two wandered the streets as aimlessly as they ever had, but more alone. Firefights broke out across the city, and though they wondered what was happening, they always gave the gunfire a wide berth. Temperatures outside were brisk. No one returned to the Karling estate. Those who were able to flee the city had. Those who could not held onto the thin hope that everything would soon return to some form of normalcy. The thirty-first of October greeted the boys with no gunfire, no yelling soldiers, only emptiness.

"Ready yet?" David called into the room.

He was answered by a grunt and James' face appearing in the doorway. "Just have to get my shoes on," James said.

James' thoughts drifted to Mackenzie as he slowly tied his shoe. He remembered waking up in the church. David had been at the small door that allowed the priest entrance to the pulpit.

"What are you doing?" James asked.

"Unlocking it," David replied.

"Where did you learn to pick locks?" James asked through a yawn.

"When you've got Hell for a life, you pick up a lot of odd skills," David whispered back and swung the door open. A dark, narrow stairwell lay beyond.

"James, can you go scout ahead while I wake Mackenzie?" David continued.

James shrugged. "Sure," he said, and made his way down the small set of stairs. They turned right at the bottom and a short passageway led to a doorway just behind the altar.

As he waited, he watched one soldier move away from the windows, sit down on a pew, and begin to treat a wound on his arm.

"How's it going?" David asked after he had arrived at the bottom of the stairs with Mackenzie.

James answered then turned to survey the room again. The soldier still sat on the pew. He busied himself with bandaging his wound, but as he did so, he paused. James could not see what had caught his attention and wondered what could be so interesting.

James swore after the man had reached to pick the thing up.

"What's wrong?" David asked. He was now beside James and peering out into the room as well.

"We've been found," James answered.

"Found?" David said.

James responded by pointing toward the man. Smoke flowed from between his fingertips as he inspected the still smoldering cigarette.

David cursed under his breath. "That's mine." David swore again. "My cigarette. Dropped it. Damnit. Mine."

"Come on, James." David's voice broke him out of the memory, and he realized his shoes were tied and he was staring blankly at a spot on the floor.

~~~

"Where are we going?" James asked after they had walked for more than half an hour.

David stared forward tiredly. "East." His voice was emotionless from fatigue. "Maybe west. South. North." He yawned. "You know."

"Tired?" James asked. It was freeing to talk to someone else. These days he would not even talk to himself. He was afraid of what nightmarish phantasm would form on the tip of his tongue. There was something he knew that he did not want to know. There was something inside him that he could not, would not, speak.

James knew if he spoke it even as a whisper, it would come out as a shout. And everything would be thrust into the open. And that which was just a thought in his head would become reality. No longer could that night at the church have perhaps been a hallucination or delusion he dreamed up for whatever godforsaken reason. but another could say they remembered exactly what he did.

"No. I'm not tired." A yawn followed David's words.

After several blocks of silence, James spoke. "So, we're going east then?"

"East." David nodded but gave no further explanation.

"Where east?" James asked.

"The marina," David answered with a nod.

"Why to the marina?" James asked.

David looked over to him. "Don't like the marina?"

James sighed. "I don't like water," he said.

"We don't have to go to the marina," David spoke in calm silence, but he was angry. He had been for a week at least, not at James, but himself. He had pestered Mackenzie about going out at night. He had led them to the church. If not for his insistence, Mackenzie would be alive. It was his fault, and the friendliness of James made him feel guilty. He did not feel as if he deserved friendliness. No, not *friendliness, not friendship, punishment.* "There's nowhere else to go," he continued. "Unless you want to go back to the church. Let's go to the church instead, shall we?" David's voice was acidic.

"Not to the church," James answered.

"Then to the marina," David replied.

"I said I don't want to go."

"God! Seriously, James? Go where you want to! I'm not your friend!" he yelled. He shook his head at the other boy and himself, and then quickened his pace and became silent once more.

~~~

James watched as the other boy continued walking in front of him. He and David were not friends. Mackenzie had been David's friend, and James and David had tolerated each other's presence for Mackenzie. Now, with Mackenzie gone, with the Karling estate vacated, going out at night was the last normalcy James had in life. It was the last shred of good, but he knew he could only lie to himself about this being normal for so long.

At first, when David had once more become silent, James tried to excuse David's outburst, but the words of David sat heavily in his chest. The smoke trailed from the man's hand once more. Though the cigarette was invisible, that smoke was easily translated. "Mine. Dropped it. Damnit." Mackenzie burst into his thoughts. "Cigarette. Mine."

That cigarette, James thought. *If it weren't for that cigarette.*

329

And the thought grew old and festered as they walked. It rotted and turned into anger. He looked at David a few yards ahead. *I'm not your friend!* David's words were slow and hate-filled to James, and James could not stop the anger from flashing into a tooth-grinding, fist-clenching rage. The emotion overtook him, and in a red fury, he rushed headfirst into the other boy's back.

~~~

David took a sharp, futile breath inward as he fell to the concrete and his face barely hit a fire hydrant. His chest and face hit the ground together. His nose twisted, and blood trickled out. He felt the other boy on top of him. He heard the other boy grunt angrily and then felt a strong yank on his hair. James brought all his force down on David's head, and David's nose smashed into the concrete. Eyes watered. Blood flowed from his nose, and the skin on his right cheekbone felt as if it were going to tear.

~~~

Crimson filled James' vision. He had read of bloodlust but thought it had only been a piece of literary fiction. He thought it was something dreamed up by some old doddering soldier to paint a more complex picture of war. Now he felt it. Rationality was expelled from his mind, and every piece of his being was caught up in the movement of his body. He was so consumed with irate red, he did not expect David to fight back.

But the boy under him scooted to his hands and knees. In one swift motion, he put his upper body under himself, causing James to be thrown off balance. David tucked his legs and rolled forward. James was thrown to his belly. In less than a moment, David was on his feet looking down at the other boy.

"Up. Up," David said. "Let's have a real fight." David set his feet and put his open hands in front preparing to react. He watched as James pushed himself up and, before gaining his balance, charged.

As they met, David grabbed one of James' arms, sidestepped, and threw the charging boy onto the ground. James gave an angry snort, picked himself up, and charged once more. Again, David threw him to the ground. A third time he stood up. David laughed and brought his hands up in the fashion of a boxer. James rubbed a new abrasion on his face and cursed. With a yell, he moved quickly towards David, threw a mighty punch and missed completely.

"Telegraphed that one, Jim Bob. I saw it coming a mile away." Anger seeped into David, and he relished every syllable of the sentences. The pain was being replaced by fury, and he was glad.

James stepped forward, swung as hard as he could, and once again missed.

"Did it again," David mocked. "Will I have to explain how fist fights work to you?" James charged again. This time David did not throw him down but sidestepped and sent a hard fist into his stomach. James bent double and gasped for breath.

"First thing," David said. "You keep on doing the same thing. That's not going to work. Second, I know what you're doing before you do it. Your hands are okay, I g—" James lunged again. Distracting himself as he spoke, David was caught off-guard, and James hit him squarely in the solar plexus, knocking the wind out of him.

Okay, David thought. *Ready to be done with this.* He grabbed James around the head with one hand, formed the other into a fist, and slammed the fist into James' face. James fell to his knees and covered his face with his hands to protect it. David brought his foot back. He kicked the other boy as hard as he could in the groin.

~~

James screamed. His hands dropped from his face to his groin. David's foot slammed into James' chest. James collapsed onto his back. He squirmed. He coughed. Snot ran from his nose. The abrasions on his face burned. His groin felt as if it had been relocated to the center of his belly. He wheezed. Pain shot through his chest up into his shoulder. Through the pain, James heard David swear at him, call him a name, but he did not hear what it was. He then saw him shift in an odd manner. Before it could register in James' mind, David brought his foot down as hard as he could on James' hand. James heard a pop and felt pain at the joint.

He cried out and swore at the other boy. He closed his eyes. He squeezed them closed, harder and harder, until purple fireworks filled his vision. James screamed between his teeth. He heard another curse from David. The pain ebbed, his eyes relaxed, and he opened them.

James sat. Pain shot through his hand and up into his shoulder. He looked around, but David was nowhere in sight. He cursed again and yelled at the boy. "Where are you!?" *How dare he leave me out here?* he thought. *That son of a . . .* His nostrils flared. His lips curled. "I'm going to beat him like a dog," he said. He imagined himself beating David senseless, beating him until he cried for mercy, beating him until he sounded like an animal, beating him until he passed out, until even after he passed out, beating him to the edge of his life.

He wanted David to suffer. He wanted to watch him die.

THIRTY TWO

"We've always gotten along quite well. He's an interesting person. Some odd habits. He always carries around a knitted chess board."

– Jack Viccor –

David looked down before he left James and saw a pathetic pile of human sprawled on the ground. He thought to send one more vicious kick into his head. This thought was accompanied by a stream of profanity directed at James.

But he did not do it. Memories flooded his mind. Words overpowered his fury, *It's my birthday,* and he felt sick to his stomach as he imagined himself bringing his foot back the way the man had. He became sick as he heard the thudding of the boot. James was vulnerable, his head exposed. He had started the fight, but David walked away

---

334

instead. His feet moved steadily until they brought him to the foot of a large window.

David looked at the dark panes of glass. He could not see it now, but he knew that if he were inside and if even the slightest light shone through this window, he would see the image portrayed clearly. Above him, standing at least fifteen feet tall, was Christ. He wore a robe that covered his wounded side, but the holes in his hands and feet were visible. His eyes were open, and he looked stoically down upon the pews. The image was humorless, unhappy, and apathetic. *What have you done to me?* it asked, and David was glad he could not see it.

He had unknowingly brought himself back to the church. The place that had once been a bastion of life was now no more alive than the ghetto. Many good things had begun to rot. Two weeks ago, his bones felt strong. Now they felt as if someone had taken them out of his body and charred them until brittle. He had been at ease, but a cruel laugh of the torturer filled him. His once-supple muscles ached, and since that night, exhaustion had overtaken him.

Slowly, he moved behind the church, to where the event had occurred. Tentative, he ran his fingers across the stones. They were rough. He suddenly noticed that he no longer felt guilty, and the tension in his fists and face was gone.

The body was a silhouetted lump on the ground. It lay face down. He had a fleeting hope that at any moment it would stir or twitch and show some sign of life, but what lay before David was as still as a rock. The clothes did not flutter. The hair, covered in mud, stuck every which way. The shirt was torn as if someone had grabbed the collar on either side and lifted. His belt was gone (someone had already taken it), but his pants were left alone despite being new and undamaged. David looked to the feet. He swore. They wore only socks.

Vultures, David thought. *He should have been buried in shoes.*

Buried? David swore aloud and sat down next to Mackenzie. He grabbed the far shoulder and paused. The body was icy-cold and stiff. David sighed through his nose. He did not want to see the face. He did not want to, but something compelled him to. As he turned Mackenzie onto his back, David winced as he saw the empty eyes staring up at him.

As David looked away from the eyes, he closed them with one hand, and with the other, he brought his friend up into a defeated embrace. "You saved me, Mack. And I couldn't save you from anything," he said as he remembered Mackenzie's grip on his forearm after he had awoken him in the pulpit.

It all made no sense to David. The word "death" seemed more like a placeholder than an actual reality, but here it was in all its terrible hurt. *A week ago, laughing, joking, talking, and now you're gone. How?* David asked.

David laid him back on the ground. He did not want

to look at the body. It looked like Mackenzie, but it wasn't him. It was the same hair and muscles and bones, but it was no more his friend than a photograph.

It was at this time that he heard the moan of distant planes. David did not care. He did not even look up. He continued to stare down at the body. He felt as if he should do something, pray, bow, salute, something, but he did not know what. As he thought, he pulled off his shoes and put them on the other boy. They were a poor, dirty replacement for Mackenzie's, but they were better than nothing. "I should really bring you inside the church and sit you down on a pew, so you look like you are alive from the back," he told him as he finished tying the second shoe. "It'd really freak some people out." A small, sad smile curled up his face. "I'm going to miss you," he continued. The smile broke.

~~~

James' eyes squeezed together in fury, blood filled his face, and his vision filled up with a dark, rich red. He had been defeated, and defeat had made him ashamed. And how dare David make him feel ashamed.

Following fury, his eyes finally opened. He expected the glare of several streetlights, but the streetlights did not shine tonight. Turning from side to side and finding everything pitch-black, he looked up at the sky. The nasty, dark orange, akin to the color of dirty, slushy snow, had faded to a calm black punctuated by pinpricks of stars.

Pain shot from his stomach to his sternum. He winced and continued to stare at the stars above. Wounds were still there, physical and emotional. Some were abrasions. Some bruises, some broken bones. Although the stars did not fix them, they made the pain bearable.

He tried to drag himself up to a sitting position. Crying out in pain, he failed and fell onto his back. Something must have happened to his arm or wrist as he fell; pain started at the center of his hand, branched out to each of his fingertips, and crawled its way back as a throb to his elbow. He took in a slow breath, winced, moved his hands underneath himself, and pushed up more slowly.

Without using his right hand, he stood to his feet. His legs were fine as far as he could tell. One of his pant legs had rubbed rough against his thigh, causing a friction burn, but besides some bruising, his legs were as good as they had always been.

James took another look up at the stars. Looking back down at the city, he sighed. The world was a fuzzy gray. Off in the distance, a single light flickered on and off, on and off; and as James moved forward into the darkness, his eyes focused on this flickering streetlamp. The bulb blinked on for a long moment and then flickered off and on erratically until it went dark altogether.

Without a thought, James stopped and waited for it to flicker again. His eyes darted to look at the darkness around him and returned to the spot the light had been (or at least where he thought it had been). It may have been a trick of the eyes, but for a long moment, James thought he perceived a rusty-hued specter of light hanging up in the air.

Then the specter disappeared. He looked up at the stars, but they had been covered by clouds, and the little wan light they did offer was no better for seeing than the glow of the streetlight. The gray of night turned black, and any features that he had been able to perceive in half-light faded altogether.

Then he heard something, a whispered voice that seemed to say his name. James spun around in circles but in the darkness was unable to see a thing. The air grew colder and a tickling tingle crawled up his spine. Fear seized his whole body. Adrenaline coursed through his veins. Without thought, his legs propelled him forward in fear.

He ran at full speed until he broke out of the darkness into a neighborhood with shining streetlamps. Sweat soaked his hair and dripped off the tip of his nose. Breath was expelled from his mouth in a cloud of steam. He stared at the sharp shadows on the ground as he tried to piece apart logical thought from muddy emotion, but his mind was not filled with thoughts or emotion. It was filled with disorder, disorder layered upon disorder. Blood rushed through his ears, that mad percussionist beating relentlessly on a bass drum. Soundbites of thoughts would zoom from the back of his mind to the front before disappearing into the darkness.

His body held the same disorder. Pain hammered his head. His ankles were sore from running. His legs stung from the bruises. He had a stitch in his side. His lungs burned, and his hand still throbbed.

The streetlights stretched out uniformly along each side of the road like silent sentinels. Each cast a gray light on the center of the street. He looked up. The city sky had rediscovered that ugly orange glow. His head began to clear as he turned his eyes back to the road.

The silhouette of buildings in the distance brought back memories of certain areas of the city. He imagined each street in his mind. *If I can get somewhere I know, I can make it back home*, he thought.

Home? he repeated the word in his mind. *Okay*, he conceded.

He turned in circles to gain his bearings, and up it loomed before him.

It was no longer a church to him. It had become something else. It was a memorial. "The biggest gravestone in the world," he whispered as he reached out his hand and ran his fingers along the rough, stone blocks.

"I would bless you, but I am not a priest." James stood silent after speaking. Silence was the best thing he could think to do. He needed to stay silent for that death. Silence could begin to combat the noise accompanying the death. A word spoken would break that sacred silence. *Sacred . . .* James would have never considered anything sacred, but this one thing, if only in his mind? He understood it had to be.

James closed his eyes. His tears had been spent, but the feeling remained, a deep, dark, empty loss. Nothing good came of it. It had no meaning. It had no dignity. James' thoughts bubbled in his mind. *The world means nothing, comes from nowhere, is going nowhere. It began with darkness; it will end with darkness.*

There is no faith. There is no hope. Eat, drink, be merry; tomorrow you die. All is pointless. Everything is meaningless. There is no love. There is no God.

"I'm not a priest, but I'll try a blessing." James heard the voice from behind the church. David stumbled over a few lines of Latin before returning to English. "Ladies and gentlemen, stand and meet your new king." The last line was whispered and half-lost in the night air, but James was certain of what had just been said.

James walked toward the voice. He turned the corner to see the familiar figure of David. He was hunched over something on the ground.

So, that's the spot, he thought.

David looked up. He nodded to the standing boy in greeting, no anger, no animosity.

James nodded back. The prior fiery emotions had died, but a cold ash of bitterness still sat in the center of his heart.

"I wasn't planning on coming here." David looked down at the body. Each word seemed to be chosen delicately, as if he was picking something out of a thorn bush.

"Yeah, me neither," James replied. Instead of looking at either David or what lay at his feet, he looked over at the cold, dark stones of the church.

"Someone took his shoes," David said after a moment of silence.

James glanced down at Mackenzie's feet; they were shod. "Those are mine," David said. "I, uh, I couldn't leave him with bare feet. There was something wrong about it."

James nodded.

The boys shared another moment of silence, longer this time.

"I was just about to bury him," David said, subdued. "If you want to do any, you know, um, last respects or whatever you call it, uh . . ."

"Yeah," James replied and finally forced himself to look down at the body. Continuing to look, he sat down, legs crossed, opposite David.

The skin was pale; the color had gone out of his cheeks. The limbs appeared wooden; the face looked like a mask. It was the boy in some sense. It was the same cells, same fingerprints, same bones. Same hands. Same feet. Same eyes. *Same flesh, but even asleep Mackenzie showed his personality.*

James wanted to tell him that whatever state he was in, wherever that state was, he would be fine, everything would be good from now on. But James did not even attempt it. He knew Mackenzie could not hear him.

"I'd like to put one of my shoes on him," James said, finally breaking through the thick silence between them.

"Yeah, I feel like that would be right," David replied. Reaching down to the feet of the body, he pulled off the right shoe. As David undid the knot on his shoe and tied the laces of his shoes together on the left foot, James yanked off his own shoes. After unlacing both, he shoved the right shoe on the right foot with a certain degree of difficulty and finally fit them on the rest of the way. He then proceeded to tie the shoe onto the foot and tie the other shoe onto the first one's lace.

James looked up; David had already finished.

"Are you ready to bury him, then?" David asked.

"No. What was that thing you said before?" James replied. "It was in another language," he clarified.

"Um, Last Rights. It's in Latin, and it's Last Rights," David answered.

"Can you say it again?" James asked.

"Sure." David paused. He looked down, and closed his eyes. His fingers drew a cross in the air as he spoke.

"*Per iseram sanctam unctionem et sunam pimam misericordiam, indulgeat tibi Dominus quidquid per.*"

James closed his eyes as well. David said ,"Amen," and looked up.

"Ladies and gentlemen, stand and meet your new

king," James said before opening his eyes and looking back at the body.

"Amen," David whispered.

"Okay," James said. "Let's get this over with." He stood up. "Have you picked a spot?" he asked.

"See the tree?" David asked.

James nodded. "Yeah," he said.

"I was thinking that would be a good spot."

James nodded again. "Yeah, me too." He was the first to stand and reach the tree, but David was the first to kneel and begin to dig the grave.

At first, David used his hands. His fingertips pressed into the supple grass and lifted chunks of sod up out of the earth. He continued to use his hands to scoop a few more times, but the gravelly soil he had not expected bit into his soft skin. He searched around until he found a sturdy stick that would not break, and it was at this point that James knelt and dug.

"We should really burn the tree down in the spirit of Mack," David said.

"I was thinking that we should burn down the whole neighborhood," James answered. "We could burn him, give him that blaze of glory he always wanted to go out in."

Then the boys spoke no more. David wondered if James had the same thoughts on his mind. *But he didn't go out in a blaze of glory, did he? Funny how that ended up. Funny?* The hole was now the size of three medium-sized dogs.

The digging was much easier. Making it wider would be simple and quick.

There was never anything funny about it. David scooped another handful and wiped the cold sweat from his forehead. His feet were cold, almost numb with cold. He lifted out another scoop. The tips of his fingers were raw. A few more scoops and the grave would be complete. It was shallow, but it was deep enough to bury a body and keep it buried.

David stood. James looked up at him. "That's enough," David said. "Let's go get him."

"Okay," James replied. It was only a few steps over to the body. The boys bent at the knees. David grabbed Mackenzie's coat at the shoulders, and James grabbed a leg of his pants with each hand.

James swallowed. *But no*, he thought, *nothing is okay about this.*

"One, two, three, lift."

The head lolled backwards onto the ground. The midsection sagged and dragged as they took the first few steps forward.

No. The word was a weak cry in James' mind. *No, no, no. This is not how it's supposed to be.* James caught a glimpse of the bobbing head out of the bottom of his vision. He swore coarsely. *No*, he thought. The word was now a pain-filled whine. His stomach knotted, turned, and rose into his throat, fear and disgust and sadness all rolled into one.

He swallowed in a futile attempt to force the emotions back down from whatever abyss they were born.

"It'll all be okay," they had told him when his mother never returned. Over and over again the word was repeated.

"It'll all be okay."

"Everything will go back to normal."

"Okay."

"Okay."

And when they said it, he had believed it. But it was not okay. Yes, he still smiled and laughed and felt pleasure, but there was always something deeper that was not happiness, whether it was anger or sadness or confusion or fear. He was not happy; it seemed a lifetime since he had an unadulterated happiness. He could never forget the pain; it was never just a memory.

How could it ever just be a memory? he thought.

He sighed as he felt the weight of the body pull his arms down. *How could it ever be normal again?* he asked himself. *Or maybe this is what they meant by normal.* His hand released, and the body thudded into the shallow grave. *Hell, if this is normal, there's nothing "okay" about it. Something is very wrong with normal.*

The people's words had been followed by rationalizations. And each time they began their rationalization, he had wanted to give them a piece of his mind.

"There is a reason for this," they would say.

Oh, really? he would reply.

"There's always a reason," they would answer.

Then show me a reason in this. Show me the plan. Show me some logic, because this all doesn't seem so logical to me. It doesn't seem reasonable to me.

Why do they always have to find a reason? Why do they always have to assume they understand something that I don't? No, their reasons were never for him.

Today he was allowed his hurt, and a different word screamed through his mind: *No!*

No. Nothing more and nothing less. Like one tortured, the word filled his mind. This terrible thing had happened, and he could do nothing to change it. *No!* he screamed and writhed in his secret pain.

No! In utter pathetic realization of his impotence, he scooped the first handful of earth onto the body.

James caught a scent of something terrible. David cursed. It was the body; even in the cold weather, decay had set in. James tried to ignore it. He tried to drag his mind away from the smell, away from the corpse, away from the church, but every hiding place he had within himself was filled with it, and he was forced to feel the pain to every, last terrible drop.

James scooped another handful of dirt and tossed it on the body. It fell in a clump, hit the chest with a thud, and bounced off to the side of the body. Staring at the clump, he rubbed his hands together to clean them.

Ashes to ashes.

347

The dirt dried and floated down to the ground as dust.

A hand grabbed his shoulder followed by another hand on the other shoulder and started to pull him off the ground.

~~~

Another shell hit, closer this time, and David's desire to abandon James grew inside like an inferno. But he did not leave James. David swore and swore and swore again, but instead of fleeing, instead of saving his own skin, he tightened his grip on the other boy.

"Let me go!" James shouted.

"We've got to get out of here!" David screamed back.

"We've got to bury the body," James answered.

"Don't you hear the bombs? Don't you feel them?"

"But we've got to bury the body," James answered again.

"No! Someone else has taken up the job." David yanked at the arm.

"I'm not coming. I don't care."

"Oh yes, you are." David was mentally determining the best way to beat the other boy senseless to save his life.

"We're dead if we run; we're dead if we stay," James responded.

David gritted his teeth. He tightened his hand on James' forearm until his fingers burned with pain and brought the other hand back above his head. He was about to punch James in the nose but was not able to complete the action.

THIRTY THREE

"Rather than expend the manpower, the nation saw bombing
its own cities as the best response to civil uprising."
– Samuel Judah, *American Autumn* –

Everything happened so quickly that it all blurred together for James. He yelled, and that is all he remembered clearly enough to place correctly on the timeline, but then there was the hand on his wrist, the fist flying toward him, and the deafening explosion that knocked him from his feet. Dust, dirt, and debris flew everywhere. Several large rocks smashed into his torso and legs. When the shockwave hit, he swore his whole body was pressed between a vice. Every muscle ached. Every bone felt bent to breaking, his brain ready to explode out of his skull.

Then he was on his back, breathless, face soured with pain, and more and more aware of the injuries inflicted by the flying debris. First, he felt his shoulder: a large chunk of concrete had hit the edge of it and glanced off, and, although it did not break any bone, something had torn. Second, he felt his feet: the socks and skin had been tattered by the flying grit, and both feet burned like fire. Finally, he felt the sharp pain in his legs, a throbbing, relentless pain. Peeking up he saw the origin: a barb of metal had lodged into his calf muscle.

James wanted to wait. He wanted to wait until that darkest moment before the sky's transformation from black to blue with the coming of dawn. To wait until high noon. To wait until the next evening's dusk. To wait until the bombs stopped, until he felt the sharp pang of hunger in his belly and his limbs began to waste away, his muscles atrophy, and he became skin and bones.

He turned his head to look over at where they had begun to bury the body. The tree was no more than a stump. The shell had done quick work in changing it to splinters. The body did not exist at all. Another shell hit.

Guess Mackenzie got his blaze of glory. James looked at the sky. Through the rocket's red glare he saw a few stars and caught the movement of David off to his left.

"Okay," James yelled, "he's buried." James shifted, and the barb in his leg sank deeper. He winced.

James saw David yelling, but he heard the other boy as if from a distance. David did not wait for James to reply. He glanced over at the tree and the body. "Looks like they have done our duty for us," David screamed over the roar, his dark joke betraying a real surprise. "You wounded or anything?"

James, wincing, pushed himself up to a sitting position and nodded. "Shoulder, feet, legs," he yelled out to the other boy. His stomach twisted, and he felt the need to throw up.

David looked down at the leg. "Aw." He scratched his head. "We could try to take it out," he yelled, but. "No..." He shook his head. "Jimmy, can you just walk with it in? I just, the blood, the bleeding . . . you'll bleed out, and—"

James pushed himself to a sitting position and nodded. "Okay," he said. Preparing for the pain, he took in a deep breath, braced against the ground, and blew it out through his teeth. He swore to himself and shook his head. *This'll be fun*, he thought and a moment later pushed up with his hands. A harsh, biting pain shot through his shoulder. He cried out. His arm crumpled under his weight. James swore again.

"Here." James, face pressed against the pavement, heard David speak from behind him. Slowly rotating, he was surprised to see a hand reaching out to help. Once more he rolled into a sitting position, accepted the hand, and found himself up on his feet. As his calf flexed around the metal, his leg immediately throbbed with pain.

"You going to make it?" He must have shown some displeasure on his face for David to ask the question.

James took in a slow breath. *Are we both going to make it?* he asked himself before nodding to David. "Don't have much of a choice, do I?" He breathed out. *This'll be fun.* He could barely stand, he could not imagine walking, but he nodded again. "Yeah, it isn't too bad," he yelled over the shelling.

As David moved, James looked over at him. James did not see a single scratch on the other boy. When David was already fifteen feet away, James took his first pain-filled step forward on tentative legs.

Why can't my feet just be torn to shreds and my shoulder destroyed? He thought that if there was a God that the whole pain thing was overdone in this case. *In any case, really,* he amended. *The whole world is insane with pain. If God is good, then it just doesn't make any sense. Pain, pain, pain. If—now that is an important word because we could be dealing with the devil. Of course, pleasure doesn't make sense either, especially if we are saying it is good and we are dealing with the devil, because if God is not good, what is? If God, that is. And if no God?*

The bombers continued to rain down fire and explosive death. There seemed neither rhyme nor reason to their targets. To the boys, the entire affair was arbitrary, as if the bombing crews had done their job for the day and, having some left over, suggested, "Let's use the extras."

Unless the intention is terror, James thought. *Then it all makes perfect sense. Maybe terror is the intention of existence. And God and the devil are one.*

"Ladies and gentlemen, stand and meet your new

king." He whispered the words. They seemed like natural closure to his thoughts.

David moved ahead quickly, and James struggled behind, gritted teeth, pain-soured face. Somehow, to his own surprise, he managed to keep up with the other boy. The shells continued to fall from the sky. He did not want to die today, but, in some sense, he welcomed it. He felt like a child who had fallen into water; a child, who, unable to swim, is slowly consumed by dark, cold depths. Farther and farther he sank and choked on the unbreathable liquid of sorrow. This sea compressed him smaller and smaller until he almost disappeared into nonexistence. But he did not disappear into nonexistence. The strand of who he was grew shorter and shorter, but, as if by some cruel joke, it was never snuffed out.

He would not, could not, kill himself. Never. But if by chance a shell happened to explode too close? *Bye-bye, James.* Darkness filled up his vision as he confronted his own thoughts. He shuddered.

No, he did not want death. He wanted to struggle against this infinite empty he saw before him, but he was discouraged. He was beaten down. He was tired. It all already seemed so long, and his strength failed him a little more each day. He wanted death because life was so difficult, *but who really wants to die?* he thought.

It was the second time an explosion knocked him off his feet. It hit in the street. It paused for a moment. In exhilarating terror, he watched the shell for a millisecond as it rested, docile on the ground, and before he was able to take another step, it exploded in a blinding-white flash. Up became down. Down, up. Right, left. Left, right. The next thing he knew for certain was that he had landed face-first on the ground, and the metal had sunk deeper into his calf.

Unable to take another moment of the pain, he reached down, grabbed the chunk of metal, and tore it out of his flesh, along with a large chunk of muscle and skin. He cried in uninhibited anguish, and tears poured down his face. James looked down at the wound through tear-blurred eyes. He had created a nasty gouge. Blood seeped from it like a stream, quickly soaking every inch of his tattered socks.

He noticed David's absence after he had torn off his partially blood-soaked pantleg and tied it tight at the wound. He had been screaming in pain; why was David not? His eyes searched the rubble around him, but he did not see the other boy. *How far ahead had he been?* The thought raced through his mind. *Fifteen yards or so?* It could have been that far; it could have been farther. *Was he off to the right or straight ahead?* James moved toward where he had last seen David. His eyes turned down to the ground and scanned the rubble. His feet quickened. He did not see even a faint silhouette of a human body under the debris or dust. He had to be there somewhere. A hand or a foot or something.

A hand! He saw it over a small hill. It stuck up and

out and seemed to grab the ground underneath. David was covered in a layer of dust and debris.

"David," he said and swallowed. He feared the body was already rigid in death.

The eyes blinked open. "David, you alright?" he asked. David responded by turning his head and looking quizzically over at James. "Are you alright?" James asked again.

"I . . ." David looked at his surroundings, confused. "When the bomb exploded, something hit me . . . in the head." He reached up and pointed at his forehead. He looked at James again. His eyes were glazed over. "I just want to stay here."

"Hell no!" James yelled in response. He grabbed the other boy and yanked him up to his feet. "I'm not dying tonight. You're not dying tonight."

"Today." David pointed to the east. James looked over; he saw the beginning of a sunrise on the horizon.

"Today. Whatever. Now, where are we going?" James answered.

David looked around. "Hell, I don't know anymore," he said apathetically. "Ooh." He swore. "Jimmy! I can't see out of my eye." He looked at James. "Iya..." He started to sway. "I think I'm about to pass out." James felt the weight of the boy as he slumped toward the ground.

"No!" James cried, bringing him to his feet.

David chuckled. He paused. A look of pain washed over his face. He bent over at the waist. Vomit showered the pavement. James felt it splash onto his feet. He winced in disgust and once more brought David to his full height.

David shook his head slowly. It bobbed up and down like a baby's. "I can't." He shut his eyes. "It's all spinning," he croaked.

"We need to go." James pulled him forward into a slow shuffle.

David continued to shake his head. "Nah." He breathed out.

"Come on!" James almost yelled the words.

David did not respond. His eyes remained closed, and he slowly slid closer to the ground.

"At least tell me where we are going!" James' voice broke into a yell.

David swayed back and forth. His eyes opened, flitted toward James, then turned to look back to where they had come as if he could see the smoldering church. "Come on!" James coaxed.

"Too complicated. Just leave me alone, Jimmy. Go away." The last two words sounded like the screeching bass voice of a dusty, old crow.

James turned his head. The early dawn cast a pale-white light on the uppermost walls of the buildings. It may have been merely a trick of the light or the shadows or his eyes or his mind, but he thought he saw the steeple of the church smoking like a snuffed candle. He looked only a moment, then turned his eyes back to the east and the fiery white of the blinding sun. David was not going to be any help. It would be up to him to save them both.

For all their running, they had not gone far. What had seemed like ten miles in the dark was barely half of one, and he still knew where they were.

David slumped onto his arm. James looked at him. His eyes were closed, his breathing heavy. James' hand came up to his face in a sharp slap.

"Stay awake," James told him. "You'll die if you fall asleep with a concussion." He was not sure if the information was true. He had heard it from George, yet he still did not want to risk it.

David's head bobbed up. His eyes creaked open, and he stared blankly over at the boy. His eyelids quivered and threatened to shut. "Okay," he said. "Let's get out of here."

November 1st was announced with explosions. They both heard them from the distance like puffs of air from a compressor valve or the distant beat of a bass drum. These were not like the first handful of sloppy, random shells that fell. These fell with military precision. Bombers lined up like soldiers in formation on the skyline. Each ran along a longitudinal line. Already they rained fire down, tearing up the countryside and, despite the early morning light of the sun, painted the sky with flame. Sky red, countryside black, James guessed they had less than an hour before they would reach the city. The buildings would be blown to bits, and the city razed to little more than an inch in little more than an instant.

"Doom. Doom. Doom." Their voices spoke over the fields and pastures, each second their cries louder and more powerful. The air raid siren droned, and James felt like prey. He felt like a cornered animal who hears the predator drawing near.

Fear played on David's face as well. He heard the thumping of the shells in the distance, felt that sense of the enemy closing in, that faceless, metallic, untouchable enemy on wings. The inevitable was upon them, but they never imagined it would arrive so soon. In this race of life, death was hard on their heels, but they could not give up. Something within them would not allow them to lay down and die. *Run!* one of them thought. "Run!" the other cried. Yes, they ran, despite their injuries, despite their fatigue, despite their sorrow, despite their fear. They ran until their legs threatened to collapse under them. They ran until after their legs should have collapsed. They ran until both were barely able to breathe. Their feet pounded until their joints were sore. The hot sweat poured from their pores and turned cold in the new November air. Their sides that felt as if they were about to burst. Cold, panting, wet, tired, sad, suffering, they ran, shells impacting the cooling earth closer every moment, shells bursting in their ears more loudly every moment until, more terrifying than a mythological monster, their explosions entered the city.

James wanted to cry. He had tried so hard. He had run so fast. He had pushed himself beyond any breaking point he had ever thought he had, but it seemed like it did not matter; they would not make it. For all his work, he would fail. He would fail, and there would be no more chances.

What is it? he thought. *A mile more?* He was not certain, but it did not matter. A block, a mile, two, ten. They had only moments, and moments were not long enough. He swore he could feel the heat of the explosions. He could hear nothing else. After each shell hit, he was stuttered on his feet and almost fell over. They were too close, and there was not enough time.

James felt a sharp jerk on the back of his throat. David knocked him off his feet and toppled onto him. James' hands scraped against the sidewalk.

"We're here!" David screamed in his ear, already getting to his feet.

James shook his head. They were not home yet; this was not it.

"We don't have a choice." David grabbed James, and both moved from the sidewalk, down the manicured garden, and to door of a mansion.

The door flung open. Screams filled the foyer. A man dressed in the formal attire of a household servant burst through the doorway, almost barreling them over. He carried a small box.

Looters, James thought as he followed David into a massive atrium with a high, arching ceiling like a cathedral. Servants rushed about every which way. Some fled out of the house. Some carried stolen objects. Maybe if he had seen it all on the big screen of a motion picture he would have laughed. The servants seemed to dance about whichever way in a comical manner, but it only made him feel sad for them. The whole affair was pathetic. The looters, certain of their financial gain, would run outside only to be reduced to dust along with their plunder. Those hiding would either be crushed under the building, eventually suffocate, or starve after they were buried. He felt the most sympathetic for those who ran filled with mindless fear.

The boys moved from the doorway through the atrium of the mansion. They stumbled over several servants. Shells hit across the street, deafening both boys and knocking everyone in the house off their feet. After picking themselves up, the boys struggled past a group of dazed servants and into a long corridor. As they ran down it, James watched David as he turned his head back and forth to peer into the side passages. Finally, he turned left. When James turned, his realization that they had entered a stairwell came too late. He ran into it. He met no step below his foot. He felt a shivering terror and crashed into the back of David and sent them both sprawling down the long wooden steps.

Hell. Hell. Hell. Hell. The word filled his mind. He swore. He swore again. *No time. No time.* He struggled to his feet. David was somewhere. He must be somewhere where they had fallen, but James did not see him. They were in a basement of some kind. There were no windows. It was cooler than the hall or the atrium. The ground was carpet covering a concrete base, and though normal lights were arranged as in any other part of the house, it seemed darker. Duller was a better description. The whole place, though clearly kissed by money, was depressed and slower than the main level.

James calmed himself, and he saw David unmoving on the floor. James grabbed him and tried to pull him up, but his limbs flopped about. *A dead man*, James thought. The body was still warm. *But soon (too soon) the heart will stop beating, the muscles will relax, bodily fluids will release to be followed by rigor mortis, and finally decay.* He started to walk backwards, pulling the body along with him with great, frustrating difficulty. A woman somewhere above in the mansion was screaming. A man yelled in an angry voice. James had always heard that disaster and difficulty brought out the best in people. The anecdote seemed untrue; all he seemed to see rise to the surface was humanity's rotten core.

James pulled the body another fifteen feet until he reached a door. He released one hand, freeing it to open the portal, but as he did, his other hand slipped, causing him to fall onto his back.

James grunted. He sat up. He looked at the other boy, feet and legs toward him, waist oddly twisted, one arm behind the head. James waited for him to wake up, but the boy did not so much as twitch.

"Another day, another corpse," he said, returning to

his back. "Corpse, corpse, corpse." For all the terrible meaning of the word, he found it fun to say.

"There have been a lot of corpses throughout history," he continued out loud. "So many dead"—*dead, death, corpse*—"bodies, and they all had lives like me. For thousands of years we've been dying, and nobody alive cares. Weird how we go on living as if there weren't so much death." *Hell of a lot of death.* "Hell of a lot of Hell.

"And almost six months ago everyone talked about this time as a new dawn for the nation, for humanity. We discovered a light, they said, and the ignorance of our fathers will be dispelled.

"Ashes to ashes. Dust to dust. Ignorance to ignorance. We've gone from night to night, and what we've mistaken for the twilight of dawn is the setting sun of dusk."

He breathed a sigh. The shells impacted outside. *They are louder than before.* They shook the mansion and he heard debris hit above his head. The blasts grew louder. An inconsumable lump of fear sat in his throat; the beast was upon him. It was time for the explosion to tear him limb from limb. He breathed out a prayer to a God he was not sure existed. *Idle chatter.* The words went through his mind. *It won't matter. It's not like a prayer will fix anything.* The thought overlapped his whispering until both his thoughts and his lips arrived at a duplicitous but specific *amen.* It was a plea to fix an impossible situation as well as an agreement with himself that his request was worthless.

"Amen," he said again, not sure what he meant by it this time.

The basement filled with the sound of explosion after explosion, each hitting the ground like heavy raindrops falling on a tin roof, and, as his whole body tensed, bracing for one to tear into him, the lights blinked out into darkness and pieces of heavy plaster fell on him.

Already the air was thickened with heat from the hot bombs. All exits had been sealed, and no way was left to escape. Not even a tendril of light reached down into the darkness. He was trapped, trapped in a simple and suffocating black.

THIRTY FOUR

———

"Mackenzie's mother moved to the United States at 16, married Mr. Leland Ulysses Jacobe, and had a child named James (after her father who died in a concentration camp) Mackenzie (after Leland's grandfather) Azriel (after his mother's grandfather who died at the end of a Nazi pistol) Jacobe (the origin of the surname has been lost to history)."
– James Anderson –

He did not know how long he slept, and when he awoke his whole body ached. "David?" he asked into the silent darkness. "David?" he asked again and turned onto his side. "David?" He reached out to the other boy as he rolled onto his belly. His brow knitted. "You're still warm." James sat up. He scooted himself over to the supine boy. "You're breathing?" he said. He bent his ear down to David's mouth. He was breathing, barely.

"David, you're alive." He fished a lighter out of the

other boy's pocket and lit it. Its flame illuminated little more than his knuckles. He held it above the other boy's head. "This isn't going to work." He let it snuff out. "I've got to find something." He moved away from the body on all fours, sweeping his hands back and forth. "You would have never been my first choice to live. You wouldn't be my fiftieth choice, but Hell, at this point you have no idea how glad I am. Ah! Found something." The lighter flickered and the cloth, a piece of curtain, flamed to life. He crawled back over to David and held the piece near his face.

"Oh!" He drew back. His face pinched in surprise. He brought the burning cloth near David's face again. With teeth bared, he took a breath in through the side of his mouth. "Ouch." He reached out and touched the skin on the edge of a deep wound that ran from the crown of David's head to his cheekbone. James flinched. "That's bad, David." He shook his head. The flame blinked out. "And back in the dark. And you are going to have a nasty scar if you wake up. If . . . If you don't, I'll be alone again." He sighed. "Alone again," he said matter-of-factly. "Just like the poem." He said the words in the rhythm of verse. "Now how does it all go? 'Alone once more. Alone again. I've lost my friends, and they're all dead. Alone. Alone. Alone in day. Alone in dusk. Alone in dark, a brittle husk. Alone a-land. Alone a-sea. Omnipotent, but still not free.'" As if he were impatiently interrupting the words of another he followed it up with, "I'm hungry."

"You wait here, David. I'm going to see if I can find some food."

He stood up and stretched his hands before himself to find his way in the dark.

"I hope you make it David; I really do. It seems everyone dies but me," he called over his shoulder at the spot where David lay. "I think it is about time my turn comes up." He found no opening in the first wall and moved to the next one.

"Or maybe I won't die." He spoke like a preacher, but underneath, if one listened attentively, a person could hear the gentle but beaten spirit of sorrow. "Maybe I'll just go on living forever. Forever and ever. I'll never die." He paused to scratch his head. "Odd to think about going on forever, going on age after age, era after era, and all the while watching everyone around you grow old and pass on." He felt the next wall against his fingertips and repeated what he had done before. Still, he found no door. "And all the while you remain a step away from decay. I suppose it would have good aspects. There would be plenty of time to learn; I could master a million things. I could go everywhere, see everything the world has to offer." He reached the third wall, a brick wall, and felt across its rough surface carefully until he stumbled on a door frame. Before stepping triumphantly through the portal, he traced the frame with one hand. "Of course, everyone would die and here I would be alone." He went on as if he were a teacher explaining some abstract concept. "Death has only served to separate me from others. I'm not sure if I could or would want to go on living forever with all this dying. I feel as if I would become more and more of an outcast and each new death would press me lower to the ground. You'd have to be a god not to go mad." He became silent. The whole thing was beginning to depress him, and he did not want to think of it anymore.

He searched the basement, and although he found several other rooms, he returned to David without food.

"We don't have a lot of room to move around, Davey." Part of him wished that David could hear the diminutive use of his name; another part simply wished the other boy could hear. "I'll give you a lay of the land as I see it, or I guess I would say 'feel it.' When you first walk into the hallway . . ." He paused. "Didn't we start out in the hall, David? How did we get into this room? Strange. Hmmm. Well, I'll have to figure it out. Okay, you step out into the hallway and run into disappointment on your left and pain straight ahead. I've got a collapsed hallway filled with bricks on the left and a doorway with big sharp splinters of wood sticking out. Some of the splinters are large enough to kill a man.

"After you've been significantly discouraged, and either avoided death or been mortally wounded, you—spirit certainly broken and body most likely maimed—move down the hallway to the right. Be careful to walk in the center of the hall as best you can because there are six more doorways like the one you were first impaled on. If you make it past these, you come to a *T* in the path. The *T* once was a cross, but rubble blocks the way forward, so the only other options are right, left, and back where you came from.

"So, let's go right. Right has little to recommend because five feet down the hall, the hall ceases to exist. Back to the left. Shortly after the *T* are three steps up onto a higher portion of the basement. Why is it higher?" James shook his head. "No idea. Most of the rooms in this hallway are blocked as well, but I did find three open. They didn't have anything of value in them, but I still found them. This final hallway is long and mostly worthless, and it dead-ends at an intact wall. Smells like smoke.

"I could use a smoke," he said. If he could see anything he would have stared into the distance, but only the darkness was available to him. "I didn't find any food. I'm going to try digging some of those rooms out tomorrow." He yawned. "I'm exhausted," he said as he lay his head down on the hard, carpeted floor.

He awoke halfway through the night, bunched up in the fetal position, shivering. He tried to fall back asleep, but the cold crept into his fingers and toes and up his arms and legs until it reached his chest. James was soon on his feet, certain there was a far more pressing need than food. He was not sure how long he lay there resting, but he knew that he did not feel rested at all. He felt more exhausted than when he had lain down.

"Maybe I'll die," he told the other boy as he wrapped

his arms around his chest and started stomping his feet to bring circulation back to his legs. It was only a few stomps before he started breathing heavily. *Why am I so tired? I've got no energy at all*, he thought. "Fire," he said. "We need fire. I think I'm freezing."

He reached out for the doorway and grabbed the molding at the end of it; his arm shivered. After exiting into the hall, he did his best to navigate to the doorway directly across from his room but stabbed his hand on a sharp piece of wood sticking out. Too cold to react, still trembling, he tried to break the wood, but the pieces were too big. He tried the other doorways, but it was not until the third on the right that he found any wood loose enough to slide out of the rubble. Soon he returned to the room and dropped wood and searched on all fours for paper or cloth to use as kindling. He found none and was forced to tear a sleeve off his shirt.

Sheer luck aided by dry wood allowed the fire to latch a tiny tongue onto a small scrap of lumber and spread over the rest of the wood until he had a small-but-warm fire.

James crouched down next to it as soon as he saw the flame and put his numb hands over it. Even though it gave off little warmth, the thawing was accompanied by pain that seemed to have a source in the marrow of every delicate bone of the hand and wrist. He grimaced but did not draw away, even after the fire grew and the pain intensified.

"If I can find more wood, I can keep it going," he said.

"But first . . ." He fell onto his butt and put his legs on either side of the small fire.

Even though the room warmed to livable levels, the fire died to little more than embers before that deep-seated cold left his body completely. A large part of him wanted to sleep, but another part kept whispering in his ear telling him to get up, find some wood, and get the fire going again. "Otherwise you won't be waking up from your sleep," he said.

James took another look at the fire and finally stood to his feet. He exited into the hallway and returned with a large armful of wood as the last pile of embers was starting to grow dark. He dumped the entire armful onto the fire, and, without waiting to see if it would snuff the fire, lay down and immediately fell asleep. He awoke to the warm, healthy crackle of a few of the larger pieces still burning.

His stomach moaned. His throat was dry. He rubbed his tongue across his plaque-covered teeth, wondering how long it must have been since he brushed them. His lips stuck together. His face felt stuffy with the exhaustion of morning. His mouth opened in a wide yawn, and he got up to his feet. His arms stretched high over his head. He looked at the fire and knew he would have to get more wood.

"And find something to drink," he mumbled. "And something to eat." He moved toward the door.

He made his way around the T of the hallway to the first of the six doors and began digging. He could not begin to measure the time he labored. There was no sun to reference whether it was day or night. All he had was the ever-same blackness.

He guessed it had been several hours by the ache of his muscles and the tiredness he felt. He had found no food; he had found no water, but he had been able to collect several armfuls of wood, which he brought back to the room and set in a corner away from the fire.

After stoking the fire, he sat down and began to take a good tired look about the room. *Lucky we happened to be in one of the three intact rooms in the basement. Luck if we live, coincidence if we die.* "A very cruel coincidence, too," he said aloud.

"But how can it be cruel if it is a coincidence?"

James jumped. He did not say it. He did not recognize the whispered voice. He heard a laugh.

David? he thought. He looked over at the other boy. His eyes were shut. He looked the same as he had before. "David?" he asked.

James heard no response. He scooted over to David and looked down at him. It had only been his imagination.

THIRTY FIVE

"I don't feel great. I'm a small man thrust into a cosmic situation."
– James Anderson –

His "days" (anytime he was awake he called day) seemed to go in circles, seemed to be the same thing over and over again: he woke up, added wood to the fire to keep it going while he worked, cleared out more and more of the other rooms, and slept until he awoke to begin a new day. It was three more "days" after he had heard the voice before he found any food. One of the rooms he had begun to dig out was larger than expected and looked odd to him. Its countertops were metal, and its floor was tile. *A kitchen,* he suddenly realized. *A kitchen!* A kitchen meant food. A kitchen meant a faucet. A kitchen meant survival.

James did not stop to rest even after he grew tired but continued to dig. He uncovered several large stoves and countertops, drawers full of silverware, measuring cups, stirring spoons, and pieces of devices he had no idea the purpose. Then he uncovered the refrigerator, a stainless-steel giant with two large, thin, vertical doors. His hands excitedly grabbed the handles and even though he knew the other boy was unconscious he yelled out, "We've got food, David!" *Food!* he thought as he reached through the darkness into the fridge and stumbled upon a bottle of milk. *Water and food all in one*, he thought. He reached to take the cap off, found none, and took a long swig of the semi-sweet colloid. He smiled as he drank, and the milk spilled down the edges of his mouth. He took the bottle away from his face and let out a satisfied sigh. He had never liked milk. He had never found anything good about it. It had an odd texture. It had a disgusting taste. It did not quench a person's thirst. He put the bottle back to his mouth and took another long drink. He sang an ode to milk this day. It was as sweet as honey. It quenched thirst better than a mountain spring. It curbed hunger, stopped starvation. He dropped the bottle from his mouth again and let out another satisfied sigh. He laughed again, wondering how a drink, a fat-filled, white, semi-solid drink that he had once hated so much, could feel so much like Heaven or be the thing to save his life.

Immediately he had more energy. His mind seemed clearer. His muscles, stronger. Triumph swelled in his chest, and he had never realized that something so simple and straightforward as survival could feel so fulfilling.

He cleared out the rest of the kitchen over the next few days. Besides the refrigerator, he found a pantry half full of an assortment of different canned goods and dried foods. He found four water taps, turning the knobs of each one after the other and finding that only one worked and that only barely. It came out in a dribble, like water falling from the ceiling of a cave. *Better than nothing*, James thought as he plugged the sink drain to let it fill up slowly. For now, he could survive off milk and the water and juice in the canned goods, long enough to allow the sink to fill.

James considered relocating to the kitchen, using the stove as a fireplace, but he feared David would not survive the move.

The next week, James cleared another two rooms. They now had food, drink, and firewood but still had no way out. Each new room was a dead end. Each new room did not have so much as a window covered by rubble on the outside.

Another week passed. Their food supply dwindled. James, between his long, intense bouts of despair, cleaned only one more room. He had done three of six and he had nothing to show for it. By his fifth day of the week, he was done and went to bed until what must have been Sunday. Resting did not help. It only worsened his mood.

On Sunday, he considered eating all the food and killing first David then himself to hasten the inevitable, but he did not for a reason he did not know. Instead, he got up, ate a handful of food, and moved to the next room.

He had already moved up the line of rooms on the left of the hallway; it seemed logical to start clearing out rubble from the farthest one on the right. *I move up, then down,* he thought to himself, grabbing the first log he felt and throwing it down the hallway.

Up, then down. I go up, then down. Reminds me of water, like waves, like being on a boat. Like life. Up and down. Ups and downs. Wave and trough. My life goes up. My life goes down, but it seems like it has kept going down. Up and down, down, down. Down from the wave into the trough, but the wave curls over and sends me to the depths.

"Out of the frying pan and into the fire." He tossed another log into the hallway. He had already hollowed an area large enough to sit inside. He felt for another log, grabbed it, and threw it into the hallway. He reached up and rubbed his eyes. His head leaned up against the smoothness of a board and his eyelids closed.

Up and down, wave and trough. A piece of metal clattered into his pile of scrap. He had almost cut his hand as he grabbed it. *Down and up.* "Another day, another sliver, another piece of wood to burn." *But all around so even ups are somehow down.* A handful he had collected fell to the floor. *Down and up and every way.* He grabbed a piece of wood and tugged, but it would not move. *The worlds a stage, and life's a play.* "You're so profound, Shakespeare." He got a better grip on the piece of wood and tugged harder. His hand slid along the lumber, and slivers stuck into his palm. He swore and gripped it again. "Yeah, sure."

Wave and trough, and trough and wave. Another tug started to loosen the lumber. *Own the world, but still a slave.* He tugged again. It loosened a little more. "And now the grand finale. If I remember how it was written." He gripped the piece as hard as he possibly could. *A whirlwind, a tinsel crown.* He yanked, throwing his entire body backwards this time. *Down and up, and up and down.* The piece dislodged. It slid out quickly, causing James to lose his balance and fall backwards. "Up and down and all around." He looked at the piece of wood that had fallen into his lap. *Lucky,* he thought. *If it would have hit my head, I would probably be in the same fix as David.* He looked up. "Now what is the name of that poem? Reply to Ozymandias? Never read the one it was replying to though. For some reason Mackenzie had said the reply was more relevant than the original. But what do you expect from a guy who likes to read into the colors of walls the author chose for the room? 'The walls are white: purity. The wall is gray-green: pain. The wall is bright green: envy. The wall is orange like fire: cataclysm. The wall is dark green: a shoot coming up out of the ground. The wall is a chaotic mix of reds: war. The wall is ivory: power. The wall is complementary colors: confrontation. The wall is black: death.'" He laughed at the absurdity of it then added, "The wall is gold—"

He paused. Something was sliding, like wood upon wood. No, it was not one thing, it was many things sliding, and they were close by. It was right in front of him. He cursed and tried to feel his way back through the door but was too late. The sliding became silent momentarily, and he felt the heavy pile of debris fall on his legs, pinning them to the floor. James cried out in pain.

His first desire was to call to David, but he knew the other boy could do nothing for him, so James tried to move his foot back into a natural position. He screamed again. The thought crossed his mind that he should have done what he had planned at the beginning of the day: *have one last gluttonous meal then kill David and myself.* "Only the inevitable," he said through gritted teeth. "Now it is going to happen anyway."

He was angry. He had tried so hard. He had fought so hard to stay alive, not only in this world of darkness, but in that world, that was now crumbling into memory. He felt like a mother whose only offspring are stillborn infants. He felt like a faithful wife whose husband laughs at her fidelity as he tells her once again of his unfaithfulness. He felt like a father who only months before had the joy of a newborn daughter and now held her as she gasped for her last breath in his arms. And the doctor cracks a joke.

He had fought so hard and for what? To die still struggling like a mouse under the blade of a sadistic child? No matter what he did, no matter how hard he tried, no matter his pain and suffering, it did not seem to make a difference. *Try, try again, but failure is the inevitable outcome.*

"No use. No use," he mumbled. He cursed. He opened his mouth and inhaled. He felt tears in his eyes, and he felt pathetic. "No," he said clearly. He would not cry. He would not mope. He would not succumb to feeling sorry for himself. He swore again. He gritted his teeth in anger; a fire leapt into his chest.

"No." He shook his head. "No," he said again. "I can't die today. I refuse to die today. I've made it too far. I've fought too hard. No! This cannot kill me. This is not my time to die." He felt a surge of energy and pushed up on the wood a final time. It moved: barely, only a fraction of an inch, but it moved. He paused, unsure of what to do, before he pushed the debris away and off himself as quickly as he could. The debris stayed in the air only a moment. James scurried away from the falling pile as fast as possible, but a piece caught his foot and the pile fell back on his leg mid-shin.

A string of profanities filled his mouth as a scream. He hit the heels of his hands against his forehead. He groaned and brought two tight, white-knuckled fists as hard as he possibly could against the ground. "I wish I could just kill someone!" He said the words in a frustrated, irate crackle. He turned his head to the side, so his face rubbed against the dirty ground. He yanked on his foot. "Why does everything have to be difficult?!" He yanked again; his foot did not move. He growled and yanked once more, sighing angrily as he let his body relax. His patience was no more than a frayed fabric. "Never get a break. The basement, then the cold, then the food, then this debris." He put up his hand to shield his eyes. "Now this goddamn light!"

THIRTY SIX

_____

"He is gone. And I am here, searching for something I've lost,
and I can't remember what it is."
– James Anderson –

"I've been able to move some rubble out from the east, at least what I think is east. That is where the light comes in first. The sun rises in the east and everything?" No one responded. He did not expect a response today. Sometimes, when he was busy at a task and asking something into the thin air, he would stop and wait for someone to answer the question. Sometimes he would get angry that he was being ignored and ask it several more times before he realized where he was.

"It has to start snowing pretty soon. It has to. I think the snow is going to cover the hole. I need to find something long and skinny to poke a hole in it when it happens, like a pole or something. The snow'll insulate us so that'll be good, but I don't think we are going to get out that way. I've cleared a lot of rubble away, but I've run into a brick wall."

"And we've got to get out; food is running out, barely getting enough as it is. I'll die from starvation soon if I don't get any more." He felt his stomach with his hand as if it would soothe it somehow. The sharp pang of hunger had gone away, and the steady, raw ache of starvation replaced it. Soon he would be dead without food. He could already see his ribs. His arms had thinned as muscles atrophied. "I'm so hungry, hungry and cold, hungry and cold and bored. Bored. I've got to get out of this basement or else I'll go nuts. Although, talking day after day to yourself seems nuts to me." He sighed and wondered if this was Hell. He then quickly dismissed the thought until the alien nature of his existence seemed to warrant the consideration again.

Eventually, he would drag himself away from these thoughts and would search the basement for more wood to add to his dwindling stockpile. Finding little, he would return to the room, allow his fingers to feel the few cans of food he had left, and finally move over the other boy lying on the ground.

The winter solstice had gone by. The days had shrunk into darkness, and finally, once more, begun to grow long again. He had developed a way to measure time by placing a large pot in the sink to see how much it filled up before the sunlight disappeared from the crack in the wall. David had yet to awake. James did not want to lose the other boy and found he was able to dribble water down David's throat to keep him hydrated. But David could not eat and had become skin and bones.

"I'll save you a can just in case," James said. He threw a can into the corner. "Hope you like peaches." He found another can and started rolling it between his hands on the carpet. "What could I use to break apart that wall? I could try one of those pots, the little ones, kind of like a hammer." James paused to think, tired of his own voice. "I'll try it tomorrow. Too tired tonight." He laid down next to the small fire and closed his eyes. Thoughts drifted through his head like cumulous clouds. An hour passed, another hour. More thoughts floated through his mind. He stood ever on the edge of sleep without ever plunging even an inch into that dark lake. His eyes opened. He sat up and looked around the darkness.

"Going nuts, David. Can't sleep." He rubbed his face from his forehead to his chin with one hand. "I am going insane. It's like, I don't know. It's aggravating. I want to tear out my eyes, tear down that stupid wall." He let out an angry sigh.

He glanced at David. "Trade you. You can stay awake; I'll sleep. I'm going on a week now. Twenty-four times five plus... plus a few; forty-eight, ninety-six, one hundred twenty? Like a hundred and twenty-three hours of being awake. Wonder what the longest it is that someone has been awake. I wonder if a person would fall apart, like your arms fall off and then your legs. Then your eyes fall out. And then your tongue. Your lips and teeth."

"Probably explode." James did not say the words. They did not leave his lips. They arrived in his ears as the sound of a voice that creaked like an old unused door hinge, gravelly and low.

James jumped. He felt acid-fear in his gut and he waited for the voice to say something else until he was sure it must have been his mind. He waited longer, still scared. He was sure he had heard that voice before and started to doubt his own opinions on the existence of demons, devils, and specters.

James sighed. The voice had not spoken for several moments, and, although his heart still held a type of hesitant fear, he began to believe it was a trick of his brain as before, a result of being alone for such a long stretch of time. He believed this until it spoke again.

"You got a problem or something?" The same gravelly voice asked.

James jumped again and cried out in fear. The voice in the darkness laughed.

"Who are you?" James asked.

"Put some wood in the fire; it's cold in here," the voice answered. "I wouldn't mind some food either."

James nodded. "David?" he asked.

The voice laughed weakly. "Please, kill me if that question is serious."

"I'm serious." James' voice rose another octave.

"No, it's not David, it's Robert Dalimore."

James did not respond.

"Food, Jimmy," David said impatiently. "I wouldn't mind some food before I die."

"Ah, yeah, sure." James reached out, found a can on the ground, and placed it in David's hands.

David felt it carefully and then spoke. "Oh, yum. I love metal. I'll just bite the top off like a deranged beaver."

"There's a can opener. Just shut up." James grabbed the can from David's hand.

"It's cold in here, Jimmy."

"I can't do anything about that." The can opener bit into the soft metal of the lid. "We're almost out of wood, can't spare any."

"How about water?" David said.

"I can get you that. Here's your meal," James answered.

David shook his head. "Jimmy, no. I'm not going to be able to sit up to eat this. I . . ."

James face flushed with embarrassment for the other boy. He swallowed and looked down at the silhouette of his face. He did not want to speak. His ears burned. He listened to the creaky sound of David's breathing. A wave of empathy hit him, and he felt the cold feeling of watery eyes. *Pathetic*, he thought. The word floated through his mind as if he were realizing something important, not as a judgment but a sympathetic realization. *All I'd have to do is slip my fingers around his throat. And just a little squeeze? How long would it take? Not too long. Shorter than a person would think?* His hands twitched as he imagined the soft skin against his fingertips. *He'd be gone in seconds. David gone.*

"I can't sit up," David continued.

"Uh, okay. Yeah, one second, David. There's a spoon around here," He held up the can with one hand and searched the ground until he found a spoon behind his back. "Can you lift your head?" he asked. David's head came up half an inch and fell back to the floor.

"One second," James mumbled. He grabbed the small wad of rags he was using as a pillow, propped David's head up with it, and snatched the spoon from the ground once more.

THIRTY SEVEN

"I still ask him questions and am surprised by his
silence. Something in me doesn't understand he is gone."
– James Anderson –

James turned from his back to his stomach for what
would now be the seventeenth time. David knew; he had
been counting. James turned again, but David was not sure
he cared any more. He had given up on sleep after the
tenth turn. After several more turns, David heard a sigh
followed finally by silence, and David thanked God and
allowed every part of his body to rest limply on the ground
and sink into the first sweet dreams of sleep. Then James
groaned, turned to his back, and began to mumble under
his breath.

David's eyes flickered open. James groaned and
mumbled again.

"Jimmy?" David said.

"Hmm?" James turned over again. The noise was like a file across David's teeth.

"What's your problem?" David asked.

"I, um, uh . . ." James sighed and turned again.

"You keep on turning over." David said the words slowly.

"Oh." David heard the other boy adjust and turn his head. "I can't sleep. We're out of food. And that stupid wall won't even chip. I've tried hitting it with everything I can think of." He swallowed, and David sensed he was afraid to say what he thought.

"What's up?" he asked.

"Probably going to die in here. We won't last much longer," James answered.

David laughed, a breathy laugh.

"Why are you laughing?" James asked.

"It's because"—laughter overtook David as he spoke—"it's because—" laughter once more.

"What?" James asked, his voice rising higher than before.

David took a deep breath in and sighed out tiredly, and continued to speak, his words broken by laughter. "You," he said.

"Me?" James replied. "Okay?"

"You." David nodded his head. His eyes closed hard, and a big smile spread across his face.

"What about me?" James was becoming impatient.

"It had to be you," David continued, his face still scrunched together.

"It had to be me?" James echoed.

"It had to be you," David repeated.

"Yep, you already said that," James replied immediately after David spoke.

"You." The word squeaked out of David.

"Has anyone ever told you you're an idiot, David?" Clear annoyance filled James' voice.

David continued to laugh.

James sighed. "I'm going to bed." He turned over.

"Hell if you are," David answered. "If you won't let me sleep, I won't let you sleep."

"Are you going to tell me why you're laughing?" James asked.

"Jimmy, of all the hundreds of thousands of people who I could have been stuck underground with, I ended up with you."

"I accepted our living situation a couple weeks ago," James replied without inflection.

"Yeah?" David replied.

"Same day I accepted Mackenzie's death," James answered.

David laughed then sniffed as if he were entertained and sad all at once. "James?" he asked.

James turned over to face David. "Hmmm?" he said.

"How did you hit the wall?"

"Um, what do you mean?" James responded.

"Did you hit the mortar? Did you break the mortar?" David asked.

"I hit the wall," James replied.

"Do you know that a wall is made up of a lot of bricks?"

"Yeah, I'm not an idiot," James answered.

"Then you know that the mortar is easier to break than the brick; it's softer. You can pull the bricks out if you break the mortar. Probably could use the handle of a pot and stab it."

"You think that would actually work?" James asked.

"Yeah," David answered slowly, nodding his head.

James let out a long sigh through his nose. He swore, and David heard footsteps around the room.

"Where are you going?" David asked as he heard James move out of the room. The other boy did not respond, and within a few moments, David heard the distant *tink, tink* of a pot handle on the brick and mortar.

David called again. James, once more, did not respond. David heard a long string of curses and smiled. The metal continued to *tink* into the wall.

THIRTY EIGHT

––––––––

"And then there was quiet. And then there was peace."
– Unknown –

When David awoke, he noted that something had changed. The noise had stopped. The noise, noise, noise: it had gone from constant to nothing. He heard no more breaking of boards or clattering rubble or even muffled curses from the other boy. He heard no howling wind or pattering rain. James did not stomp. He heard not a yell, not a word, not a whisper. Everything had settled into silence. It was as if the final shot of a bloody battle had been fired.

His head rested slightly to one side. The muscles of his face were relaxed, and the brisk air nipped gently at the soft skin stretched over his cheekbones. The pain in his head had healed to little more than a stinging itch. The wind picked up as he listened, and it began to slap something gently against the mansion. He heard the quiet sound of droplets falling into water. He felt refreshed; everything had settled, and now, finally, his soul.

The wind eventually stopped hitting whatever it was hitting against the house, but the water continued dripping, and his ears focused on another sound. *A bird?* he wondered and continued listening. *No. Birds.* He paused and laughed to himself. Not one of the sounds the birds made was a stereotypical "tweet." Each had its own song. Together they were like a symphony of some very high-pitched woodwinds, not playing together but somehow creating music more beautiful than David had ever heard. More birds joined the symphony. David closed his eyes and leaned his head to the other side. His smile grew larger; he could feel its warmth spread across his face. "I wonder what birds match up with what songs," he said.

"Hey, David, who are you talking to?" James said. David had been too distracted to hear him enter the room. The other boy seemed in a good mood.

"Just myself," David responded. "I was listening to the birds sing. I was wondering which song went with which bird."

"Hmmm, interesting," James replied with a big smile.

"How's the wall coming?" David asked. A lump of fear rose in his throat. He wondered if James had finally gone mad.

"Do you want to go see what birds sing what song?" James asked.

"What?" He could not tell if the other boy was joking.

James laughed. "It'll be a little walk, but I can help you get there." James laughed again. David felt a hand grip his arm and drag him up to his feet.

"Did you get out?" David asked, preparing himself for disappointment and unsure whether to laugh or cry in joy.

"Wait and see," James responded. David had already found his balance, and James helped him stumble out into the hallway.

"Watch yourself as you walk. There are some sharp things sticking out of the walls, metal 'n stuff," James mumbled, but David did not have time to process what he had said before they were halfway down the hall.

"We got out?" David asked, about to burst from excitement.

James laughed again but did not respond. When they turned left, David saw it, a white light streaming through the doorway and the dust and hitting the hallway wall. It was bright, blinding, and clear. And David could not help but laugh. It was a quiet, suppressed laugh that finally overtook him and transformed into a full, ringing laugh of joy from deep within him.

They turned the final corner, and David saw a hole large enough for both to fit through. He looked at James. His face was filled with a smile, a look of hope, a look of elation, a look of accomplishment, of joy. And finally, James broke into laughter as well, deep, soul-sprung laughter that consumed him from his skin to the marrow of his bones and even deeper.

Together they walked out into the freezing but fresh air. Pure snow covered everything. Goosebumps rose on their exposed skin. Their eyes squinted in the light, and each was quick to wrap their free arms around themselves for warmth. But they did not care; they stood out in the snow for fifteen minutes, not dressed for the weather, laughing until they could laugh no more.

And then they were silent and looked out at the city. The devastation brought on by the bombs was covered by snow. Poor and rich, none were spared.

David turned to James. "So, what day are you guessing it is?" he asked.

"It's January first."

"January first? You sure?"

"January first," James replied. "Welcome to 1977, the new world."

THIRTY NINE

———

"As even shadow or shade, Oh, dearest friend, return."
– Aurelius Schiavone –

Relief swept through David and James as they saw Mackenzie's smile. The gunfire faded for a moment, but the relief was short lived. They were filled with even more pain, and both rushed forward as Mackenzie collapsed into the dirt. They felt his warm blood staining their hands as they turned him over. As they looked down, though they did not see Mackenzie smile, a look of satisfaction still filled his face.

"You've been shot, Mack." The words tumbled from James mouth.

Mackenzie laughed gently. "To Hell with getting shot." A small smile curled up on his face. His voice held not a drop of fear or anxiety.

"We've got to get you out of here, get you home,"

David answered. He spoke more calmly than James, though only barely.

Mackenzie brought up a hand and waved the comment away. "It'll be fine. Everything'll be fine." He sighed as if tired. "Trust me."

"That was stupid, a stupid thing to do," James replied.

"You weren't shot, were you? Either of you?" Mackenzie asked.

Both shook their heads. "Why did you do it? We could have found another way out of the church," James continued.

"I did. I had to," Mackenzie answered. "And isn't it obvious why? Did you ever imagine anything different?" Mackenzie breathed out a laugh. Neither of the other two responded. "I was fated to do great things, but I've always had a desire to turn fate on its head." He laughed again. "How bad am I anyway? I don't feel any pain?"

David studied the blood pooling on the ground, but James was the one to respond. "We've got to get you home, Mack. Get a doctor. And then you'll be fine. You'll be fine." James sighed.

Mackenzie smiled at him. He shook his head gently. "You're a terrible liar, James."

James let out a long sigh. He allowed himself to understand what was happening. Though he was a poor liar, he had convinced himself everything was going to be fine because it had always been fine, and since it had always been fine, it would continue to be fine. The sun rose each day; therefore, it would rise the next.

But...

"This is awful, Mackenzie," James said. He felt his throat tighten.

Mackenzie answered calmly, as if relaxing on a warm afternoon and discussing some philosophical minutiae. "A matter of perspective, I suppose. I thought it was worth it." He coughed, and his voice grew weaker. "I thought," he took a strained breath in before continuing. "Best decision of my life." He pushed a strained breath out.

James heard a sniffle from the otherwise-silent David, and though he did not look to see him speak, James could hear the deep pain in his voice. "This is the end," David said. The usually detached David seemed deflated and exhausted.

"No," Mackenzie strained the word out. "It's not an end, David. Not an end, more of a beginning, hardly an end." He took another labored breath in. "We'll talk about endings in twenty years. Better yet, seventy. That leaves a long road ahead of . . ." But Mackenzie could not finish his words. He had run out of breath and had to take another long breath in before continuing.

"I'll sleep well tonight. Sleep. The thought's rather wonderful. I'm not going away. I'm going back, back where I belong. Home." He exhaled. His body relaxed.

The other two stared down at him, helplessly.

"What a year. What a year," Mackenzie continued, barely able to speak the words.

"Almost another New Year's Eve, Mack," James answered him. "We'll stay out all night. All three of us." The boy knew he was convincing Mackenzie of nothing. He was only lying to himself, trying to convince of himself of something different than what was clearly reality, but it was not working at all.

Mackenzie shook his head at the comment. "No, James," he said. "We won't."

Mackenzie became silent for long moments after that, and the other two could only tell he was alive from his breath rattling in and out and his soft inspection of each of them with his eyes.

Finally, after many long moments of waiting, he opened his mouth, and at barely a whisper, he spoke. "Either . . . either of you . . . have a . . . cig-cigarette?"

James searched every pocket of Mackenzie's coat. He found a pack in the left pocket, pulled it out, and flipped it open.

"James," David said.

"I've got a cigarette for—"

"James," David repeated.

James glanced at David. The anguish on the boy's face seemed to reach and grab him. The last thing he wanted to do was look down.

"He's—" James nodded before David could finish. He did not have to hear the words. He understood full well.

Gone. James finished the sentence for him, and finally, facing reality, looked down at the boy. The last sigh of life that escaped him seemed to go on forever, and the light in his eyes faded, from twinkling fire, to a wan flame, to ashy, unseeing nothing.

EPILOGUE

———————

"Ladies and gentlemen, stand and meet your new king."
– James Mackenzie Jacobe –

Excerpt from *Of Wars* by I. A. Stonewall

The war ended in time for Christmas, December 24, 1998, 4:14 in the afternoon. A light snow drifted down through tops of the pines that stood as ancient sentinels just outside the hospital window. The sun slowly sank on the horizon with deep oranges and purples, bright yellows and vibrant reds. The messenger was no more than a boy, not a day older than twelve, not a day younger than eight. His soft knocking at the door would have been missed if it had not been for one of the older patients who, after three straight days of complaining of the draft blowing through the cracks of the windows, was attempting to "weatherproof" the room, an activity which had fortunately placed him near the entrance.

The official conclusion of the war was an anticipated event in the ward. We had stockpiled an assortment of dried fruit and liquors, and one of us was skinning a white-tailed deer to prepare for the festivities soon to arrive with long-awaited unconditional surrender.

We were sure the battle of Southfork would be the last. We could sense it in our bones. The closing shot had been fired, the smoke cleared, and a man on foot in a tattered military dress uniform, followed by an entourage of trucks, tanks, and infantry, searched for signs of the enemy leader.

A minor wound I had suffered the first day of battle, having become gangrenous and requiring amputation, placed me on one of the first trucks to leave, only allowing me a moment to glimpse General James Mackenzie ("Mack") Jacobe. I saw him at a distance. I knew it was him by both the descriptions I had read in the papers ("a man of stoic posture who moves with a slight limp that he takes great care to hide") paired with the respect others afforded him as he moved about the empty battlefield. I watched until his shrinking silhouette was swallowed by the amber sunset.

It was already completely dark when I was rolled under the lights of the operating room and put under for surgery. The next morning, upon awakening in a morphine euphoria, I vaguely remember someone telling me that the enemy general had disappeared and Jacobe along with him, leaving the war uncertain still.

For the first month, we all crowded around any stranger who walked through the doors of the ward, our questions about Jacobe always ending in frustrated disappointment. Some of us held out a week or two longer, and the last two or three optimistic gave up hope of any news by the end of the second month. The earth continued to grow colder. Many individuals made their way into the ward one way or another, but new faces now went unnoticed.

As the boy entered, none but the old man gave him any heed. No one noticed as he, teeth chattering, face flushed with cold, moved from the door to the stove and was given a cup of black coffee.

The boy's message was hesitant, tempered by the sorrow of defeat. He said the enemy leader had been killed, but so had our own, that he had watched as the bodies of both were loaded onto stretchers before a guard had shooed him away. One had been shot in the chest, the other in the head. Those last two shots, as one poet has put it, "had rid us of a demon and robbed us of an angel."

Dinner that night was unaccompanied by celebration. The sun abandoned us, and each sat silently in the light of the bulbs shining sickly from the ceiling. The ward was filled with the hollow sound of silverware on metal mess kits. Christmas was now to be paired with another holiday, one not of celebration but of sorrow-filled memorial.

After dinner, some spoke softly next to the stove, but most remained silent. Eventually, each went to bed, one after another, until the ward was filled with the sound of snoring and heavy breathing. Always preoccupied with far too many thoughts at night, I was one of the last to succumb to sleep, a chaotic, sickly, restless sleep.

When I awoke, the ward was completely black. The hot fire had turned to cold ash in the stove, and the cold had crept through the cracks in the walls, under our blankets, and into our beds. The door swung open. Several silhouettes carrying a stretcher stepped into the room and obscured the light of a lantern that someone was attempting to hang on a high hook outside. A current of cold air swept in, and I brought my legs up to my chest and wrapped my hands around my knees as I watched a thick and formless clump of mud fall from the boot of one of those who had entered. They were followed by the hourglass figure of a female in a duffle coat and heels snatching a knit beret from her head.

After the men had moved across the room, as they gently shifted the new patient from the stretcher to the bed, the woman pressed a stethoscope against his chest.

While one of the men started to wrap the patient in blankets, the taller of the two clanked open the stove door and noisily began to stack logs on top of each other and use match after futile match until a small fire had latched onto the wood. The doctor said something to the first man in an inaudible mumble then stood up and moved out of the door in the same stately way she had entered. The two men followed her out.

I looked over at the new patient. He was in his mid-to late thirties. His nose bent in the fashion of one that had recently been broken. A thick, bristly beard grew from his emaciated face. His glistening forehead sat under an ugly, matted head of thinning hair. His face was deathly pale, his lips purple. His eyes twitched as his head turned from side to side in a fit of nightmares. Another soldier. Another patient. Another victim so late in the war.

I stared at him for several minutes and then rolled onto my back, thanking God the tall soldier had started a fire. Quickly I fell back into a peaceful, transcendent sleep, thick with warmth and dreams.

The ward cheered significantly on Christmas. Moods brightened, partially due to the passing of time, partially due to the alcohol consumed; and by the end of the night, the ward was in an uproar. Most woke with hangovers the next morning, making the day after Christmas far less enjoyable than the holiday itself. The rest of the days passed quickly towards the New Year.

I woke up early the morning of New Year's Eve. My body was stiff, and I dragged myself to the stove to sit a while before bundling up and relocating outside to smoke. The morning was bitterly cold. The sun barely peeked over the horizon. Sitting in the dusky dawn light I was at peace with the world and in a mindset I had not experienced since I was a young man. Others began to wake up around seven and move about the ward. One stoked the stove. Others prepared food on a makeshift range in the corner. Surprisingly, two started preparations for the celebration. Around half past seven, I grew too cold and retreated to the relative warmth of the ward.

Festivities began quickly. As soon as the patients pushed both tables together and placed the food upon them, everyone sat down and fell into eating.

"Do you think it could be Jacobe?" a voice broke the silence. Everyone peeked over toward the bearded man on the bed.

"Nah! Jacobe isn't that young," was the first response.

"But the war's been over, no one's been shooting for a long while," the first patient responded.

"It's the tail end of the war," an older soldier replied. "Some guy in the middle of nowhere is probably hiding out with a gun shooting any boos he sees walking by. Besides, didn't you hear the boy?"

The discussion continued.

Jacobe. Jacobe. As they spoke, the name would not leave me alone. The thought of the man would not leave me alone, his legend. It is said he came from nothing. It is said he descended to Hell to battle with a demon. It is said he is the friend of the eagles and can tame any animal. It is said that he fended off hundreds of soldiers single-handedly. It is said he cannot die, that no matter who goes against him, he cannot þe slain in battle. It is said he never died, and many believe he has survived into the new millennium and this new today.

His titles and nicknames reflected his renown: "The Foreigner," "The Bear," "The Hammer," "The Final Judgement of God," "Reaper," "The Son of a New Era." Each person has a new title for him that they hope might catch on, but none were powerful enough to replace his own name: Jacobe.

In less than a year that name had spread across the world, and he was no longer just a person; he was an icon, the tidal wave of a revolutionary idea.

"Why don't you just ask him when he wakes up?" I said after the argument dragged on past its first hour.

That seemed to settle the matter, but although I barely spoke during the conversation, even after the meal had ended, part of me held some hope the wounded man in bed was Jacobe. Like an itch I could not scratch, it burned in my mind as we laughed and told stories and announced our both serious and joking New Year's resolutions. Even as we focused on the clock and started counting down to the New Year, it would not go away.

I remember watching the coffee percolate the next morning in silence. I filled up my cup and sipped. *Bitter, bitter,* I thought. The war was over, and I was beginning to remember comforts of my youth; I had not seen sugar for at least five years. I looked at the clock, 7:00 A.M. I had at least two hours before any other patients would begin to stir. I turned around and started toward a chair I had placed by an east window specifically for mornings such as this. The chair was empty, but the ward was not completely asleep. Someone had grabbed one of the wheelchairs and placed himself next to my seat. I did not recognize the person from the back, so I started to survey beds to determine who it was.

The man who had arrived Christmas Eve was not in his bed; the enigma had awoken.

"May I sit?" I asked him.

He nodded as he stared off into the distance at a patch of tall pines as if he were looking for someone. He looked tired, tired as if from a great weight of sadness.

As I settled into my chair he spoke. "It's a nice hospital." The sadness seemed to be a theme within every word he said. "It doesn't feel like a hospital," he continued. The sadness was one that stretched deep into his soul.

"We've been here for several months, in recovery or rehab or not having anywhere else to go, and it's become more of a barracks than a hospital. Started to add personal touches to the place." I sat in silence a moment before continuing, "So, where were you in the war? I mean, why did you end up being injured so late after Southfork?"

"Travelling for months," he said. "I was one of Jacobe's bodyguards. We ran into the enemy general three days before Christmas. He was all holed up ready for a siege. Took out most of our squad single-handedly, shot me in the chest."

"Did, uh, Jac—" He shook his head before I could finish my question.

"He got shot in the head a couple minutes before I was shot. Last thing I remember before passing out was someone cussing up a storm. Going on about how they were going to burn the mother-effer alive."

"Should have done it in the first place," I said.

"Jacobe wouldn't let 'um. Wanted the general alive." The man again stared into the distance as if he were looking for something.

I watched him in silence. Finally, he looked at me. He looked at the cup in my hand.

"That coffee?" he asked.

I nodded and smiled.

"There any more?" There was less tension in his voice, "I don't think I've had a good cup of coffee since the middle of the war," But it had not broken out above the sorrow.

"Sure, sure." I hopped up, moved across the room, and retrieved a cup. He took it, looked down into it for a moment, and then he took a sip.

"Well, I guess that it will be a little while longer before I get some good coffee then, eh? Don't have any cigarettes, do you?" he asked.

He smiled, a genuine smile, a forced smile. I laughed and nodded.

He turned to me and stuck out his hand. "David Amore," he said.

"Why do you stand at my grave and cry? I am not there. I did not die."

– Unknown –

Author's Note

I hope you enjoyed my debut novel, The Ninth Hour. As a self-published author, I am very dependent on the support of those who enjoy my work. If you did enjoy this book, and are looking forward to future installments, the best help you can give me and any other self-published author is to write a review on Amazon. If you would like to support me in another way, you can check out my website at danielpoppie.com, sign up for my newsletter, and tell your friends that you enjoyed the book. Thank you for your support.

More by this Author

"Jones"

As a self-published author, I have the freedom of creativity. You probably noticed this in how the book was written itself. Part of this freedom involves the choice to include supplements that flesh out the *In Memoriam* world. As a gift to you, you have received a code to download a free copy of the short story Jones. Because it becomes difficult to keep a book focused when juggling several different complex stories, to bring you into the world of *In Memoriam* more fully, I have opted to include supplements and serial stories along with the main storyline. Jones is the first snapshot story that dives into this world from a different perspective.

Coming Soon . . .

"Uncreated"

The United States has fallen. Mackenzie is gone. David and James find themselves coming out of the ground with civilization stripped from the city and devastation in its place. A story of survival, perseverance, and grit, *Uncreated* continues the *In Memoriam* story.

About the Author

Daniel Poppie is a student on the oddly long path to becoming an English teacher. He is also the host of podcast How to Write Good, a writing podcast that doesn't talk about how to write. He occupies most of his time by doing homework, blogging, podcasting, and writing. Dan also enjoys hiking, camping (the type that requires you to hike into the middle of nowhere), sailing, learning new things, art, and coming up with too many goals for most to be fully realized. Dan does not like shopping. Dan lives with his wife in southeastern Wisconsin. Visit his website at danielpoppie.com to stay in touch.

www.ingramcontent.com/pod-product-compliance
Lightning Source LLC
Chambersburg PA
CBHW030913050726
47498CB00003BA/727